KEEP BREATHING

By Len Serafino

ALSO BY LEN SERAFINO

Back to Newark
Sales Talk

Keep Breathing
© 2013 Len Serafino
All rights reserved

ISBN 978-0615827537
LCCN 2013942246

Author's Note

For Frank Euston
In memoriam

Chapter 1

Miracle Morgan woke up in an agitated state. He was confused and frightened. Something or someone was strangling him. He could feel his heart beating hard against his chest. He was gasping for breath. And yet, there was something familiar about all of this. He willed himself to calm down. He went rigid for a moment and opened his eyes for the first time. Yes, it had indeed happened before. The same thing happened just last week. He reached for his neck and felt the oxygen tubing, tightly wrapped around it, not once or even twice, but three times.

He knew instinctively that the tubing was also disconnected from his oxygen concentrator, the machine his doctor ordered for him. He wasn't getting any of the nearly pure oxygen he so desperately needed. He sat up and got the tubing from around his neck. He felt exhausted but he stood so he could find the connector at the end of the long line of tubing and place it back on the concentrator's oxygen outlet. He had to run his hands along the tubing and follow it to the other bedroom where the concentrator sat. That done, he shuffled back to his bedroom. Now he just had to sit still for maybe ten minutes. The oxygen level in his bloodstream, vital to his wellbeing, would return to normal, or something close to it, now that the concentrator was giving him oxygen again. His head would clear and he would begin to feel better. He checked the clock on the nightstand. A quarter to eight. Day or night? He wasn't sure. He looked toward his bedroom window for confirmation. A bit of sunlight peeking through the blinds told him it was morning.

An hour later he was shaved and dressed. Too tired to stand up long enough for a shower, he had settled for a sponge bath.

His doctor had also ordered portable oxygen cylinders he could use when he left his condo. He checked the cylinders to see how many were full and how many were empty. Three full and three empty, not bad. He checked these things at least half a dozen times a day, as if some thief was likely to sneak into his condo and steal them if he wasn't constantly on guard. Although he knew he was being paranoid, he also knew from the other patients he met at his pulmonary rehabilitation sessions that everybody who depends on supplemental oxygen has the same fear. Without those tanks he was homebound, tethered to his concentrator with its fifty feet of tubing. It was that simple. And fifty feet didn't take him very far. He could roam around the small condo, moving from room to room, tied to his concentrator, but there was no way he could leave the house, not even to get the mail without his portable cylinders.

Miracle shook his head. The mail; he hadn't shuffled down to the mailbox for at least two days, maybe three. He wasn't sure which. And neither his daughter Melanie nor his son Brian had stopped by to retrieve it for him. He grabbed the handle of the wheeled carrying cart that held a full cylinder. Thirty-six inches long and heavy enough that just pulling it made him tired, he rolled it to his front door. He removed his nasal cannula, the source of the precious oxygen coming from the oxygen concentrator and switched to the cannula that was attached to the cylinder. He braced himself for the walk to the mailbox. It was exactly 76 feet away and it was on a slight decline from his two front steps. That was the easy part. What he dreaded was the walk back to the condo which of course had a slight incline plus the two steps he had to climb to get back into his home.

His mailbox only held a few items; some of them advertisements which he dropped immediately into the conveniently provided trash can that sat next to the mailboxes. He didn't bother to look at the rest. He stood and stared at the parking lot and the front doors of the condos that surrounded him, trying to work up the nerve to make the hike back to his own. He knew from experience that by the time he got to those two steps, the last barrier between him and his recliner, he would be totally spent, mucus filled, gasping for breath and coughing.

It was the first day of summer and the temperature was a perfect 80 degrees. He reveled in the mild breeze, his tall, thin frame braced by the handle of the oxygen carrying cart. His car, a fully restored, astral blue, 1950 Packard Clipper Custom, was parked directly in front of his place. With its front vertical windshield seam down the middle, its long hood, capped by a swan ornament and its sloping back, the Packard was a thing of beauty to Miracle. It was the last remaining vestige of his former wealth. He loved the car more than anything he had ever owned.

Although spaces weren't assigned, the neighbors had the good sense to leave that space for him. It was only when a visitor showed up, there to see a friend or perhaps a lover, that his space might be taken. In spite of his rapidly declining health he still tried to get out of his condo every day at lunch time for his usual medium-well hamburger, catsup only, and sweet potato fries. If another car happened to take his space while he was gone, he would park his directly behind the vehicle and go inside.

He didn't park in front of the car that took his space to be cantankerous. He left his keys in the Packard's ignition and put a note on his windshield describing his situation, asking that his keys be returned once his car had been parked in its rightful spot. Eventually word got around the complex and it usually worked out fine. Sometimes he didn't even bother to leave a note anymore. Occasionally, the owner of the blocked car would come out and blow his horn if he didn't see Miracle's note or someone hadn't already explained what was going on. Miracle would wave him to his front door and ask the other driver to move his car out of the way so the driver could back his own car out, then park Miracle's car and return with the keys.

Miracle had been doing this for the last three months, ever since his oxygen requirements went past six liters per minute. As his doctor had told him several times, once his oxygen reached that point, he would find it increasingly difficult to be active at all. Yet, Miracle knew of at least two people who needed more than six liters per minute who were still driving. His own needs were now upwards of eight liters per minute but it didn't stop him. It slowed him down considerably of course. But he found ways to compensate. He grudgingly accepted the reality that it was best not to walk any farther than absolutely necessary. For the last couple of weeks he was up to eight liters per minute even at night, a sure sign that his disease was going from bad to worse. A couple of times he felt like someone were actually suffocating him. Panicked, he even cranked the setting up to ten for awhile. Again, not a good sign. The numbers would never go down again, only up. He knew he probably shouldn't be driving. Still, he drove. He needed to hold onto what little freedom he had for as long as he could.

Only once had somebody, a guy named Nate, given Miracle any lip over his parking routine. When Miracle asked the guy to come to his door so he could explain, the guy said, "Hey old man, come and get your car out of my way yourself. This ain't no valet parking establishment."

Miracle shook his head. "I would, but I can't. I'm not well."

"You're gonna be a lot worse you don't get over here. I'm not foolin' with you."

Miracle tried to explain. "I have pulmonary fibrosis. I can't walk very far without oxygen."

"I don't care if you got cystic fibrosis, uterine fibrosis or halitosis. Get your ass over here and move your damn car."

It dawned on Miracle at that moment that the man was probably drunk. One of his neighbors, Mrs. MacBrien saved the day. She had just pulled into her space across the way and as she got out of her car, she heard the commotion. As soon as she realized what was happening, she walked over to Miracle's car, got in and moved it. She stayed in the car until the unruly character drove off. An hour later, the man's girlfriend, who lived a couple of doors down, heard about what happened. She rang Miracle's bell and very apologetically explained that she had just had a nasty breakup with the man. No one was sorry that Nate was never seen at The Arbors of Glen Ridge again.

As soon as he got back into his condo, Miracle walked the cylinder cart to the spare bedroom and switched back to his concentrator. Once that was done he dragged himself back to the living room and sat down to catch his breath. He reached for the mail but it wasn't there. Damn, he thought, I left it on the bed. He wasn't about to get it now. He would check it later.

To give himself something to do while he caught his breath, he surveyed his condo. He could see his tiny kitchen from his living room. The wallpaper in the kitchen had a very 1950s look with a bold and colorful floral design selected by his daughter, she said, to cheer him up. The pink, blue orange and red flowers matched the dark wood cabinets well according to Melanie. He had hated it when she showed him the design she picked but now he found it comforting. In spite of the retro wallpaper, the fixtures in the kitchen and bath were completely up to date brushed nickel. All of the countertops were Bismarck Brown granite.

His living room had built-in rows of bookcases on each side of a gas log fireplace. The bookcases were filled with mementos of vacations he took in Europe and South America more so than books. He usually gave his books to the local library after he read them. He traced his concentrator tubing to the door to his spare bedroom that he had set up as a combination office and guest room when he moved in. As it turned out he didn't have guests and he didn't need an office. His oxygen concentrator sat in that room rather than his bedroom to reduce the noise level while he slept.

The former owners had updated the 1,100 square foot unit a bit beyond what the neighborhood called for, but he was happy with it. What had mattered most when he bought it was the simple fact that it was compact. No more walking than necessary was his number one goal.

He heard his front door open. Before he could say a word he heard his son's voice.

"You're not watching porno, are you Dad?"

"No. I'm just sitting here rewriting my will. I just took you out of it again."

Brian, the same height as his father, inherited his paternal grandmother's red hair and green eyes. He was a good looking kid, better looking than Miracle. "Sweet, I can get a job at Starbucks as a barista. College is a drag anyway."

"What are you doing here Brian?"

"Glad to see me?"

"Always! Just surprised to see you when you probably should be taking final exams, speaking of college."

"Did that last month. Did you forget?"

"Sadly, it seems so."

"How come you're out of breath?" Brian asked, well aware of the answer. His father had been a healthy, active man. Seeing him like this was always a surprise no matter how many times he saw it.

"I'm dying. Did you forget?"

"Touché."

"Just went out to pick up the mail." He was about to ask his son to retrieve it from his bedroom but something, an intuitive thought, stopped him.

"Oh. Hey, Melanie's on her way over. We're having a family meeting."

"We are? What for?" Miracle was wary now.

"Let's wait for Mel. She should be here any minute. Is there a cold beer in the refrigerator?"

"No. How about a Coke? College boy or not, it's too early to have a beer."

Brian smiled at his father. He realized that one of the reasons for his inability to come to terms with his father's illness was that the old man still sounded like himself. Sitting in his recliner, he actually didn't look bad in spite of having lost more than 40 pounds. He was skinny in the way an older sick person looks skinny, but he still had a full head of steel gray hair. His pale blue eyes completed the picture of a man in control of his life. His appearance changed dramatically when he stood up though. He was hunched over, unable to come fully erect anymore. Standing, he looked like a much older man than his 60 years.

The doorbell rang, the door opened and Melanie sang out. "It's just me, your one and only daughter."

"Join the party," Miracle said, "Looks like we have a quorum, so let's get this meeting started."

"Daddy, please, I just got in the door and I'm thirsty."

"Brian, get your sister a Coke while you're at it," Miracle called out. He reached for a tissue and blew his nose. He was doing that more every day it seemed.

"Are you out of breath?" Melanie asked.

Miracle wished his kids would stop asking that question. It was, more or less, his natural state of being now. "I just got the mail. It takes a minute or two to catch my breath."

"I see. Where is it? Anything interesting come today?"

"Had you been here sooner, you could have saved me the trip and you would know what was in the mail."

"I'm sorry."

Miracle looked at his daughter. She was 35 already, he thought, still pretty but like her mother, she was beginning to look more like a middle aged woman, prematurely in his opinion. She was almost a foot shorter than her younger brother Brian. In fact, in spite of having the same father, neither of them looked like him. They both took after their mothers.

"I wouldn't be out of breath either," he added. "Not that I'm blaming you."

Brian walked in and handed his sister a can of Coke. They exchanged glances. Something passed between them and Miracle saw that. What were they up to?

Melanie cleared her throat and spoke up. "Dad, I was talking to the people at the hospice. They really don't think you should drive anymore. They think it's time you stopped. So do I, and so does Brian. You might have an accident."

"Really?" Miracle said. "Then maybe you two should stop driving. You might have an accident."

"Seriously Dad, it isn't safe with the oxygen and all. You might hurt yourself or even someone else."

"Listen kids, I'll know when it's time to stop driving. It's not up to you or the hospice people to decide that."

"Don't be like that dad," Brian said, pushing his long hair back. "It's for your own good. When you need something, Mel or I can get it for you."

"Like my mail? Listen, I'm going to keep doing what I'm doing for as long as I possibly can. It's not like I'm driving into Manhattan. I only drive within a three or four mile radius to get the things I need. And I need to get out of the house now and then just like anybody else would. I won't be a prisoner in my own home. And nobody, not you or the hospice can make me stop."

"You're right dad. We can't make you stop," said Melanie, "but the hospice director told me that they are going to cut way back on the number of oxygen cylinders you get so you won't really be able to drive anyway."

"They can't do that," Miracle said, worried now.

"Actually they can. I met with Doctor Cardoza and he agrees. He's changing your prescription," Melanie said, a tiny note of triumph in her voice.

"What gives you the right to meet with my doctor?"

"I always go with you when you see him, right?"

Miracle sat quietly for a while pondering what he just heard. There was no point in arguing with his children. He would get this straightened out with Cardoza and the hospice after the kids left. "Drink your Cokes and get on with your business, whatever that might be. I want to take a nap."

"I'm sorry Dad," Melanie said, her voice a whisper.

"Me too," said Brian. "We'll get you whatever you need, promise."

Miracle waved them off. They sat in silence for a while. Brian took another couple of gulps to finish his Coke and stood up. Melanie stood too. "I'll call you tonight," she said.

After they left, Miracle walked into the bedroom and checked again to see how many cylinders he had left. Not that it mattered considering what he just heard. He picked the mail up off his bed and placed it on the bureau. He really did need a nap. Sleep though, wouldn't come. He knew Melanie was doing what she thought was right but she was way out of bounds going to see Doctor Cardoza behind his back. He hated himself for thinking what he was thinking but he couldn't help it.

Maybe Melanie and Brian figured that if he was homebound, with nothing to look forward to, he might slip away sooner. He already had too much time on his hands. The joke was on them though. They believed, like everyone else did, that he still had money. The thought tickled him a little. Only he, Miracle, knew how little was left. By the time Melanie and Brian were done fighting each other, there might be just enough for Brian to finish college. And whatever Melanie and her goofball husband Vincent were hoping for, probably a new house, it wasn't going to happen.

Miracle wasn't born into a family with a lot of money. His father John owned a print shop on Frelinghuysen Avenue in Newark that afforded them a decent living. All that changed when his father got a stock tip. An old friend with connections on Wall Street told him to buy stock in Walt Disney's company because they were about to announce a new theme park in Orlando, Florida. This was in October of 1965, a month before Walt Disney himself announced his plans. Mr. Morgan had about twenty grand stashed away which was earmarked for Miracle's education. Years later he would say he never knew what possessed him, but instead of buying stock, he bought two huge parcels of land in the area where the theme park was to be built. He even took a second mortgage on the building that housed his print shop to get enough cash to make the deal. Then he just waited for the announcement. As expected, the value of the land skyrocketed. Just like that, the Morgan's were multimillionaires.

As the only child of John and Celia Morgan, Miracle inherited everything when they died. Everything, it turned out was just over four million dollars, what was left of the estate. His parents had given him a nice starter package of course, handing him a quarter million the day after his graduation from the University of Miami in Florida. By the time he was 32 both parents were gone and he had the whole bundle. Over the years, charitable giving, high living, foolish investments and two marriages whittled down his small fortune to practically nothing. All told he had maybe fifteen thousand in the bank. As he did with his cylinders, he counted it, or at least reviewed his statements, frequently.

Now thinking again about what his kids were about to do to him if he couldn't persuade Doctor Cardoza that he was capable of driving, he felt an overwhelming sadness. Since his diagnosis three years ago, he would get depressed now and then, but he worked hard to fight it. The way he saw it, his time was very limited. Why waste it feeling sorry for himself? He had quickly learned that the best way to beat the blues was to move. Even if, under the circumstances, moving meant nothing more than shuffling from room to room. He sat up and stretched. He stood and walked over to the bureau and picked up his mail. He shuffled his way into the bathroom and took care of business before heading for the living room and his recliner.

He sat in his chair to look through his pile of mail. There were some bills, a book club offer and a post card from yet another realtor. He looked at the airbrushed photo of the realtor and smiled. As a man who once sold real estate he still marveled at the stupidity of glamour shots. Where do ideas like this come from? Is that mug supposed to put a homeowner in the mood to sell his house? He shook his head. The next item was a letter. He noticed his name and address were hand written. Even before he read the name on the return address, he knew who it was from. It was Marcia Lacy. He sat and stared at the letter for a moment. Just as he started tearing open the envelope, his cell phone rang.

"This is Miracle Morgan."

"Really? I was hoping it was Jennifer Anniston."

"Ray Rosario. Wow, what kind of trouble are you in?"

"When have I ever been in trouble? The closest I ever came was when I got engaged and I only did that a couple of times."

"How long has it been Ray? I haven't heard from you in what, two years?"

"Can't be that long paisan. Didn't I see you in November? Oh, wait, no, not then. Maybe it has been that long."

"Where are you? Monte Carlo? Marco Island? Montpelier?"

"How about Mt. Prospect Avenue?"

"You're in New Jersey? Really? Why?"

"Don't sound so shocked. I did grow up here too you know."

"And you're back here to do what? Atlantic City I could see, but Newark?"

"Never mind all that. I'm in town for a week. I have a couple of meetings set up in Manhattan. I was thinking about stopping by. Is that OK?"

"Do you even know where I live?"

"Aren't you still in Livingston? Big house, pool in the backyard?"

"Not anymore. I guess it's been more than two years, Ray. I live in Glen Ridge now, in a condo. After Wendy died I sold the house in Livingston and moved here."

"Yeah, Wendy. When she died, I was in London. Couldn't get out of there in time for the funeral. I hope you got my note."

"No note, Ray. It's okay though. She wasn't too fond of you."

Both men laughed. Neither of Miracle's spouses liked Ray.

"Well, I still feel awful about that. I really couldn't get here," Ray said. "Like I said, I was in London doing some crazy retrospective on Wimbledon. Wound up staying for six months. Are you doing okay?"

"Me? Well, we have a lot to catch up on my friend. I'm glad you're in town. What time are you coming over here?"

"Uh-oh, that doesn't sound so good," Ray said.

"Never mind that. What time, Ray?"

"Let's see, it's about 10:30. How about if I come around lunch time? I'll take you out to lunch. I'm buying."

"No later than noon. If you don't mind, pick up a couple of sandwiches, and we'll eat here. Here's the address."

Ray Rosario had been Miracle's best friend for many years. They grew up together in the same neighborhood. In fact, they were born on the same day in Saint Michael's Hospital in Newark. They went to the same grammar school and the same public high school. Both played on the tennis team. Miracle was good enough to make the all county team but he wasn't in Ray's class. Ray was an incredible tennis player. He went undefeated in both his junior and senior years, winning the state singles championship in both years. Together, they won the state doubles championship their senior year.

While Miracle was enjoying college life as the prototypical frat man in Miami, Ray was busy becoming a tennis pro. He was that good. He earned a tennis scholarship to Stanford, but only played one year. He wanted to turn pro and make some money. He won a couple of big matches, beating two tennis icons in early rounds of tournaments in Great Britain. Although he never actually won a tournament, he got a lot of mileage out of beating top ranked players.

For a long time, they managed to get together at least once a year, usually at a tennis function wherever Ray was playing or teaching. Eventually though, Ray and Miracle drifted apart, getting in touch once a year to wish each other a happy birthday. Some years they would find a way to catch up during the Christmas holidays. A lot of the distance between them was the handiwork of Miracle's first wife Sandy. She hated Ray. She told Miracle he couldn't be trusted, he wasn't welcome in their home. She didn't even want him attending their wedding, but Miracle put his foot down. Ray was his best man.

As far as Miracle knew, Ray made a living as a tennis club pro. The year he beat the then first and second ranked players, he was considered a dark horse candidate to win Wimbledon. Incredibly, he made it to the round of 16. He was playing so well that beat writers were predicting he would make it to the finals. He was young and impetuous, and like most young, athletic men, he felt invulnerable. Then, the day before his next match, he got injured. He had been playing a pickup game of Rugby, a foolish act, typical of Ray. He hurt his right shoulder so badly that he needed surgery. The doctors did their best to repair it, but there was too much damage. He would never be able to raise his right arm enough to produce a good serve, certainly not good enough to play professionally ever again. He was out of the tournament; his career on the professional tour was over. He moved around a lot after that, always warm weather locales, usually moving on after he wore out his welcome. And he always wore out his welcome. When he wasn't hustling club players he was hustling the married women who adored his good looks, good humor, and even better, his ability to fix even the worst backhand.

When he still had lots of money, Miracle would stake Ray when he was in between things. In fact, the last half-dozen times he saw Ray he had loaned him money, usually around $1,500 and rarely more than five thousand. Miracle understood that Ray was using him, but when he had money, he didn't care. Miracle felt he had been the luckier of the two, at least until he was diagnosed with a dreaded lung disease. Helping his pal didn't bother him.

After Wendy died, the calls and visits just stopped. Neither

Miracle nor Ray made the effort. Both men understood in the way only lifelong friends could grasp, that it didn't matter how much time passed. They would be there for each other when the chips were down.

Now Ray was back in town. What was he up to? Well he probably needed money again knowing Ray. Like his kids, Ray was in for a surprise.

Miracle checked his watch. It was already after eleven. He was still tired. Every day now the fatigue seemed to get worse. He wanted to get up and straighten out the place, but he couldn't muster the energy to get moving. He picked up Marcia's letter again and opened it. It was hand written in a very careful scroll. Miracle remembered that Marcia had been a calligrapher for a while. He had long ago forgotten just how good she was. The letter reminded him. Then he started reading. He soon forgot about how pretty her handwriting was. Marcia's letter made him sick. He didn't have to check his pulse oximeter, the tiny device that measured his blood oxygen level, to know it was down and still dropping. He could barely take a breath.

Chapter 2

Ray Rosario was about to ring his friend's doorbell when he noticed that the door wasn't completely shut. He opened it and stuck his head in. "Anybody home?" No response. "Miracle?"

"Is that you, Ray? Come on in." Miracle struggled to his feet and made the journey over to the front door where Ray and a young woman were standing. Ray looked good, sporting a salt and pepper beard that looked more like he hadn't shaved for a few days than something he cultivated. His tan, befitted a tennis pro; and although his hairline had receded some since the last time Miracle saw him, Ray was sporting a rather longish ponytail.

"What's with this?" Ray asked, tugging gently on Miracle's nasal cannula.

"Long, sad story with an ending so depressing you don't want to know."

"Seriously? You have emphysema? You never smoked!"

Miracle waved him off. "We'll get to that later. Who's your friend?" He almost said, is this your niece? The woman was probably close to Melanie's age. But Miracle knew better. He would have been happy to tweak Ray, but he thought his comment might embarrass Ray's companion and Miracle simply couldn't abide that.

"This is Tara Ridgley. She came up here with me from Florida. She's never been to New York. Can you believe that? She looks thirteen years old and she's never seen the Empire State Building." Ray had no problems embarrassing people.

"Nice to meet you, Tara. I'm Miracle Morgan."

"I know. Ray sort of told me that on the way over here."

Miracle started to feel short of breath. Just standing and

chatting was too much for him. He motioned them into his living room. He pointed them to the couch while he settled back into his recliner. There was a brief silence which made the sound of the concentrator with its rhythmic hiss seem louder than it was. The silence made Tara uncomfortable. She felt like an intruder.

"Maybe I should wait outside," Tara said. Miracle smiled. He liked her.

"Don't be silly, Tara," Ray said. "From the looks of things, you may be needed any moment." Then to Miracle, "Tara's a nurse."

Miracle really looked at her then for the first time. She was very pretty. He had lost all interest in things sexual, but he had to admit this girl was sexy. She was wearing shorts; sandals and a black T-shirt with the word "celebrate" spelled out in rhinestones. Five feet, nine inches tall, she had long legs, a bit thick at the top. Before he got sick, Miracle would have found that appealing. And she had blonde hair and blue eyes, another plus.

"What kind of nurse are you," he asked.

"The regular kind I guess," she said. Miracle didn't have the energy to banter. He turned to Ray.

"You won't believe who I heard from."

Ray shrugged, "Who?"

"Marcia."

Ray stared at Miracle as if waiting for the punch line.

"You remember Marcia, Marcia Lacy."

Ray said, "Oh, sure. How could I forget? The love of my life and yours. Red hair and green eyes. She was a hippie back then."

Ray's comment irritated Miracle more than he let on. Marcia Lacy really was the love of Miracle's life. Marcia set the standard for every woman he met. When they broke up, Miracle was devastated. It didn't take long for him to realize that no woman was going to measure up to her. Marcia understood Miracle in a way that no other human being ever had.

She was gentle and yet, on matters of principle, she was, in her own quiet way, unwavering. She wouldn't argue. She would listen patiently, her green eyes unmoving and then, simply shake her head no if she disagreed with what you said or didn't approve of what you were selling. She could spot the weakness of an argument, and in a few short sentences, calmly point them out.

And she was beautiful; her red hair ran straight down her back to the top of her lovely ass. Above all, she seemed totally unaware of her beauty, her charisma or her bearing. She was someone who's opinion of you mattered. When Marcia cut him off, Miracle was lost. Now he looked Ray squarely in the eye.

"We were all hippies back then."

"Not you," Ray said.

"Right, not me. You knew her for what, a month? Love of your life. Excuse me Tara, but keep this guy at arms length."

Tara rolled her eyes in agreement.

Ray laughed. "So what did she say?"

"She wrote me a letter."

"And?"

"It was complicated. Anyway, I'm really glad you're here. You can help me sort out a few things, kind of like when we were kids."

When they grew beyond the boyhood playground stage and were teens struggling through the storms that would evolve into manhood, Miracle looked up to Ray. In part because Ray was the better athlete, but Ray was also supremely confident of his abilities in those days. He was street smart in a way that Miracle wasn't. When Miracle had a problem or worry, he went to Ray. Ray's parents were divorced; his father had spent time in prison. As the oldest child in the family, Ray just sort of took over. Many years later, Miracle would understand that Ray was faking it, that Ray's confidence was simply a better choice than putting his tail between his legs and crying.

"Hey, I'm just glad I'm here. I wanted to get together anyway," Ray said, a bit surprised but quietly reveling in the opportunity to play his old part. Ray was well aware that Miracle and he had long ago switched roles. Miracle was the one dispensing help, which of course usually meant money.

"You asked about this," Miracle said, pointing to the cannula in his nose. "I'm dying. I have idiopathic pulmonary fibrosis. I'm a hospice patient. Can you believe that?"

"What the hell is idio-whatever pulmonary fibrosis?" Ray asked.

"I knew it," Tara said to no one in particular. Then, turning to Ray she said, "You know what? We forgot to pick up something for lunch. I saw a couple of places just before we turned into Miracle's development. Give me your keys. I'll go get us something."

Ray handed her the keys. Obviously, the two men needed to talk. She was in the way. Miracle appreciated the way she was handling herself. Ray wasn't quite up to speed. "Don't rush," he told her. "Look for something special."

"Got it, Ray," she said, again rolling her eyes.

As soon as she was out the door, Miracle started to talk. He had a lot to say. "Ray, this letter I got really shook me up."

"What the hell could shake you up more than dying? Are you sure you're dying?"

Miracle took a few breaths. "Yes, I'm sure. Now bear with me. I can't talk too much. I have to rest to catch my breath."

"Okay, sure," Ray said. Instinctively, he reached for a cigarette. He had been dying for one but Tara never let him smoke when she was in the car with him. Now, he really wanted one. He saw Miracle staring at the pack of cigarettes in his hand. "I guess I shouldn't smoke in here," he said.

Miracle fixed him with a look as if to say, what don't you understand about my situation? "It will be easier if you read the letter. Then we can talk."

"Let me have it." Ray got up from his seat and walked over to Miracle. He took the letter. He could tell Miracle wasn't sure if he was doing the right thing. "You sure about this paisan?"

Miracle nodded. Ray sat down again and started reading.

Dear Miracle,

It's been so many years since we have seen each other. And now, after these many years have passed, I have a few things I need to share with you. I know I broke your heart once. Now I fear I'm about to do it again. Not long before I broke it off between us, I found out I was pregnant. We were so young and I was so scared, but one thing I knew for sure in spite of everything else, I did not want to trap you into anything. I had no desire to play out that tired cliché of a shotgun marriage. I loved you very much and still do. But you were so wealthy, and I had nothing but my art. Our son's name is Jagger. (Yes I named him after Mick.) There have been times that I wanted so badly to get in touch with you but I didn't want to burden you. I honestly believe I made the right decision.

I'm sure you must be curious about Jagger. He is 38 years old and the light of my life. He was such a beautiful baby, Miracle! Unfortunately, we soon found out he has a low IQ and is mentally challenged. It wasn't anything you or I did. Doctors have assured me hundreds of times it just happens sometimes.

Life hasn't been easy for Jagger and me. Sadly, my life as an artist did run true to the cliché. I have always been a starving artist, you might say. I have always worked though, and I have been able to take care of Jagger, at least until now. Miracle, I am very sick. I don't have much time left, according to my doctor. I won't trouble you with the horrible details, other than to say that in just a few months, perhaps sooner, I will be gone.

That is why I am writing to you. Our son needs to be cared for. He is not able to live independently. I have explored group homes that take in those without means and they are just awful. I'm sure you can imagine what life would be like in one of these places. Miracle, I am praying that you can find it in your heart to

*care for Jagger. I hope life has been kind to you all these years.
Perhaps you have the means to take Jagger into your home. If that
isn't possible, maybe one of your children, if you have any, could
provide a home for Jagger. He is very sweet and usually compliant.
He can perform what the health care providers call activities
of daily living. He even has a part time job bagging groceries.
If living with you isn't possible, maybe you have the resources
to place him in a private, homelike situation where he will be
properly cared for.*

*I'm sure all of this is quite a shock. I apologize profusely for
the mess I am laying in your lap, but I love Jagger so much. As his
mother, I need to prepare for when I can no longer care for him.
Miracle, if caring for Jagger isn't in the cards, I will understand.
You need not worry about me making any trouble for you or your
loved ones.*

*I hate what I must be doing to you, but I simply must reach
out to you for his sake. Here is my contact information if you
decide to get in touch.*

*Marcia Lacy
Garden Estate Park
4444 Indian Trail
Bonita Springs, FL*

*I think if you met Jagger you could see for yourself how
special he really is. The choice is yours. I know you'll make the
right one whatever it is.*

*With much love,
Marcia*

When he finished reading the letter, Ray sat still, trying to
take it all in. No wonder Miracle was a wreck. "How the hell did

she find you?" he asked.

"My guess would be Google. You might be the last guy in America that Google couldn't find, but the rest of us have no place to hide anymore."

"And I intend to keep it that way paisan. So, what are you going to do?"

Miracle shook his head. He wiped his brow with his arm. "No idea. In the shape I'm in what can I do? I'll probably be gone before Marcia is."

"Yeah, but suddenly you have another kid? Do you believe her?"

"Marcia wasn't a liar," Miracle said.

"How can you be sure? They were crazy times, Miracle, free love, LSD and booze, lots of it."

"I just know she wouldn't make up a story like that," Miracle said.

"Maybe not. Maybe she really thinks he's yours, but who knows? In any case, obviously you're in no position to take in a 38 year old retard," Ray said. "I assume you can send her some cash to help her out, right?"

"I have to think about all of this, Ray. And don't call the kid a retard, okay?"

"Got it, I didn't mean anything by it. I think it's a shame really."

"What's happening to me? I can't breathe, my kids are trying to keep me locked up in this condo, and now I have a child with special needs on my hands."

"What do you mean your kids are keeping you locked up? Why would your kids do that to you?"

"What I mean is they're trying to keep me from driving. It's another long story," Miracle said. They sat listening to the concentrator for a while. Ray drummed his fingers on the arm of his chair, and Miracle reached for a tissue to blow his nose again. Neither man seemed to know what to say next.

After another full minute of silence, Ray spoke. "Before Tara gets back, tell me what this pulmonary fibroids is."

"It's pulmonary fibrosis. It's a lung disease, and there's no cure. One doctor described it as the difference between a wet and dry sponge."

"What the hell does that mean? Ray asked.

"It's not an exact analogy, but picture your lungs as wet and pliable when they're healthy, the way a normal sponge works; you know, soft, it absorbs water. It can be wrung out, and its still soft."

"OK."

"Now, imagine you throw that sponge out in the back yard in the hot sun for a few days. It gets dry and eventually, brittle. That's what's happening to my lungs."

"And there's no cure?"

"No. I heard Marlon Brando died of the same thing"

"Wow." Ray sat there gently wringing his hands for about ten seconds. "Did you get a second opinion?"

"No point, really. After you've had lung biopsies and a couple of bouts with collapsed lungs, you'll take your doctor's word for it. Anyway, I'm screwed and that's that."

"What about one of those lung transplants? You hear about transplants on the news all the time."

Miracle nodded. "Yeah, I looked into that. I was in the hospital for a week. Went through a battery of tests, but I have other problems. My heart's not so good and I have high blood pressure, among other things. Bottom line is, I'm not a good candidate. A friend of mine works at the transplant center. You probably remember him, Carl Andrews."

"Yeah, Carl. Colored kid, lived around the corner from us right?"

"Right. Well, the colored kid runs the transplant center. He's in charge of the whole thing. He looked me up when he saw my name on one of the 8 million forms they make you fill out."

Ray laughed a little. "What did he have to say?"

"He came to see me about an hour after I got the news. It's interesting the way they tell you." Miracle tried to use a deeper voice than normal to mimic the doctor who gave him the news, but couldn't quite manage it in his condition.

"He said, 'Mister Morgan, we have some disappointing news for you. Our tests indicate that the likelihood of success in your case is small. Transplantable lungs are very precious. They're hard to come by. We have no choice but to reserve them for patients who have the best chance for survival. I wish I had better news for you.'"

"Jesus, Mary and Joseph. So what did Carl say?" Ray got up and walked into the kitchen. He helped himself to a bottle of water. "You want one?"

"No. He said he was sorry, that he tried to influence their decision. But, he said, doctors love doing these surgeries. And, you'll love this, they can only be sure they can keep doing them if they have a high batting average."

"I'm really sorry, man," Ray said. And he was.

Miracle nodded again. He was out of breath from talking so much, but he had a question. "What's the story with Tara?"

"Tara? She's really a nice girl. I met her in Miami. She just moved there, maybe six months ago."

"Is that where you live now, Miami?" Miracle asked.

"Yeah, Miami Springs actually. I have an apartment there. Anyway, I was hustling a few business dudes, younger guys who just knew they could blow me off the court. She watched me take her boyfriend for $500," Ray said. "I could tell she was enjoying the beating I was giving him."

"Then what?"

"Same as always, I guess. That night I saw her in the bar alone and bought her a drink. She told me the guy was just a casual acquaintance."

Ray went on to tell Miracle that Tara once had dreams of being an actress. When that didn't work out she went to nursing school. She had been married once but only briefly. The husband turned out to be the type who liked sex in the morning and slapping her around after dinner, by which time he was drunk. After a few months of this, when she realized his promises that it would never happen again only seemed to whet his appetite for the next time, she left him. Always restless, she moved around a lot. "Right now she's working per diem in one of the Dade County hospitals. She turns down assignments she doesn't think she'll like. This younger generation has such a different outlook on life than ours did," Ray said.

"Well, you were ahead of your time then," Miracle said, a smile on his face.

"Perhaps. Anyway, being a nurse, it isn't hard to find steady work. When she does work, the money is good, especially with the overtime pay. And, she's careful with her money," Ray said. "She told me she got tired of Los Angeles -imagine that, and decided to try another city. She took a nice break once she got to Miami before going back to work. Smart kid."

According to Ray, they got along well in spite of their age difference. She was charming and also amused by the way he made his living. He said nothing about whether they had been intimate. When he was younger he always made a point to do that. Miracle was too polite to ask, even though he knew Ray wouldn't be offended by the question.

"How are you getting by?" Miracle asked.

"Tennis lessons mostly. I get away with charging $75 an hour."

But he made his real money hustling the better club players, wealthy guys who thought they were hotshots. First, he would let it be known he had gone to Stanford on a tennis scholarship. He played a year before turning pro. This impressed the guys sitting around the bar at the golf and tennis resorts where he worked. Eventually, he would get around to mentioning that he had beaten both Rod Laver and Arthur Ashe, two of the world's greatest players at the time. Not in the same tournament of course, but it was during the same summer. He let it be known that he had been considered a dark horse favorite to win Wimbledon that year, that he might have done it had it not been for a freak accident. Now all of this was true, but he told it in a way that made him seem tired, a washed up old tennis pro, and a guy who saw himself as still great. He deliberately developed an annoying way of letting the other players know it. As he pointed out to Miracle, it made him a tempting target.

Invariably, someone would ask, "Is that why I hardly ever see you serving out there?"

Ray would nod solemnly. Then came the hook. "Doesn't matter. I could still beat any one of you hackers, even if I let you serve every game of every set."

As Ray told it, there would always be at least one guy who took the bait. "Wait, are you saying you could beat me even if I serve every game? I'd like to see that."

"Well, maybe not every one here, but you I could take."

"Right. What a bull shitter you are," the mark would say.

"I'll be here tomorrow morning, if you want to give it a try," Ray would answer.

"You're on," was music to Ray's ears. The next morning he would lay down the rules.

"Look," he would say, "No matter what happens, you are playing a pro and I will give you some pointers just by being out there with you. So, if you want to play me, my time is money. It will cost you $500 for the match, payable in advance. But, I'll tell you what, if you win, I'll waive the fee." And the con usually worked in spite of the fact that he was dealing with very successful businessmen, Wall Street types, doctors and lawyers. None of them could pass up the chance to put this ponytailed clown in his place. Sometimes, the mark would even up the ante.

"How about this, old man. If I win, you pay me $500." Naturally, Ray would seem to hesitate at first. Then he'd say,

"What the hell, sure." Never missed, he said.

Miracle thoroughly enjoyed the story. "You never change, do you? Do you always win?"

Ray nodded. "I've lost a few times, but not many. Losing once in a while is good for business actually."

"How do you beat them?" Miracle asked. "They're all so much younger."

"What was my claim to fame as a player, even back when we were in high school?"

"Your return of serve as I recall," Miracle answered. Both men laughed.

"So what are you really doing in New York?'

"I came to see you, Miracle."

"No meetings in Manhattan?"

"Nah, I'm broke, Miracle, but I have an idea for my own tennis pro shop. I'm tired of traveling my friend. I've seen and worked every tennis resort from Naples to La Jolla, most of the Caribbean islands, South America, and the best Europe has to offer. I even did a winter in Dubai. I'm tired of the life, man. As much as I hate to admit it, it's getting harder every day to beat these young guys."

Miracle waited in silence for what he knew was coming.

"Owning my own business would solve my problems. That's for sure."

Then, Tara walked in with the sandwiches.

Chapter 3

    Miracle Morgan was a good man, definitely the kind of man that other men liked having for a friend. For one thing, he was generous with his money, generous to a fault. Left to his own devices, his tastes were simple. A good meal, a decent glass of wine and casual, off the rack attire suited him. His one extravagance throughout his life was cars. He had a thing for them, especially cars made in the 1950s. His favorites were the offbeat models. Rather than say, a classic 1957 Chevy with the distinct tail fins, he would go for an aqua marine, 1953 Nash Rambler which was what he drove while he was in college. Normally, these cars wouldn't be terribly expensive, but he was only interested in having cars that looked like they just came out of the showroom, so he paid top dollar. As soon as he graduated from college, just two days after he deposited the check his father gave him, he bought the car he had long hungered for: A 1958 Edsel Citation, a two-door hard top. He drove the car for a couple of years, enjoying the comments he got from friends and strangers alike, until someone plowed into the Edsel's passenger side doors totaling it. The car had been parked on the street where his girlfriend lived. The young woman's father, on his way home from a local tavern, drunk, as usual, did the damage. Miracle always suspected the old man did it on purpose. He didn't like Miracle and he made no bones about it. He resented Miracle for his money and for being a college boy. That was what he called him, in fact. "Oh, I see the college boy is here again," was as close to saying hello as he ever got. Regardless, when it turned out the father had no car insurance, it lead to an ugly argument between Miracle and the girl, and that was that.

He was unique in another way as well. He felt an obligation to give to charity. He got this trait from his mother, Celia. She was a pious woman. Even before they came into money, she sponsored children she found through magazine ads looking for donations for deprived children. When she reached 30 kids, her husband demanded that she quit. She could keep the 30 she had, but that was it. For her part, Mrs. Morgan was never comfortable with the sudden wealth the family realized from the land sale. To her way of thinking, all that money was getting something for nothing. Even worse, she was terribly troubled in a way her husband was not. The source of their fortune, after all, was an illicit inside tip, not hard work. So, Miracle followed his mother's example. He gave money to charities; he did this in small quantities even before he had money of his own.

He could have lived his entire life, gradually giving away his fortune, but he had a knack for finding women who could more than make up for his indifference to the finer things in life. He met his first wife, Sandy, at a Blood, Sweat and Tears concert in Brooklyn in 1973. A friend had put them together and suggested they meet up at the concert hall.

Miracle wasn't too interested in Sandy. She was very thin, her hair cut extremely short. He thought by the look of her that she would be a prude. As he found out that first night in the back seat of his friend's Oldsmobile, he had no worries on that score. As they got to know each other, he began to appreciate Sandy's intelligence. She was a third year law student at NYU with big plans for a future in the Justice Department. Her dream, she said, was to be a Supreme Court Justice. She was sure that by the time she was ready, the high court's glass ceiling would already be broken, probably more than once. She had a softer feminine side too. When Miracle got around to telling her he preferred women with long hair, she grew it long, just for him.

Not that any of it was enough for Miracle to commit to her. He was only 23 years old. Sandy, who was two years older, had other ideas. She knew about Miracle's wealth of course. And, she was savvy enough to realize that having a few million dollars would make everything easier as she climbed through the ranks at the Justice Department. Miracle's money wasn't exceptional. Sandy understood that. Obviously, it didn't put them in a class with the truly rich, but it would be enough to give her the opportunity to live and play where the moneyed played. This is not to say she was only after his money. In fact, she was genuinely fond of Miracle. And Sandy had a plan. By the time they were dating for six months, she brought up the subject of marriage on a weekly basis. Sometimes, she was direct about the topic. Other times she was circumspect, mentioning for example, that her cousin had just landed a job in a jewelry store in Manhattan. Miracle would listen politely, and even nod in apparent agreement. His only comment on the topic of marriage though, was, "maybe someday."

After three months of planning their future without Morgan's help, Sandy upped the ante. Without telling him, she stopped taking the pill. On the one year anniversary of their first date she informed him she was pregnant.

Miracle was beside himself when he heard the news. But, steeped in the traditions of the Catholic faith, he agreed to be married. Sandy was thrilled. As soon as they got settled in a nice two bedroom apartment, she set out to have the best of everything. It didn't matter to her that Miracle's money, at the time he had just under $200,000 in the bank, wouldn't last a lifetime. She knew he would eventually inherit more. She was sure she would make a decent salary herself. Anyway they wouldn't need as much once they got established. So, just four months after moving into an apartment in West Orange, they purchased a three bedroom Colonial in toney Short Hills, New Jersey, complete with the fine china, and furnished in large part by Baker Furniture. She also had to have a Mercedes, which Miracle gave her, but he hated the pretentiousness of it all. When Melanie arrived, she got the best crib, clothing, toys and naturally, a nanny from Sweden. Miracle did all of this to make Sandy happy. He felt that more structure would motivate him to find himself.

When he met Sandy, he was working at a car dealership selling Buicks. It wasn't his dream job by any means, but he always got a kick out of being around cars. He particularly loved selling the sleek Rivera model. A few of his customers were young women. He casually dated a few of them after selling them Regals. Then he learned the downside of dating customers the hard way, when one girl decided she hated the color of the car's interior and wanted him to use his influence to let the dealership swap a gray cloth interior for one with leather at no additional charge. An argument over seat covers ended that romance.

Still, he loved cars. Selling them was one way to be around them constantly. In fact, Miracle did some of his most creative work when he was selling cars. He was constantly looking for ways to attract buyers. After a particularly long week of standing around the dealership waiting for people to show up with little success, he found a clever way to get Buicks in front of people with money to spend. He hooked up with one of the biggest home builders in the state, and persuaded him to let Miracle park new Buicks in the driveway of model homes on weekends. He would be standing there with the cars. At first, the home builder thought Miracle was crazy.

Why, he wanted to know, would he give people a choice about how they would spend their money? He wanted them to buy houses, not new cars. Then Miracle told him the second part of the deal. The owner of the dealership agreed to give a new car to one of the people who bought a new home during the contest, selected by a random drawing. All the builder had to do was chip in 50% of the dealer's cost for the car.

The winner would have to be present at the drawing, which would be held at six o'clock sharp on a Saturday night at the dealership's showroom. The new suburban development, made up mostly of large, upscale homes, was huge. There were more than 100 entries during the so-called contest period. Even if a lot of people showed up, all but one was destined to be a loser. But, at least some of them might be infected with new car fever. That could mean more sales.

The promotion turned out to be a big hit. The builder's traffic doubled which boosted home sales, and Miracle sold 23 cars to customers who had seen the new cars while shopping for a new house. It was so successful that other dealerships got in on the act with other builders.

Another thing Miracle did was go out to the local mall and put handwritten notes on the windshields of attractive vehicles parked in the massive parking lot. The note was simple, something like, "I am interested in buying your car. I'll give you $2,500 for it (this was the 1970s,) as long as it runs as good as it looks." Of course, the amount varied by make, model and year of each car.

The offer was always generous. He made sure to include his name and number on the note. That strategy didn't produce many leads, but a handful of people called. One or two actually traded in their cars for a new Buick. Before he could see what really worked and what didn't though, the mall's manager called the owner of the dealership, a Mr. Kenneth Gibson, and complained about it. He insisted that they stop annoying mall customers with such tactics. Gibson quickly agreed they would discontinue the practice. He feigned ignorance that it was going on, but he congratulated Miracle for being so aggressive.

One afternoon, Miracle made a mistake that nearly cost him his job. A prospect stopped in, dressed in a suit and tie, and asked to see the Buick Century. He picked a white one, and asked if he could take it for a spin.

In those days, dealerships would sometimes let customers take a car for a ride without sending a sales representative out with them. Of course, they always got a copy of the customer's driver's license before handing him the keys. Eager to oblige, Miracle let the guy go out but forgot to get the necessary information. All he knew was the guy said his name was Dan.

The guy drove the car off the lot and didn't come back. Closing time came and went. There was no sign of Dan or the white Buick Century. Now this was not entirely unheard of. Occasionally, a customer would take a car home and bring it back the next morning. In fact, many times, dealers encouraged customers to do just that. They figured that once the customer breathed in that addictive new car smell, got the feel of sitting behind the wheel, and let his neighbors see him driving it, he was hooked. A whole day of that would overwhelm even the most disciplined buyer.

But the next day, a Saturday, there was still no Dan. No call, nothing. The dealership was closed Sunday of course. Promptly at nine Monday morning, Miracle's sales manager explained the situation to the owner of the dealership.

"Are you kidding me?" the owner asked.

"Should we call the cops?"

Kenneth Gibson had owned his dealership for 33 years. He was a heavy set guy, head shaved, with a salt and pepper beard. He had seen a lot of wild things happen over the years. He stood there, silent for a moment, considering the question. Then he shook his head. "Not yet. Maybe he'll be back. It's never happened here before." He scratched his beard. "I've been told this kind of thing happens once in a while."

Just then, the receptionist paged the sales manager. He picked up the phone on Gibson's desk. "There's a Mr. Phillips on the phone. I think it's that Dan guy who took our car," she said.

Gibson picked up the phone and spoke with Phillips.

"Just wanted you to know I have your automobile here. I didn't run away with it or anything. My mother was rushed to the hospital Friday afternoon. I've been with her ever since. I guess I forgot all about whose car I was driving," he said. "My mother gets out of the hospital tomorrow morning. Can I return the car as soon as I get her home? I'll come right by the dealership, promise."

Gibson was so relieved he quickly agreed to the customer's request after jotting down the caller's driver's license number and address. "Mr. Phillips, we expect to see you first thing in the morning." The next day it got to be noon, and there was still no Dan and no white Buick Century. At three o'clock they got a call from the State Police in Florida. The car was found sitting in a Publix parking lot in Miami. The dealer's license plate was in the trunk.

Gibson didn't fire Miracle, but he wasn't the fair haired boy of the sales team after that.

Not that it mattered, because after marrying Sandy, she pushed him to get out of the car business and into something she felt was more respectable. So he took a job as a management trainee in one of the local banks which pleased Sandy. He also asked his parents for an advance on his inheritance. His parents weren't crazy about Sandy. They agonized over his request, theorizing that a refusal might put an end to the marriage, an event they would have welcomed. In the end, they gave in and gave him another $250,000 to cover some of their spending. As Mr. Morgan put it, "How do we know the next one will be any better?"

Fortunately, Sandy was by no means lazy. True to her word, soon after she got her law degree, she found a job working in the Essex County prosecutor's office. Sandy worked hard from the start, putting in long hours and at least a few hours on weekends. But life didn't quite work out according to her carefully thought out plan. She got assigned to a complicated securities fraud case that involved a Newark based, multi-national firm and its powerful and well respected CEO. She was in over her head, but she pursued the case with a vengeance hoping to make a name for herself.

Instead, the case blew up when a well coached and well connected witness for the prosecution suddenly recanted. She wasn't fired, but the CEO, who wasn't the type to forgive and forget, had enough friends in state and federal government circles to ensure that Sandy's dreams of working for the Justice

Department were delayed, if not derailed.

She was never the same after that. She didn't relish her work anymore. Eventually, she recognized the fact that Miracle would never rise to a powerful position in the bank or anywhere else. In any case, the mere thought of rubbing elbows with bank tellers and assistant managers at Christmas parties gave her migraines. She and Miracle went through the motions, bonded by their love of their daughter, but neither of them got much satisfaction out of the marriage. During their last few years together, Sandy was often critical of Miracle's seeming unwillingness to make something more of himself. Ten years in banking got him the ubiquitous vice president's title. Sandy belittled him for that too. That's when Miracle decided to make a change. He hated banking. He took real estate courses at night, passed the test and started selling real estate.

Sandy was horrified by his choice, embarrassed by his new profession. "You might as well sell cars again," she said. As far as she could tell, he showed homes in between golf and tennis outings. Of course, by then, he had inherited the money she long ago counted on, but none of that mattered now. Their relationship was beyond repair, and they both knew it. For Melanie's sake they went to marriage counseling for a while, but neither of them cared enough about the marriage to work on the problems, which were only made more vivid by counseling. As Miracle confided to a sympathetic co-worker, "There was never any chemistry to begin with."

Finally, after 12 years of marriage Sandy filed for divorce. She took a generous one million dollar settlement and moved on. She got custody of Melanie; that was what mattered most to her. In exchange for the generous settlement, she agreed to cooperate when Miracle sought an annulment through the Church.

Two years later, Miracle married again, this time to Wendy, a vivacious brunette with all the physical attributes that Sandy lacked. She had curves in the right places, was the way he explained it to Ray. He met Wendy on the tennis court during a mixed doubles tournament at his club. He was still a good tennis player, and enjoyed the game, maybe more than Ray did. As it turned out, Wendy was in real estate too. She worked harder at it than Miracle did. Miracle found her to be charming and thoughtful. He genuinely cared for her. And she too enjoyed the good life. The difference between her and Sandy was that, while Sandy loved theatre and the opera, Wendy's idea of the good life involved parties, travel and taking classes in exotic subjects. She insisted they try kick boxing, Indian cooking and classes in scuba diving for starters.

When Miracle met Wendy she was half-way through a class on animal training focused on tigers, bears and lions. Wendy made Miracle feel alive in a way that Sandy couldn't possibly have done. After dating for just seven months, they were married. Ray, who had been Miracle's best man when he married Sandy, stood up for him again.

From all outward appearances, observers couldn't be faulted for suspecting that Wendy married Miracle for his money. Like Sandy, she spent extravagantly. She was a bit flirtatious too, but what people around them didn't grasp was that Wendy truly fell in love with Miracle. Maybe she wouldn't have given him the time of day had he not been wealthy. Still, she was smitten immediately with his tall frame, good looks and charm. That first day on the tennis court, she marveled at his athleticism and his good manners.

Brian came along a year after their marriage and it cemented their relationship permanently. Miracle was happy with his life and his marriage to Wendy. He settled in and finally became comfortable living in upscale surroundings. He spent time with Brian and he made time for Melanie. As he moved through his 40s and 50s, he would occasionally feel guilty about not having tried to build a career or a business like his father had done. Such thoughts never lasted long though.

He did make one half-hearted attempt to open a video store

soon after Brian was born. He got the store up and running and saw a profit in his first year. It was all down hill after that. He lost interest and lost his investment in the process. He had no regrets. His father worked so hard for so many years. Miracle thought it was pointless to work that hard. The old man never gave up his business, even after he profited so well from the Florida land sale. It was his single stroke of genius. He kept right on working. He never enjoyed the money and what having it might do for him. Miracle was determined to avoid that fate.

No, he was happy selling homes. As soon as he shut the doors of the video store, he got back into real estate. Between his earnings and Wendy's, they were bringing in enough income to hold their own without having to dip into what was left of his inheritance too often.

As they grew older, Wendy became less interested in hosting parties and making trips to Paris. She began to think about Brian's education and their eventual retirement. She started putting a little money aside. She didn't tell Miracle what she was doing. He was too careless with money, and he was such a soft touch, always lending money to that deadbeat friend of his, Ray for example. Not that Ray ever paid any of it back. She put up with that because she knew she was never going to change the way her husband felt about his friend.

But one day she discovered something she knew nothing about. Miracle was a closet philanthropist. His early habit of giving money to charity had morphed into something larger. Searching for some old financial records, she found a box filled with clippings about disasters. It didn't take long to figure out that her husband was sending money, apparently cash; to people he never heard of, that had been victims of some tragedy.

Each clipping had a dollar amount written in the margin in Miracle's fine script. Amounts varied from $100 to a staggering $25,000. He sent $500 to a family in Jacksonville, Florida, victims of a hurricane. The story had been featured in the local newspaper.

When a tornado wiped out a small town in Tennessee, he sent $15,000 to a family with 9 children. That particular tragedy he discovered in one of the real estate news letters he subscribed to. He even sent money to a 97 year old man who was about to be evicted from his apartment.

All of this was done anonymously through his attorney, except for the smaller amounts which he handled by sending cash in unmarked envelopes. Wendy was flabbergasted by what she saw. Miracle had never mentioned any of this to her. Over the next few days, she cross referenced these amounts with their income tax returns. She was mortified to see he had claimed none of it. She confronted him and he quickly confirmed her every suspicion. He was unapologetic, saying, "Are we lacking for anything important?" That's when she started socking away money she knew they would need in their so-called golden years.

Wendy's instincts were right, of course. Even though she curtailed his giving and insisted they take the tax write off, the money dwindled. Then, Miracle got taken for a ride by an investment advisor in 2006, just three months before Wendy suffered a brain aneurism and died.

It happened without warning. She was home alone, doing the laundry. She suddenly felt lightheaded and immediately afterward there was an excruciating headache. She picked up her cell phone to call Miracle. She pressed his speed dial number but that was as far as she got. It was over quickly. When Miracle returned home from a dental appointment, he found her on the floor, her phone still clutched in her hand.

Miracle was devastated by her passing. For months afterward, in spite of a noted neurologist's assurances, Miracle worried the investment losses were the reason she had the aneurism. She had been so angry because she had been opposed to working with this particular advisor. He extracted a huge fee for his advice, but when the investment soured, he got off scot free. "There are never any guarantees," he said.

What was left of his money sat in a portfolio heavy with stocks and mutual funds. Of course he lost nearly all of that, including the money Wendy saved, when the market crashed in 2008.

A life insurance policy on Wendy that she had insisted they buy helped. It paid for Wendy's funeral, and covered the cost of Brian's first two years at NYU. After Wendy died, Miracle lost all interest in his former life. He never dated, and he cut off all but a few of his friends. He did his best to guide Brian, who would soon be headed to college. He remained close to Melanie too, but he was lost without Wendy.

He continued to sell real estate, but the market was so bad he was barely scraping by. He still played tennis at least once a week. It was the one thing that continued to hold his interest. He was no longer a member of a private tennis club though. Wendy had seen to that after she found out she was living with a one man Rockefeller Foundation. He had switched to the public courts to save money.

It was on the tennis court that he started to notice that something wasn't right. Just seven months after Wendy died; he began to notice it was taking longer to catch his breath after playing an extended point. His muscles and joints ached even when he wasn't playing tennis. Then he developed a persistent dry cough he couldn't seem to shake. He was otherwise in good shape. Playing as often as he did, he couldn't understand the long recovery time. Then he noticed that he felt tired for a couple of days after playing. Friends suggested he was suffering from the stress of being a widower. That, plus the responsibility of raising a teenage boy as a single parent, one had who just learned to drive, was sapping his energy, they said.

He desperately wanted to believe his friends, but his body was telling him otherwise. Even long walks were becoming a strain. Climbing steps was a serious chore. After another month of struggling, he finally went to his doctor. She performed a complete workup, but she couldn't find an explanation. She sent him to a pulmonologist. Doctor Cardoza was very thorough. Still, it took him two months to finally diagnose the problem. Miracle had idiopathic pulmonary fibrosis, a disease without a cure. The doctor informed him in an unemotional, clinical tone that he had three to five years to live. That was three years ago.

Chapter 4

"So did you two get to reminisce about old flames and flameouts?" Tara asked while she was putting the roast beef sandwiches on plates.

"Not quite," Ray said, "It would take us at least three days to get half way through the flames. Less than ten seconds though to remember we never had any flameouts."

"Until you met me."

Miracle laughed, but then started coughing a little. It was one of his biggest fears that he would have a coughing spell and be unable to catch his breath. Finally he said, "Lets eat lunch and then you two have to go. I have to get some rest."

"Sure. We're heading back to Florida tomorrow morning," Ray said. "Maybe I can stop by again tonight and finish our conversation."

"Without me," Tara added. Then she looked at Ray. "You're so sophisticated Rosario."

"Don't come tonight. I'm already exhausted right now. By evening, I'm barely coherent. What time's your flight?" Miracle asked.

Ray took a bite of his sandwich. He shrugged and looked at Tara.

"Our flight is at noon," she said.

"Then stop by in the morning around 8:30. But Ray, things are different now. There's no way I can help."

"Help with what?" Tara asked.

Miracle took a bite of his sandwich. The three of them sat in silence until finally Ray spoke up. "Don't worry about it. I'll stop by in the morning anyway."

After they left, Miracle picked up the phone and called Doctor Cardoza's office. The receptionist told him the doctor wasn't available, so Miracle left a message. Tara had cleaned up after lunch which he was very grateful for. He no longer had the energy to do even simple tasks. Any exertion was difficult. He realized that Melanie and Brian were probably right to insist he stop driving. The last time he went out, just three days ago, he had to stop and lean against a parked car about half the distance between the store and his car. He was pulling a two-wheeled shopping cart filled with groceries and two oxygen tanks. It was too much. While he was trying to catch his breath, a woman, probably in her 70s, noticed and offered to pull the cart for him the rest of the way. He gratefully accepted, but the irony wasn't lost on him.

He took a long nap that lasted the entire afternoon. He woke up when he heard the phone ringing. He was disoriented, partly from having slept so soundly. But his oxygen saturation level went down too when he slept, which meant his brain didn't respond in a normal fashion.

"Hi Dad, how's it going?"

"Who's this, Ray? I thought I said come tomorrow morning."

"Seriously? Dad, it's me Brian. Did you talk to Mr. Rosario today?"

"Oh Brian. Ray was here this afternoon. I guess I got confused. Is Melanie here yet? Are we going to meet now?"

"Dad, we met this morning. Remember?"

"We did? What time is it?"

"It's 6:30."

"In the morning?"

"No, no. Its 6:30 p.m. Dad."

"Oh, right. Who is this?"

An hour later, Miracle was fully awake, his oxygen saturation level improved. He noticed he had voice mails. There were two messages, one from Melanie, and one from Doctor Cardoza's office. Melanie's message said something about bringing dinner. The doctor's office just said he was returning Miracle's call.

He shuffled to the kitchen and saw a note on the table. There was lasagna in the refrigerator. Melanie must have stopped by. Her note said she would be back later. He wondered why she didn't wake him up. He took the lasagna out of the refrigerator, opened a can of Coke and sat down to eat. Still tired and feeling frustrated, he began to cry. He had to face it, as bad as his life was, he was afraid of dying. He forced himself to take a bite of his food, pushing the self pity he was feeling away. Such a useless feeling, he thought.

Twenty minutes later, he heard his front door open. It was Melanie. "Thanks for the lasagna. You make it yourself?"

Melanie laughed. "You know I don't cook. My cooking is worse than Mom's. She asked about you by the way. She said she might stop by and see you next week." Miracle rarely spoke to Sandy now that Melanie was an adult. Since Melanie didn't have any children, aside from their daughter's birthday, there were no occasions that required them to be together.

"Tell your mother it's not necessary," Miracle said, "I appreciate her asking about me. That's enough really."

"If that's what you want, I'll tell her, but I think it might mean more to her than you."

Miracle got up from the kitchen table and willed himself to walk to the living room, his once tall body hunched over. He heaved a deep sigh and sat in his recliner. "Why didn't you wake me up when you were here earlier?" he asked.

"I didn't know how long you were sleeping. I assumed you needed the rest," she said. "You know Dad, Brian and I have been thinking, and we think you shouldn't live alone like this anymore."

"Why is that? You just told me this morning I shouldn't drive anymore. Now I shouldn't live alone. What's next, a nursing home? Is that where this is going?"

"No Dad. Don't be silly. I'm just saying, look how hard it was for you just to walk into the living room. What if you fall? You can afford some live in help, can't you?"

"I don't know, Melanie. How much does a thing like that cost?"

"About $150 a day," Melanie said, "I checked."

"What's that, about $55,000 a year?" Miracle asked.

"Right. You can afford that."

"I doubt it."

"My God, Daddy, how much money do you have? You never tell us anything about that."

"I know. I don't like to talk about it. Never did. I have a life insurance policy worth about $500,000. You and Brian are co-beneficiaries. Not much beyond that." He held his hand up to signal he had to stop talking so he could catch his breath. They sat there looking into each others eyes, both saddened by what was happening. Melanie was thinking about her father's condition. He didn't have much time left, but he acted like he was going to be around for years when he had only weeks according to his doctor. What had the doctor said? That he could live another three or four months but might be gone sooner.

Yet, whenever the subject of money came up, her father avoided any details. Certainly she knew about the insurance policy, but she was surprised to hear there wasn't much beyond that. And what did that mean anyway? Not much could mean anywhere from a few thousand dollars to another half-million. Her father had always had money.

Miracle spoke again. "I don't care if you want to get somebody in here. I probably can use the help. But you and Brian are going to have to cover some of the expenses. You can use the insurance to recoup what you put in after I'm gone."

Melanie thought that one over before speaking. "I know you hate talking about money Daddy, but under the circumstances, we really need to know how much money you have. I think we all need to be on the same page."

"I get Social Security every month, and I have a small annuity that pays about $500 on top of that. I have maybe $15,000 in the bank. I don't owe anything on the condo. That's worth maybe $250,000, but I might have to use that for something else." It didn't occur to Miracle until that moment that he might be able to do something for Jagger after all.

Marcia's letter upset him more than he let on to Ray. It wasn't so much that he had a son he never knew he had, as startling as that was. And, the fact that Marcia was dying too, while sad, was beyond his control. They were both dying. It was simply bad luck, a matter of fate. But Marcia's request that he help their son was another matter entirely. The fact that he and Marcia had a shared legacy in Jagger was special. In a way he couldn't put into words, Miracle felt that Jagger's existence justified the secret torch he had carried for Marcia all these years. He would never deprive Melanie and Brian of what was rightfully theirs, of course. But now he felt he had an obligation to his other son, one who needed more help in the long run than either Melanie or Brian.

For the first time since he read Marcia's letter, he felt a surge of energy, or what passed for it under the circumstances. He owned the condo outright. Maybe he could leave it to Jagger.

"What could you possibly need the house money for? I don't understand," Melanie said. Then she got angry. "It's not for that asshole friend of yours, Ray is it? Mommy told me about him and how he was always using you. Is that what he was doing here, asking for more?"

"What are you talking about? Miracle answered. "How did you know Ray was here?"

"Brian told me."

Miracle nodded. "Oh, I guess you two talk a lot. Do me a favor. Check my cylinders. Give me a count." Not that he really expected to use them again. What he wanted was to buy a little time to think. He hadn't even considered what to tell his children about their older brother, or whether to tell them anything. He just found out himself. Now he had to explain what he meant when he said he might need the house money for something else. At times, the lack of oxygen clouded his thinking. At the moment, he was fine. Since both kids were aware that he could suddenly talk gibberish, he decided to fall back on the confused, sick man explanation.

"Okay, I checked your cylinders. Nobody stole one since this morning. Now, what do you need the house money for?" Melanie asked again.

"Miracle blew his nose. He took a sip of water. "I guess I was confused there for a minute. I can't think of what I would need it for."

Melanie seemed satisfied. She started gathering her things to go. "Melanie, for what it's worth, I want you to know I've thought it over, and I agree with you and your brother. No more driving for me."

Melanie smiled, but at the same time she felt tears in her eyes. Every small step was another step toward the end of her father's life. She loved him in spite of the fact that she felt abandoned when he and Sandy divorced. On balance, he had been a good father. She hated to see him suffer like this. She kissed him goodbye and hugged him hard. "I love you Daddy."

"I love you too honey." Melanie turned and headed for the door. Miracle did his best to hold his tears until she was gone.

Chapter 5

Miracle never made it to bed that night. He didn't have the energy to get up and walk to his bedroom, just twenty feet away. He spent the night on the couch instead. An idea occurred to him just before he drifted off to sleep. He had to see his son before he died. What did he look like? If only Marcia had included a picture with her letter. He had to admit it. He desperately wanted to see Marcia too. Now that he knew they were both dying, it might be okay. Otherwise Miracle would never let Marcia see him this way, a shriveled, tired man, dying before his time.

In the years since their breakup, only once did he try to get in touch with her. That was just after his divorce from Sandy. Working on the assumption that she was still living in the Miami area, he went to the library and searched through a south Florida phone book. This was, of course, long before Google. Nothing turned up. He even arranged a business trip that would take him to a place near her last known address in Miami. He came up empty, so he hired a private investigator. The odd thing was he didn't know what he would say to her if he found her. As it turned out, he never got the chance. After a month of searching, the investigator, a retired police officer in his late 60s, reported that he had found Marcia and, as instructed, he approached her. Miracle simply wouldn't have had the courage to approach her himself if there was even the slightest chance he would be rebuffed. Instead, he instructed the investigator to ask Marcia if she would like to see Miracle. She was working in a dress shop in Bonita Springs on Florida's Gulf coast. Marcia had a message for Miracle, just four words. Leave me alone, please.

After that, Miracle let it go. The investigator had been extremely lazy, having done nothing beyond finding her in the dress shop. He was charging a small fortune for his services. Naturally, he asked Miracle if he wanted him to keep digging, find out whether she was married, divorced, in a relationship or had kids, but Miracle called him off. Now Miracle wondered if that had been a mistake. Maybe he would have found out about Jagger had he kept the investigator working.

Miracle woke up before the morning's first hint of light. His back was stiff and his nose was congested, making each breath difficult. He forced himself to get up. He struggled through his morning routine, shaving, showering as best he could while sitting in the shower chair the hospice provided. By 7:30, he was dressed. Then he called Ray.

"What time can you get over here?" he asked.

"I should be there by 8:30 or 9:00," Ray said.

"Sooner would be better. I want you to do something for me."

"I'll see what I can do," Ray said.

Miracle sat down and wrote short letters to Brian and Melanie. His penmanship, once beautiful, was now a hard to decipher scrawl. He had to start over a few times, partly to be sure he said the right things, and partly to make his words legible.

Melanie already had limited power of attorney, which she used to pay his bills. He had allowed it because he was having problems paying them himself. He would forget to pay some bills and pay others, like his real estate taxes, twice. His check book was a mess until Melanie put her foot down and insisted on at least handling his routine finances.

Miracle mulled over whether to tell his children about Jagger. He considered all the reasons why he should tell them they had a brother. In the end though, he felt no useful purpose would be served. Why burden them with the worry, however unlikely, that they might one day have a child that was learning disabled? Who knew why these things happened anyway? Sure it was possible that one or both of them would offer to look after Jagger but they were both young. They had lives to get on with. One day they might resent Jagger. No, shared DNA was not a good enough reason to burden his children. It never crossed his mind that in his compromised state he might not be the best judge of that. Nor did he grasp the idea that, considering what he was planning, it was almost certain his kids would find out about Jagger anyway.

Ray arrived promptly at 8:30.

"Where's Tara?"

Ray smiled. "In the car. She thought we should talk alone."

"Go get her," Miracle said, "This involves her too."

"Whoa, Morgan, what are you talking about?"

"Rosario," Miracle said, responding in kind, "We don't have a lot of time. Go get her, please."

Ray left the condo to fetch Tara. The phone rang. It was Melanie, telling him she arranged for the people from a company called Friendly Visitor Service to come out and assess his needs.

"Who or what is a friendly visitor?" Miracle asked.

"We talked about this last night. We're going to have someone stay with you to help you with whatever you need."

"Isn't that what hospice does?"

"No, not exactly. Don't you remember talking about this last night?"

"Sort of. When are they supposed to be here?" Miracle asked.

"This afternoon at 1:30," Melanie said.

"Tomorrow would be better. The hospice nurse is coming today."

"She comes in the morning dad."

"Oh, right. I guess it will be alright then." Miracle checked his watch. Usually the nurse arrived about 9:30 and stayed for maybe twenty minutes. He would have to get Ray and Tara out of the house before then.

Miracle was thinking quickly now and more clearly than he

had in some time. When he really wanted something, his mind worked almost as well as it did before he got sick. He realized he would need the entire day to get things in order. He wouldn't have a lot of time for the nurse and the people from the Friendly Visitor Service. First though, he had to convince Ray and Tara to help him.

"Good morning Mr. Morgan." It was Tara, dressed in jeans and a bright red halter top. Her long blond hair was fixed in a braided ponytail. She looked great.

"Good morning Tara. Sit down please, both of you," he said motioning them to the couch. "Did Ray tell you what was in the letter we talked about?"

Tara shook her head no. "I didn't say a word, and she didn't ask," Ray said.

Miracle nodded and started to tell Tara what was in the letter. He glanced over and noticed it was sitting in its envelope on the table next to his recliner. He picked it up and started to get up so he could give it to Tara to read. Anticipating him, she jumped up and took the letter from him.

"Thank you," he said.

Tara read the letter slowly. When she finished, she said, "I'm so sorry Miracle. Is there anything Ray and I can do? Would you like us to contact Marcia or visit her for you?"

"Very kind of you, Tara. Yes, there is something you can do for me. I want to see Marcia and Jagger before I die. Unfortunately, I can't fly anywhere. I need way too much oxygen for that. But, if you two would drive me to Bonita Springs, I could see them."

"Wow, I don't know about that Miracle. You're not really in any condition to make a trip like that," Ray said. He looked to Tara for support.

"A trip like that could kill you, Miracle. Maybe you could call and speak with them instead?" Tara suggested.

Miracle shook his head no. He removed his cannula to blow his nose. "Listen, I can't do this without you. My kids would never go for it, so if you say no, I'm stuck. But this is my last dying wish.

Yesterday, Ray said something about Marcia being the love of our lives. Well, she really was the love of mine. And now it turns out we have a child who needs help. I think I can help him some, and I want to see him with my own eyes before I die. I've been getting ready to die for the last six months, probably the last year. I thought I was ready, but now, there's no way I can die in peace unless I do this." He paused to take several breaths. "You know the more I think about it, that's probably partly why Marcia wrote to me. She wants to die in peace too. I am sure she would want to see me and explain."

"I don't have any idea of how to take care of you, Miracle. No way I can do it paisan," Ray said.

"That's why Tara has to come with us. She's a nurse. She'll know what to do if I need anything, right Tara?"

Tara smiled. She sat quietly thinking things over. She understood the risks better than either of the two men sitting there with her. She knew that even if Miracle just sat in his recliner he was in for a very hard time and soon. A road trip probably wouldn't be much worse than sitting around the house.

"I'll tell you what the problem is," she said. "How would we ever get enough oxygen for you to make the trip?"

"I'm getting plenty of oxygen now out of that concentrator. I can get up to 10 liters a minute," Miracle said.

Tara nodded. "What would we plug it into while we're driving? You know where we can get an extension cord 6 million feet long?"

"Maybe we can use an adaptor," Ray said, "Like we use for cell phones and GPS units."

"Ray, have you seen the size of that thing? Would you say that an oxygen concentrator requires a little bit more juice than a cell phone?" Tara said.

"Why can't we just use cylinders?" Miracle asked.

"I took a quick look at your set up yesterday. You're at 8 liters a minute now, and I'll bet it isn't always enough right?" Tara asked.

"It's not bad. My oxygen level dips in the afternoon and before bed most days, but I can live with that."

"No, you can't. Pretty soon you will need more. Let's be realistic here. The largest cylinder we can probably use is like the ones you have sitting in your bedroom. They're called E cylinders. We're going to need 10 to 12 of them a day if we just drive for 8 hours. At night you can switch back to the concentrator in the hotel room, if we can take it with us." Tara was actually considering Miracle's request.

"Well, that doesn't seem so hard to do. We can rent a van. I can even lie down in it. We'll have room for 30 or 40 cylinders," Miracle said.

"Just a minute. You're assuming we won't run into traffic, or have any car trouble. What if we get stuck in a traffic jam?" Ray asked.

"That's the first intelligent thing you've said all week," Tara said. She smiled at Ray and then turned to Miracle. "Ray's right. A lot can happen on a trip like that. There's no way we can be sure you won't run out of oxygen."

"Couldn't we call 911 if that happens?" Ray asked.

"We can do that, of course," Tara said. "But understand that if the cops get involved, we might have some problems when they see all those oxygen tanks."

"Is it illegal to travel with these things?" Miracle asked.

"No," Tara said, "But transporting oxygen can be dangerous. We get rear-ended or something like that, we're sort of a moving bomb."

"What do you mean?" Ray asked. "Are you making that up to get out of doing this? Because you don't have to do it, believe me."

Tara turned to Ray. "Try to get this Mr. Tennis pro. If oxygen comes into contact with fire, it can make it a lot bigger fast, a huge and really hot fire."

"So it's an accelerant, right?" Ray asked

"Ray, you do amaze me sometimes," Tara said.

"I did go to college, Tara, at least for a little while."

"That was long before I was born. Lord knows what they were teaching back then."

"Well, can we do this?" Miracle asked. "Please?" He fixed Ray with a knowing stare. "Ray, please don't disappoint me, okay? I mean I hate to mention it, but I never disappointed you, right?"

Ray returned Miracle's stare. "Only one time right?" Something unspoken but very tangible passed between the men.

Miracle nodded his head in agreement, "one time."

Ray and Tara looked at each other. Tara spoke. "Will you excuse us for a moment, Miracle?" With that, she took Ray by the hand, and they walked outside. Miracle could see them through the window. At first, they appeared to be arguing. It appeared to Miracle that Ray was trying to persuade Tara to go along. But Tara was shaking her head no. He thought he heard her say, "You can't do that," but he wasn't sure. It took them a full fifteen minutes to get it resolved. They walked back into the condo with grim looks on their faces.

"I don't know how else to say this, Miracle, but here's the thing. I need about $25,000 to get my tennis store up and running. The way I see it, the store plus what I can pick up giving lessons should be enough to keep me from a steady diet of Raman Noodles. Without the store though, well, I'm pretty much screwed."

"Like I said, I can't help you there. I really don't have any money left to speak of."

"Look, I know you want to get to Florida to see Marcia and the kid and all, but you're asking for a really big favor here. I mean what if you die or something on the way?"

Miracle stared hard into Ray's eyes, not quite able to believe what he was hearing. He glanced over at Tara, who was staring intently at her shoes. "What are you saying, Ray? If I don't come up with $25,000 you won't take me?"

"No, I'll take you either way, but it would mean a lot to me if you could help me out."

"With what? How many times do I have to say it? I don't have the cash."

Ray walked over to the window. He pulled back the curtain. "How much is that Packard worth?"

Miracle coughed. It was a long horrible cough. For a moment Tara wondered if he would die right there. Finally he stopped. He wiped his eyes and blew his nose. He smiled and shook his head. When it came to what he needed, Ray could be a fast thinker. "Okay Ray. If I give you the car, will you take me to Florida?" Miracle asked.

"Like I said, I'll take you either way paisan. But, my hustling days will be over soon. I need your help, that's all."

Miracle looked to Tara for confirmation. "I'll do it on one condition. You both agree that I'm in charge. We do what I say all the way down the line. Agreed?"

Both men nodded.

The first thing Tara did was ask where Miracle's computer was. He told her it was in the room with his concentrator. She used Google Earth to look up Marcia's address. What they found was depressing. They could see Marcia was living in a dilapidated mobile home, confirming Miracle's worst fears. Obviously, Marcia's life was a struggle.

There was a lot to do in the next few hours to get ready. Tara and Ray's bags were already packed. As a first order of business, Tara assigned Ray to pack a bag for Miracle, instructing him carefully in what to pack. Then she got to work getting some cash together. She told Miracle to give her his ATM card and password. Miracle looked at Ray, momentarily concerned that Tara might scam both of them.

But Ray gave Miracle a reassuring smile. Miracle was embarrassed by his concern. He handed his card and password over. "Sorry Tara, I didn't mean anything by it."

Tara laughed and patted Miracle's arm. "Your card probably has a $500 a day limit on withdrawals. We'll need enough to cover about ten days worth of expenses including our trip back to New Jersey. Do you have $5,000 in your accounts we can tap?"

"No, but I don't think we'll need that much. I don't think I'll be coming back. Anyway, we can use one of my credit cards if we need something extra."

Ray was about to say something reassuring, wanting to tell Miracle of course he would be coming home, but Tara, anticipating Ray's reaction, stared him down.

"Ray, get the rental car back to the airport and pick up a van." Tara was fully in charge now. "We're going to have to get it rigged up so Miracle can travel in as much comfort as possible."

"How do I pay for it?" Ray asked.

Tara shrugged. "Let's see," she said. "Miracle, are you up to taking a ride with Ray?"

"Sure, but I can't leave until after I see the hospice nurse. She'll be here in about thirty minutes."

While they waited for the nurse to arrive, Miracle had Ray get a strong box that was stored in his bedroom closet. He instructed Ray to open the box and look for the title to the Packard. Ray found it and handed it to Miracle. "I'm going to sign the title over to you now, okay?"

"I'm not sure that's a good idea, Miracle," Ray said. "Do you know anybody that would buy it so we don't have to drive it down there? I would hate to take that chance if I didn't have to, you know? Driving a car that old all the way to Florida, who knows what might happen to it?"

"I see your point. Actually, I do know a guy who would jump at the chance to buy it." Miracle picked up the phone and made a call. Five minutes later he had the car sold for exactly $25,000. When he got off the phone he called out to Ray who was busy packing his bag. He said, "An old friend of mine bought the

Packard. He'll be here by noon tomorrow with a check. You can start planning your pro shop immediately."

Ray walked in from the bedroom. He smiled. It wasn't a happy smile. It was his turn to be embarrassed. He walked over to Miracle. He bent down and kissed his check. The two men looked at each other, neither saying a word. No words were necessary.

The hospice nurse came and stayed fifteen minutes. She took Miracle's vital signs, and then settled in to watch a few minutes of a show Miracle was watching about Italian pastry. The chef was making sfogliatelli, a classic Italian pastry with ricotta filling. He had Ray and Tara, already back from the bank, sit with him on the couch, and introduced them as dear friends from Florida.

The nurse, a woman of considerable heft and desperately trying to lose weight, decided she had to leave because the pastry was making her hungry again.

As soon as the nurse left, Ray helped Miracle, cylinder between his knees, get into the wheelchair and rolled him down to the car. They headed for the rental car center at the airport and rented a Ford Econoline van using Miracle's credit card. On the way back to the condo, they passed an Italian bakery. "You think that nurse is in there picking up some sfogliatelli?" Ray asked.

By the time they got home, the woman from the Friendly Visitor Service was there. She was young and very enthusiastic as if she was about to tell Miracle he won an all expenses paid trip to the Azores. She told Miracle that the Friendly Visitor Service would arrange to send someone to his home every day. The visitor would fix his lunch and do some routine chores, like vacuuming and dusting. If he wanted her to do his laundry, that service would cost a few bucks more.

Miracle listened to her explain everything. He nodded politely, but didn't ask any questions. When she finished, Miracle told her he wanted to sleep on it. He promised to call her the next day around noon. By then, he would be crossing the Delaware Memorial Bridge, if everything went as planned.

As soon as the woman pulled out of her parking space Tara got down to business. "I have everything packed, except your meds. It looks like you have enough of everything for about seven days worth. Are you sure about this?"

He shrugged. "I'm sure."

Chapter 6

"How are we going to get the cylinders we need?" Ray asked. "We need about 40, right?"

"I've been thinking about that," Tara said. "It won't be easy. Oxygen requires a doctor's prescription." She turned to Miracle. "You have a delivery scheduled for tomorrow morning, right?"

Miracle nodded. "Not sure how many I'll get though. My daughter told me Doctor Cardoza is about to cut back on how many get delivered so I can't drive anymore."

"Uh-huh, well here's what I'm thinking," Tara said. "We need to get a little bit lucky here. When the delivery guy comes to the house, Miracle and I will distract him for a while. Ray, you see if you can empty his van. Just take as many cylinders that look like the ones Miracle already has and put them in our van. Then, you take off for a while."

"What if he doesn't have enough cylinders? Forty sounds like a lot of cylinders to carry around, doesn't it?"

"You mean you want to steal them?" Miracle asked.

"Can you think of a better alternative?" Tara asked. She was pacing between the couch and the TV. "That's true, Ray, he might not have that many, but it's a start. Like I said, we need to be lucky here. I need to look at the back of the van you guys picked up. Where are the keys?"

Ray threw her the keys. As soon as she left, Miracle said, "Ray, where did you say you found this girl?"

"What I said. I met her in the bar at one of the tennis resorts in Miami. She's a piece of work, isn't she?"

"She is that," Miracle said. "The question is, what is she doing with you? You're 30 years older than she is. Your interest in her seems obvious enough, but what is she doing with you?"

Ray smiled. "You mean what's in this for her? It isn't exactly how you think it is my friend. She's a good kid, high spirited and obviously she loves an adventure. I think she's still trying to find herself."

"It just seems odd that she would be so willing to get tied up with a caper like this. She just met me and she really doesn't know much about you."

"Did you just say caper?" Both men laughed.

Tara came back into the condo, a serious look on her face. "I have another job for you Ray. Go find some racks to hold the cylinders. We have plenty of room in the back of the van, but we can't have oxygen tanks rolling around while we ride."

"Where am I supposed to get them? Does Wal-Mart carry them?"

"Start with the Yellow Pages, Ray. And Miracle, you need to get some rest, big day tomorrow."

Miracle nodded in agreement. He was tired. He managed to pull himself away from his recliner and shuffle his way to his bedroom. About half-way there, he turned and faced Ray and Tara. "I just want to say thank you to both of you. You have no idea how much this means to me. And, listen, if I die somewhere on the road, just dump my body at the next rest stop."

"Don't say a thing like that," Ray said. "Our highways have enough litter on them now."

"Well, I didn't mean it literally, Ray. I just want you both to know that no matter what happens, this is what I wanted. I want to see Marcia one last time, and I want to meet my son."

"We'll get you there Miracle, don't worry about that," Tara said.

"One more thing, I need to see a lawyer," Miracle said. "Ray, see if you can get Tommy Price to come over here later this afternoon, say around 4 o'clock."

"I remember Tommy. Is he your lawyer?"

Miracle nodded. "His office is only about 5 minutes from here. Call him. His number is in my book." He gestured to a burgundy colored address book sitting on the end table near his recliner.

"What do you want me to tell him? Ray asked.

"Just tell him I need to see him. He'll come."

By the time Miracle woke up from his nap, a lot of work had been done. He looked at the clock on his nightstand and saw it was 4:45. He had slept most of the afternoon away. When he walked into his living room he saw Tommy Price sitting on the couch, waiting patiently for him. Miracle wasted no time getting to the point. He explained the situation to Tommy, about Jagger and Marcia and what he wanted done, which was to leave the condo in trust to Jagger. He wanted his will amended to specify that. Tommy would serve as the trustee.

"Are you sure about this, Miracle? It's been years since you've seen or heard from this woman. A lot can change in that amount of time. I hate to say it, but it could be a scam."

"I understand. And thanks for your concern, Tommy, but I doubt that very much," Miracle said. Ray sat there mulling over what he just heard. He thought Miracle would be better off leaving the house to him just in case. If it was a scam he, Ray, would be sure to turn the property over to Miracle's kids. He wanted to suggest it but thought better of the idea. With his track record, he wasn't likely to be taken seriously.

"One more thing, Miracle," Tommy said, "There isn't any problem doing this. Just be aware that your children could contest that part of the will." Then he took one more shot at changing Miracle's mind. "Is there any concrete proof beyond Marcia's letter proving your paternity?"

"No. But I am certain that Marcia wouldn't make up a thing like that," Miracle said.

"Your kids could insist on a DNA test you know."

Miracle had not considered that. As sure as he was about the kind of woman Marcia was, he realized Tommy was only trying to protect him. "If my kids want to do that, there isn't a thing I can do about it. I'll be gone. But I think when they see they have an older brother, they'll do the right thing. If any of this becomes a problem, you can explain everything to them. Let them know this is what I wanted. Ray will back you up. They'll understand." His tone made it clear that no further discussion was necessary. He wanted it done.

"I'll take care of it," the lawyer said. In his many years of experience, he had learned that when it came to money, there would always be a problem. He could see that Miracle wasn't in any condition to think things through. For a moment, he wondered whether Miracle really had the mental capacity to change his will. It was a moot point. He would do what his long time client asked. "I'll have an amendment to your will ready for your signature tomorrow morning."

As soon as he left, Ray told Miracle that he had indeed found the oxygen cylinder racks, bought them and put them in the van. He also stopped at a body shop and had them secured to the van's walls. "I had to slip the guy at the body shop $100 to get him to do it. When he saw it was a rental, he said no."

"Good work, Ray."

Tara had been busy too. While he was sleeping, Doctor Cardoza's office called. She pretended to be Melanie and requested refills on all his prescriptions. She said she would come by to pick them up within an hour. She waited fifteen minutes before she jumped in the van and went to the doctor's office, hoping the receptionist wouldn't ask any questions.

"How did that go?" Miracle asked.

"Well, I got them but only because I got lucky. The receptionist was smart enough to ask me for some identification, but when I explained to her that my married name was different than yours, she said she couldn't release the prescriptions."

"Then what happened?"

"I said, call my father. He'll tell you who I am. I gave her Ray's cell number. She was too lazy to look up your number so she picked up the phone and got Ray. He told her I was there just as he asked, and get this; he thanked her for being so cautious."

"I've been a con man for 35 years and you guys act like I'm some Rube who can't tie his own shoes," Ray said.

"Did you just say Rube?" Again, the men laughed.

"Was there an oxygen prescription included?" Miracle asked.

"No, sorry."

The three of them settled in for the long evening ahead. They ate some Chinese takeout and watched the history channel for a while. All of them were restless. Miracle read for a while hoping he could fall asleep in his recliner. His mind was working overtime. Sleep was out of the question.

At 10:30, Tara said, "I'm going to bed. We leave tomorrow as soon as we deposit the check for the Packard. Miracle, you'll have to write a check to Ray."

"I could just sign it over to him," Miracle said.

"No, it should be a cashiers check for the amount drawn from the bank just to be sure there are no questions. We don't want any complications," Ray said.

"Ray, it will be a cashier's check," Miracle said. "Did you think I was going to take a personal check and hand over the keys like I'm handing over 25 grand to you?"

Ray looked at Tara, and then at Miracle. "I know what you're thinking, buddy. That money really is exactly for what I told you it was."

"I'm sure it is Ray."

"Okay, but let me put your mind to rest." Ray got up and went to his suitcase. He opened it and rummaged around for the paperwork. "Here is the paperwork for the pro shop. I'm thinking of calling it Straight Sets. I've got a backer who will own a small part of the business. We already have a strip mall in a neighborhood not far from where I play most of my matches now."

Miracle waved him off, refusing to look at the papers Ray tried to hand him. "Straight Sets? When did you ever win a match in straight sets?" Miracle had his doubts about Ray's intentions, of course. There was a time when Miracle would have questioned Ray's deal; would have asked him how he could get a pro shop up and running with just $25,000, who would back him when he had no experience running a business? Now, of course, he didn't have the energy. As far as he was concerned the Packard was the price of getting Ray and Tara to take him to Florida before he died. Whatever happened to Ray's deal, Miracle would be long gone before it played out.

"What time is your oxygen usually delivered?" Tara asked.

"I don't know, it varies. I think usually in the afternoon though."

"Let's just hope he doesn't get here while you're trying to get your car thing taken care of. Timing is important now. Do you have the title to the car ready?" Tara asked.

"I do."

It rained hard that night, a seemingly endless line of thunderstorms passing through. Miracle had insisted on sleeping in his recliner. He wanted to be sure that Tara would have a bed of her own to sleep in. She protested, insisting that she would prefer the couch. Ray made the same offer but Miracle stubbornly refused. Ray slept in the small bedroom where the concentrator was. Miracle insisted the concentrator be moved to the living room so the constant thump the machine made wouldn't keep Ray awake. Miracle didn't expect to get much sleep anyway. He was right about that. He didn't get much sleep. Not only was his head still spinning as he contemplated what he was about to do, the storms kept him awake. He was resigned to the fact that a lot could go wrong on a long road trip considering his condition.

Even if the trip went without incident, he realized he was

probably shortening what remained of his life. The thought didn't bother him. He was tired of living like this, mostly confined to his condo with nothing but worsening conditions to look forward to. Television, lots of reading and the occasional visitor distracted him, but even that wasn't working as well as it had in the past. Faced with the inescapable reality that he was dying, breath by miserable breath, he welcomed the end.

When morning finally arrived, he felt weaker than usual. Both Ray and Tara had to help him get a shower. He managed to get a T-shirt on, but Ray had to help him get into his trousers. The three of them ate a solid breakfast of scrambled eggs, toast, juice and coffee that Tara made   but had very little to say to each other. It was still raining. Around 9 o'clock, the phone rang. It was Miracle's friend, Mitch, the guy who was buying the Packard. "Miracle," he said, "it's still raining hard. I'm thinking maybe we should do this tomorrow when I can get a better look at the car in the sunlight."

Miracle knew they couldn't wait another day. Every day was precious now. "Mitch, we have to do it today. This morning if possible, because I am going to be very busy tomorrow with doctor appointments."

"Then we'll do it the day after that. There's no rush." It was getting worse.

"Listen, I hate to do this to you, but I'm not going to wait until tomorrow or the next day. Truth is, I have another offer for the car. It's higher than yours, but I promised you I would give you first shot. If you want the car, be here no later than 10:30, today."

There was a long silence on the other end of the phone. Mitch had been pestering Miracle for years to sell him the car. He didn't want to lose out now. Finally he said, "Okay Miracle. I'll be there."

"Oh, and one more thing. Make the check payable to Raymond Rosario."

"Well done," Ray said when Miracle flipped the lid on his cell.

"I'm learning from the best."

Then the doorbell rang. Tara answered the door. A short, handsome young man with a well trimmed beard, about Tara's age, stepped into the foyer. He asked for Mister Morgan. He was one of Tommy Price's interns. He had the amendment to the will Miracle requested the night before. He showed Miracle where to sign, and had Tara and Ray sign as witnesses. He was obviously smitten with Tara, but she ignored him. No time for any delays.

The sale of the Packard though, didn't go as smoothly as they hoped. The buyer, Mitch, got there on time, but he took a long time going over the car. He asked a lot of questions. Suddenly, he seemed to be having second thoughts. He questioned whether all the parts were original. He wanted to know if Miracle had any spare parts, when the last tune up was done and who did it. Miracle sat in his wheelchair next to the car, patiently answering Mitch's questions while sucking down precious oxygen. Then Tara thought to send the 50 foot tubing from the concentrator through the window so Miracle could use that instead of wasting the gas from his cylinder.

Finally the guy said he would buy the car. Only there was a problem getting the money so quickly. He said he had to sell one of his other classic cars first. He offered Miracle a down payment of $2,500 to hold the car for about a week, he said.

It was getting too hot for Miracle to stay outdoors. He suggested they go into the condo to discuss the matter. "Listen Mitch, if you want the car you have to buy it today. As I said, I have another buyer."

"Well, I hate to lose the car, but I can't give you twenty-five grand today," Mitch said.

"What is the most you could give me?"

"I can get maybe $17,000 together today."

"Not good enough. You'll have to do a lot better than that."

"What can I tell you?" Mitch said.

Miracle shook his head. He was still sitting in his wheelchair next to his recliner. "I'm sorry we couldn't get this done today. I was hoping I could sell the car to someone I know would take proper care of it. I have a feeling my other buyer is going to chop it up for parts. He's been known to do it before. From what I hear, he thinks he can actually make more that way, especially considering how primo this car looks."

Mitch gave Miracle an appraising look. He hated guys who, in his opinion, mistreated classics like the Packard. "What if I could get you twenty grand by three o'clock this afternoon?"

"Make it twenty-two by 2:00 p.m. and we're done."

Mitch smiled and stuck out his hand. "I can have a check ready in twenty minutes. Spell Rosario for me."

Under other circumstances, Miracle would have balked as soon as the guy said he could have the check so quickly after all. He would have forced the guy to pay more. He had been a car salesman and a good one. None of that mattered now. He was on a mission.

At 2:15, Miracle's doorbell rang. It was the guy from the homecare company delivering the oxygen tanks. Ray let him in. The driver walked into Miracle's bedroom and saw that he had three full cylinders. "Where's the other three?"

Tara spoke up. "Oh, didn't you see them out by the curb?"

"No, I didn't. I'll be right back."

Just as they hoped, the driver placed the three empty cylinders in the back of the delivery van and pulled out two full ones. He shut, but neglected to lock the door. It was the break they had been praying for. Then he walked back into the house. "I'm taking the three empties and giving you two full ones, doctor's orders. I'll let you keep the extra one, which gives you five full tanks but your maximum is now four. When I come back in two weeks that's what I have to leave you with."

"Would you please check his concentrator?" Tara asked very

sweetly. She was again wearing the halter top, but that day, she also wore short-shorts and high heels. The outfit was obviously having the desired effect. In the meantime, Ray was busy pulling cylinders out of the homecare van and loading them into the rental van. Earlier that day, Tara made him pick up an empty and a full cylinder several times to be sure he would recognize the difference and take only full cylinders out of the truck. He took his time, confident that Tara would keep the hapless driver busy for a while. Also, he didn't want to give anyone who might be observing what he was doing the idea that it wasn't a perfectly normal thing to do. They had arranged things so that as soon as it looked like the driver was about to leave, Miracle would call Ray on his cell so he could shut down his little operation.

Tara did a great job of keeping the driver busy. She saw the name Matt on his company issued shirt. "Is Matt short for Matthew?"

"As a matter of fact, it is," he said, smiling. The guy was in his late 40s. He wore long sideburns no doubt to make him look younger, or so he hoped. Flirting with caregivers and the patients' daughters were one of the few pleasures of his work.

Tara got Matt to explain how the equipment worked, asking him how long he had worked for the company and complimenting him on his knowledge and fine manners. Still, when Ray got the call, he had transferred just 28 cylinders. With the five that were sitting in the condo, they would still be short of their goal by seven cylinders. Regardless, even if Miracle needed 10 liters per minute, they had every reason to believe they could make it to Marcia's with oxygen to spare. They were good for at least 33 hours, about a 12 hour cushion, considering how long a drive they had ahead of them. They didn't have as much leeway as Tara wanted, but it would have to do.

When the driver left the condo and got into his van, Miracle and Tara gave each other a high five. So far, so good.

Chapter 7

Mitch made it back to the condo as promised with a cashier's check made out to Ray for $22,000. He even helped Ray load the van, getting Miracle's recliner into the back. When he asked what was going on, Ray told him Miracle was buying a new recliner, and he, Ray, was buying the old one. It was left to Ray and Tara to load the suitcases and a box Tara had filled with medical devices and soft goods Miracle would need; extra nasal cannulas, boxes of tissues, an extra oxygen regulator, which was required to regulate the flow of gas from the cylinders, his wheelchair and, of course, the 10 liter oxygen concentrator.

At least ten times, Miracle asked Tara if she packed his nebulizer compressor, his respiratory medications, and his other meds. She was very patient with him. Miracle kept his pulse oximeter, which would tell him what his oxygen saturation level was, in his shirt pocket. If it fell below 85%, he would know he was in trouble. After the van was finally loaded, Miracle inspected it and nodded approvingly. His recliner was situated to minimize its movement. Still, they would have to be careful to avoid sudden stops.

"Anybody you want to call and say goodbye to?" Ray asked.

Miracle looked down at his hands while he gave that some thought. Once he was diagnosed, he gradually lost touch with most of his friends. He began avoiding them, not wanting their pity. Sure, there might be a couple of people he should call but what would he say? He looked up at Ray. "No, I don't think so."

By 3 o'clock that afternoon, Miracle, Ray and Tara were on the road. Miracle dropped his letters to Melanie and Brian in the outgoing mailbox that sat just outside his condo development. Just before they left, he ran into Mrs. MacBrien, the woman who helped out with his parking situation. She was retrieving her mail. Miracle stopped her and asked if she would mind keeping an eye on the place. "I'm going away for a few days. I have an appointment with a pulmonary specialist who is doing experimental procedures."

"Oh my! Do you believe he might be able to help?" Mrs. MacBrien asked.

"Not sure. At this point every option is a longshot, but there's no harm in trying."

"Do you have very far to go?"

Miracle was surprised by the question. He never anticipated it. Mrs. MacBrien wasn't nosy, but she was inquisitive. Instinctively, he looked at Tara who was standing within earshot of their conversation. "No, not at all, we should be back by Friday, Saturday at the latest." Mrs. MacBrien, a quizzical look on her face, promised to keep an eye on the condo.

Tara quickly got behind his chair and started pushing him toward the van. She wasn't taking any chances that Miracle might say more than he needed to say.

They made a quick stop at Miracle's bank too. He withdrew another $500 from the ATM. Then Ray wheeled him into the bank so he could withdraw $3,000 from his savings account, which left him with just under $12,000. He handed Ray the cash without a word. A deal was a deal. Ray now had his $25,000 to work with.

Miracle wasted no time checking out his recliner. He had no trouble falling asleep either. He was out cold before they reached the first toll booth on the Garden State Parkway. He didn't wake up until they were about to cross the Delaware Memorial Bridge. "What time is it?" he asked.

"We're right at 7:00 p.m. buddy. Are you hungry?"

"Yes, a little bit. I need a restroom too, pretty damn soon."

"As soon as we get over the bridge we'll get you taken care of."

Ray parked the car at the first restaurant he could find. They were in Delaware. For Miracle, actually being out of New Jersey, made it feel like it was really happening now. He took care of business and they headed to the restaurant. He ordered meatloaf and mashed potatoes. During dinner, he got a call from his daughter.

"Dad, where are you?"

"Hi Melanie," he said, his tone casual. "Out to dinner with Ray."

"Where out to dinner?"

"What difference does that make? Do you need something?"

"Dad, I'm at your condo. I brought Mom to see you. Where's your recliner?"

"Oh, that. I spilled some chili on it. Made a mess. I had to send it out to be reupholstered."

"I see. What time will you be home?"

Ray and Tara were exchanging glances, worried that Miracle was already going to have problems with his kids. They could claim he didn't know what he was doing. Tara whispered to Ray, "What if they say we kidnapped him?"

"Now, you're asking that question?" he couldn't help it. He was laughing.

"I'll be home in a couple of hours," Miracle said. "Don't worry, I have enough cylinders with me."

"I'm sure you do," Melanie said. "You took all of them with you. And where is your concentrator? What is going on Dad?"

Ray gave Tara a smile. "Stop worrying," he said.

But Miracle was beginning to worry. He had assumed when he dropped his letters to Brian and Melanie in the mail, he would be in Florida by the time they had any idea of what was going on. "Melanie, there's nothing to worry about. I'm just taking a short excursion. Now, no offense intended, but I really don't want to see your mother. Rather, I don't want her to see me like this. You can understand that. Take her home. I'll call you later."

"I'm worried about you. Mom wants to know where that nut

case Ray is taking you."

"Out to dinner. Just like I said. And I will thank your mother to stay out of my business."

"No need to get prickly Dad. We're just worried about you."

"Don't be. Really. I'm fine. I'll call you tomorrow." With that, he hit the end call button and returned to his meatloaf.

The trio decided to stop for the night just before 9:00 p.m. outside of Baltimore. They were all tired. To save money, they decided to get two rooms. They asked for connecting rooms. Ray and Miracle would sleep in one room. Tara would have the room next door. The door between the rooms would remain open so Tara could quickly reach Miracle should the need arise.

Knowing Ray, Miracle assumed that sometime during the night Ray would slip into bed with Tara. He didn't believe what Ray told about his relationship with Tara. Why else would he take a pretty young woman on a trip home unless she was providing comfort? Miracle had no objection to the arrangement. Certainly he thought Tara was much too young for Ray. Maybe because he liked her, it bothered him that she was wasting time on him. As he lay in bed thinking about it, he could see clearly now what perhaps only the dying could see. Time is precious. One shouldn't waste any of it on fruitless pursuits.

Certainly, Ray would have disagreed, strenuously so. Ray spent his entire life in pursuit of trivial pleasures. And Miracle had to admit, he seemed happier than a lot of guys he knew who had done more with their lives. Whether he, Miracle, had done more with his life than Ray, he couldn't say. Certainly considering the advantages he had enjoyed, he was in no position to boast. Just before he dozed off, he had an epiphany. He wasn't making the trip just for Jagger and Marcia. The trip was for him, a last hurrah, and one last chance to do something important and do it right.

Miracle woke up the next morning feeling very sick. He wasn't getting enough air in his lungs. He was confused.

"Where am I," He asked.

Ray looked at Tara, worried. "You're in a motel room just outside of Baltimore," Tara answered.

"Why? The hospice nurse is going to be at my condo in a couple of hours. Are we going to get there in time?"

"Oh boy. Now what?" It was Ray.

"Talk to him, Ray. He'll come around."

"What do I say to him?"

"Ray, he's right in front of you. Tell him what we're doing," Tara said.

"Hey, Miracle, we're on the road to Florida, our old stomping ground, to see Marcia, remember?"

"Marcia? Does she know we're coming?"

"No, we're going to surprise her. You want to see your son, Jagger."

Miracle reached for his glasses and put them on. "We're going to Florida?"

"Yes we are. It was what you wanted Miracle. But, if you've changed your mind, we can go back to New Jersey," said Tara.

Looking around the room and taking a few deep breaths, Miracle's head began to clear. He looked at Ray and then back at Tara. He took a few more deep breaths. He was conscious of the concentrator now humming and thumping along. "Good morning," he said.

"Welcome back," Ray said, "You had us worried there for a second."

Miracle waved his friend off. "It happens sometimes. I get a little confused. Where did you say we are?"

Ray smiled. "Baltimore, paisan."

"What time are we leaving?"

"As soon as we get cleaned up and have breakfast," Tara said. "Ray, why don't you go get us some juice and English muffins or something? You like English muffins, Miracle?

"That's fine. How's our oxygen situation?"

"Not bad. We went through 4 tanks yesterday. We have 29 left," Ray said.

"How many hours are we going to be on the road today?" Miracle asked.

Tara said, "About ten hours if you can handle it."

"I'll be alright. Where would that put us?"

Tara looked at Ray. "What's the plan mister deuce court?"

"I looked at the map. We should be near Atlanta. If we push it an extra hour or so we could be in the heart of the city."

"We're not going to push it, Ray," Tara said.

"Maybe we can just see how we're doing," Miracle said. "Obviously, the faster we get there, the better it is, if you know what I mean."

Tara nodded. "Let's cross that bridge when we come to it."

They were on the road by 8:45, Ray doing the driving. The plain white van was well equipped; fully air conditioned which had been a must. It was also customized, which was a lucky discovery at the rental car counter. The vehicle had four tan, leather captain's chairs that swiveled just enough so the front seat passenger could turn partially around and talk to someone in the backseat. The oxygen cylinder racks were attached to the interior walls of the truck on both sides of the recliner. On the floor in front of them were the medical supplies. The luggage each of them brought was put in the back against the van's back door. Ray also managed to fit a cooler he found in Miracle's garage between the captain's chairs in the rear compartment. The only complication they foresaw was getting Miracle from his seat into the recliner when he needed a rest. That challenge would require both Tara's and Ray's help.

As they rode down I-95, Tara was able to face Miracle, who was seated in the driver's side rear passenger seat, and talk to him. Miracle was looking at his cell phone. "I don't think I should turn this thing on," he said, "it's been off since I talked to Melanie last night."

"Are you sure that's a good idea?" Tara asked.

"No good can come from any calls I might get. Sooner or later, I'm sure both Melanie and Brian will be calling me."

They rode on through Baltimore, through the McHenry Tunnel toward Virginia. Miracle said, "It's been years since the last time I did this, but I made this trip a lot when I was in college."

"Did you go to Florida for spring break?" Tara asked.

"Oh no, I went to the University of Miami. I went to New Jersey for spring break several times though. Starting my sophomore year I spent a lot of time with two other guys from New Jersey that went to Miami U with me. One of them had a twin sister who was in some of my classes, as I recall. The four of us used to jump in my car and go home, not just during breaks but when the spirit moved us and we had the time. Sometimes we would miss a day or two of classes, but that wasn't uncommon back then. We'd leave on a Thursday afternoon and drive straight through. We usually made it in less than 24 hours."

"That must have been fun for you," Tara said. "Do you ever see your friends?"

Miracle shook his head. "Not for years. I really have no idea what happened to them except for Marianne, one of the twins. She was always interested in politics. She was a rabid anti-war activist during the Vietnam War. Later on she worked on Jimmy Carter's presidential campaign. Coincidentally, she met my first wife Sandy in law school, which is how I found out about her involvement in the Carter campaign. I believe she also worked in the Clinton Administration. After Sandy and I got divorced, I never heard anything about her again." Miracle was out of breath and needed to rest. He put his hand up to signal he needed a break.

"Don't worry, Miracle. We have a long ride ahead of us. Take as many breaks as you need," Tara said.

"Might be easier if I ask you some questions and you talk for a while."

"I'm afraid my story is boring, but I'll try," Tara said. "What would you like to know?"

"Start anywhere you like. Your story will lead to questions, I promise." He smiled.

"Well, I was born in Los Angeles. I never knew my father. My mother, bless her heart, was an actress. She had some roles in soap operas and did a little modeling. She never married. She died of liver cancer. Funny, she never drank. Anyway, maybe it was being in Los Angeles and my mother being in the business that got me interested in acting. That, plus just about every kid living out there has the movie star dream at one time or another."

"Did you get to do any acting?"

"I did," she laughed. "My mother had a good friend who got me a bit part in a movie nobody ever heard of. After that, it was all down hill."

"What was your mother's name?"

"Her given name was Dana, but nobody ever called her that."

"What did they call her?"

"Oh well, she had a few nicknames over the years. Mom was a colorful woman. She always had lots of friends, and there was always some drama going on around her." She smiled her head down, looking at her bracelet. It was obvious she didn't want to talk about her mother.

"What made you decide to become a nurse?" Miracle asked.

"My friend Gayle, another wannabe actress with no prospects, talked me into it. She was going to nursing school and she didn't want to do it alone. Then she decided to quit after just three semesters. She wound up being an agent, you know, representing actors. She was doing well until she met a guy, fell in love and got married. She moved to Minnesota. I haven't heard from her in a few years."

"But you stuck with it."

"Yeah, I kind of got into it and finished. Funny isn't it?"

"Hey guys, not to interrupt, but it looks like we are running into traffic here," Ray said. They were just outside of Alexandria, Virginia.

"How bad is it?" Miracle asked, straining to see through the front windshield.

Ray rolled the van to a stop behind a semi, tractor-trailer with a huge Sunbeam Bread logo on the back. "I can't see anything ahead right now," Ray said.

"I never thought about this," Miracle said. "What if I run low on cylinders?"

"We'll be fine Miracle," Tara said. "Worst case is we'll get off the interstate and find a place where we can plug in your concentrator."

Miracle was beginning to panic. "That's all well and good, but what if we run short of cylinders? How am I going to make it to Florida?"

Ray answered quickly. "We have enough for at least 30 hours, maybe more. Our trip to Bonita Springs will be less than 22 hours drive time, Miracle. Tara and I calculated all of this. Don't worry."

"That's easy for you to say, Ray. You aren't in any danger of suffocating to death." Miracle's breath rate increased. He took out his pulse oximeter and took a reading. "I'm down to 88%. It's dropping. I'm going to need more like 10 liters per minute. Did you calculate that too Ray?"

"Yeah, we did, Miracle." The traffic was still at a standstill. "That still gives us about 29 hours."

"Well that's just not enough leeway," Miracle said.

Tara took his hand and spoke to him. "Miracle, you need to calm down. Now, we can turn around and go back to your condo if you want to, that is up to you."

"Maybe we should do that," Miracle said.

"Ray, as soon as you can, let's get this thing turned around and head back north," she said.

Chapter 8

Ray managed to get the van over to the right lane only a half-mile from the exit. It took him a full forty minutes to get close to the exit. Then traffic started moving again. He turned his head toward Miracle. "Paisan, we're moving again. What do you want to do?"

Miracle shrugged. "Keep going, I guess."

Within a few minutes, they were back up to speed, traveling at 75 miles per hour. They were in Virginia now, hoping to make it to Petersburg around lunch time where they would jump on I-85. Miracle and Tara picked up their conversation again.

"So, how did you wind up with a washed up tennis pro?"

"I was in Miami looking for work. I met a guy at a job fair who happened to be a tennis fanatic. I met the king of the backhand drop shot at the club where my friend played."

"That's it? Did he pick you up at the bar? That's what he told me."

"Well, that's what he thinks happened, but maybe I was looking for him, had it all planned out, you know?"

"Did you?" Miracle smiled.

Tara smiled in return. Then she said, "Have you thought about what you'll say to Marcia when you see her?"

"You changing the subject on me?"

"I am."

"Well, I don't know what I'll say to her. Haven't had a chance to think about it actually."

But Miracle had been thinking about it ever since he decided to pay Marcia a visit. Even though he acted as if Marcia's word was unimpeachable, he realized there was no way he could be entirely sure about her after so many years with no contact between them. She had broken off their relationship very abruptly. Considering when they broke up, Jagger must have been born about eight months after the breakup. Suppose it was another guy's kid? Was that possible? He doubted it, discounted it really, based purely on his instincts, which rarely steered him wrong.

Not that he cared, as far as taking care of Jagger now. He always saw himself as an entry level philanthropist anyway. Anyway he had cared plenty enough about Marcia. He would do it for her. And, he reasoned, Brian and Melanie would be fine splitting half a million dollars in life insurance. What he wanted most, what had burned inside him just below the surface for so many years, was to know why she dumped him back then. He had been deeply in love with her. Up until about a week before she sent him packing, he thought everything had been fine between them.

Forty years later, he could look back on those times and understand that there were probably little trouble signs he missed long before the storm hit. The problems, whatever they were, like a mold growing under the kitchen sink, didn't start just a week before they were discovered. He felt he understood women, a conceit he allowed himself for years. Older now, his conceit no longer useful, he saw the error of his ways.

As much as he wanted Marcia to level with him, the problem he wrestled with was how to ask questions in a way that would get an honest answer, notwithstanding what Marcia felt she had at stake, that being Jagger's future. He certainly didn't want her to form an answer that was calculated to satisfy him just to make him more likely to help Jagger.

Why was it so important to him, especially now when his life would soon be over? The answer was simple. Marcia's decision to end their relationship had changed the trajectory of his entire life. After he met her, inspired by her passion for life and making a difference in the lives of others, he changed his major from liberal arts to business. He had no aptitude for the sciences or he would have chosen that discipline in hopes he could be in on the discovery of a cure for cancer or maybe one of the neuromuscular diseases.

He was after all, a child of the Sixties. She suggested business instead, telling him he needed to learn how money made things go. So he changed his major and planned to work for a foundation so he could raise money for a worthy cause. He truly believed that Marcia had helped him to find his purpose in life. He realized of course, that a bad breakup was a ridiculous excuse for not chasing his dreams. But were they his dreams or Marcia's? He realized that it was his love for Marcia that had lit the flame and fueled his ambitions. Without her, he was drifting. His life and Ray's had some parallels. He found it hard to fault his friend for the way he lived his life. And, the way it turned out, Marcia never got the chance to spread her wings either.

"Well, Miracle," Tara said, "maybe you should start thinking about what you're going to say to her. You'll probably see her tomorrow night. Isn't that exciting?"

Miracle gave her a long look. Her face flushed. "Sorry, I guess under the circumstances the word exciting is an exaggeration."

"No, it's not that. I am looking forward to seeing her and even getting a look at Jagger. After that, well, there's nothing but the end."

"Don't be so sure, Miracle," Ray said, turning his head away from the road. "There are some fantastic doctors in Florida. Maybe you'll get a whole new lease on life."

Miracle almost said, "well, one of us will," but he saw no point in being sarcastic. Instead, he said, "I need to make a pit stop and then lie down for a while."

Once the restroom business was out of the way, Tara and Ray got Miracle into the recliner. Tara gave him a cup of juice to sip. She also set up his battery operated nebulizer kit so he could take his respiratory meds. Less than twenty minutes later, he was sound asleep.

Ray and Tara rode in silence for a while. The sound of the tires on the pavement and the occasional vehicle flying by them provided the only diversions from the tedium of the road. The endless rows of pine trees that lined both sides of the highway punctuated the silence. Ray glanced over at Tara and noticed something he hadn't seen before. Something was troubling her. "You look like someone who was just sentenced to twenty years for a crime you wished you didn't commit."

"Do I?"

"Yeah, what's up kiddo?"

"It's good that he can sleep," Tara said, glancing back at Miracle. "He is struggling. I checked his O2 saturations and he's at 86%. If we can't get it up to 90% soon, we might have to give him a higher liter flow."

Ray was about to ask why she changed the subject, but thought better of it. One problem at a time was how he taught tennis and how he dealt with life. "We sort of anticipated he might need more oxygen, or you did, I suppose. We should be okay," Ray said. "Just in case, do you have any ideas about how we can get him more cylinders?" Ray asked.

"I might. I used to be a sales rep for Perfect Respiratory a while back."

"Sorry but that doesn't mean anything to me, kid."

"They're a huge company with locations in all fifty states. They provide home oxygen services just like the people who delivered oxygen to Miracle's condo."

"So you think you can get one of them to give us some tanks or whatever?"

"They might. Let's hope we don't have to find out."

Miracle slept all the way through to Petersburg. Even with the traffic jam, they were only 30 minutes behind schedule. Ray pulled up at a Taco Bell, but Tara told him to look for a place that offered food that wasn't spicy. "Keep it simple, Ray. I'd rather not take a chance that something disagrees with him. They wound up at Panera Bread instead. Tara woke Miracle and explained they were stopping for lunch. He was confused again.

"What do you mean stopping for lunch? The refrigerator is right in the kitchen."

Tara patiently explained where they were again and what they were doing. This time, Miracle came around quickly, but said he didn't feel well. His chest felt tight, he said. Tara maneuvered herself to where Miracle was reclining. She checked his cylinder and saw it was nearly empty. She switched to a new one. This time, she adjusted the setting to ten liters per minute. This was his fifth cylinder of the morning.

"Ray, go into Panera and get us all something to eat. We'll eat in the car and keep the motor running. When we're done we'll take bathroom breaks and then get going."

"What should I get him?" Ray asked.

"Soup, a roast beef sandwich with tomato and a large lemonade. In fact, get me the same thing."

Ray exited the vehicle and Tara followed him. "You coming in with me, darling?"

"No Ray, I just wanted to talk to you for a minute. He doesn't look good at all. I'll keep an eye on him. I turned up his oxygen. Hopefully, that will help."

"This was really a crazy idea," Ray said, surveying the parking lot.

"I know that. Now we have to make the most of it. Hurry up and get those sandwiches."

When she got into the van, Miracle was waiting for her. "Sorry you agreed to do this?" he said.

"Not at all, Miracle," she lied. "I turned up your O2 so you should feel better very soon now."

"I hope so. I can't see how I can feel much worse."

They spent the next ten minutes quietly chatting. Miracle told Tara about how loyal Ray was when they were in high school together. How Ray kept getting invited to colleges by tennis coaches eager to have him on their squad. He always said the same thing. "You have to check out my friend, Miracle too. He's a great player. You'll definitely want him in your program."

Miracle laughed as he told the story. He was a good player, but he simply wasn't in Ray's league. Some of the coaches gave him a tryout, but they could see he wasn't good enough for a top tennis program. "The nicer ones would encourage me to try a second level school. Some of them weren't as nice. I'll never forget the coach who said, 'You are doing your friend a disservice by even coming here. We both know you don't belong here. Stop wasting people's time. Tell Rosario you're not interested. You're nothing more than a distraction to him and to us.'"

"That must have hurt," Tara said.

"Not really, the guy was right. I was only there to keep Ray company." Miracle blew his nose and took a moment to catch his breath. "Let me tell you something. If I didn't have a date on Saturday night, he wouldn't go out with a girl unless she found me a friend to go out with. We would double date. And he would tell them 'no dogs,' he was that brash. And, he got away with it."

"Somehow I don't find that charming," Tara said.

"No, I guess you wouldn't," Miracle said, but he was smiling.

They ate lunch quickly. Tara barely touched hers. She said the chicken noodle soup was making her nauseous. Ray suggested that Miracle try sitting in one of the captain's chairs in the back. He also told Tara to drive so he could sit in the back next to Miracle so they could talk. At first, Miracle objected, saying Tara wasn't an approved driver by the rental car company. Ray laughed and pointed out that that was the least of their worries. Miracle shrugged and Tara took the wheel.

By the time they reached the North Carolina border, Miracle was feeling better. Eating something had helped, and he was feeling good again about his chances of actually seeing Marcia and Jagger. He and Ray had a good time too reminiscing about their childhood and catching up on the years since then. Tara was playing the radio and not really paying attention to them.

They talked about Miracle's marriage to Sandy, both men agreeing that it had been a mistake. "I knew we were in trouble when we went to that Moody Blues concert. There were eight of us and she and I sat seven seats apart," Miracle said.

"Yeah, that might be a clue that something was up," Ray said. "Did she notice?"

Miracle laughed. "Who knows? I will say she did a great job raising Melanie though."   All the talk tired Miracle out. He used so much energy just to breathe. He really preferred to listen more than talk at this stage. He was happy to turn the focus to Ray's life.

"I've always wondered, you know, you took the D Train in life. How did that work out for you?" Miracle asked.

Ray smiled. "The D Train, huh? I guess you took the A Train paisan, all straight track, no curves, from beginning to end."

"I didn't mean it that way. Listen, I had to navigate a few sharp curves along the line too. What I meant was…"

"I know what you meant. You're right, I followed my nose and that, along with my tennis racquet, took me to some interesting places. Man, I had some good times. I never told anybody this before, but I made a lot of money romancing my clients; some years maybe more than I made giving lessons."

"How did that happen?"

Ray rubbed his palms on his jeans. He opened and closed his right hand, first making a fist, then extending his fingers out straight and pointed upward. He did that to combat the arthritis he felt in his joints. "Let me say first of all, I never asked for a dime. But one day, I was in my early thirties at the time, lying in bed with this girl in her late 20's. I think she lived in Santa Monica. I know I was living in Malibu. Anyway, I mentioned that I was really short of cash and might have to move on. She turned to me and said, 'How much do you need?' I didn't know what to say because I was just making an excuse so I could move on with as little drama as possible, so I came up with the first number that came to mind. I said, 'about $2,000.' The next day she had it for me in an envelope. Well, I was always short of cash anyway but I didn't need that much. Half that amount would have been fine, you know?"

"So you told her that right?"

"Not exactly, no."

"You took the two grand? How did that make you feel?"

"Miracle, I've been through a little therapy with professional therapists and it didn't help much. Ask me something else."

Both men laughed. "Okay, did you ever feel like a scumbag taking all that money from these defenseless women?"

"Now that's much better. No, I never felt bad about it. I never asked for money other than my standard lesson fees. I think a lot of these women were pissed off at their husbands. And when being unfaithful wasn't enough, they gave me some of their husbands' money too."

"So how much do you think you made all told?"

"I don't know, thousands of dollars. Maybe not six figures, but close. One time, a real doll, a 42 year old whose husband was the owner of the resort I was working in Scottsdale, gave me thirty grand so I could open a tennis camp."

Miracle gave Ray a withering look. "Is that right?"

"Wait a minute, Miracle. There really was a tennis camp involved. I'll admit with the Scottsdale babe it turned out to be a pipe dream, but my pro shop is the real thing. Remember the paperwork I have?"

"I don't really care Ray. Real or not, you've been a good friend. Six figures huh? And that doesn't even count what you took from me."

"Excuse me for a moment. I just need to turn off your oxygen supply."

"You would be doing me a favor."

"No, you want to see Marcia first," Ray said.

83

"You would acknowledge that you manipulated these women to get what you needed though," Miracle said.

"Not at all, I never promised any of these women anything. Hell, most of them were already married anyway."

"Was the girl from Santa Monica married?"

"Let me think. No, I don't think she was."

"And she wasn't pissed when you left?"

"Who can remember? If she was, it wasn't as bad as some situations I got myself into." Ray said. "You know, it wasn't always smooth sailing. I'll never forget having to leave Amelia Island in the middle of the night."

"Amelia Island, is that off the coast of Georgia?"

"No, Jacksonville. I didn't even have time to pack"

Miracle raised his eyebrows. "The way you lived, that must have been a huge loss. You left a tennis outfit, a racquet, a can of balls, Trojans and maybe a Bic razor?"

Ray shook his head in mock anger. "I got a call from this woman; her name was Madron. Who could forget a name like that? Anyway, she called me at two in the morning and told me her husband was on his way over to my apartment with a gun."

"Wow!"

"She said he would be there in five minutes. That I should just get out. And it turned out she was right. As I was pulling out of the complex he was pulling in. The son of a bitch jumped out of his car and fired a shot at me."

"Come on Ray, really?"

"True story. I made a couple of calls and found a club in Madrid that needed a teaching pro for a few months."

"Interesting; Is Tara the latest in a long line?" Miracle asked, keeping his voice low.

Ray looked over at Tara to see if she was listening. "I thought so, but maybe I'm finally too old for this. There is something different about her. She's kept me at arm's length longer than any of the others, but to be honest, and I can't believe I'm saying this,

I'm kind of relieved."

The conversation turned to another matter that Miracle had been contemplating while they drove south. "I listen to your stories, and I can't help thinking, Ray, you sure give tennis pros a bad name."

"What do you mean by that?"

"Now don't get pissed off. It's just that in all my years of playing in private clubs and on public courts, I can't remember ever meeting a hustler." Miracle paused to catch his breath. "And I mean club players and club pros. Sure, once in a while a pro would get frisky with one of the member's wives but those guys usually get bounced pretty quickly. Bottom line though is most of the people you meet in tennis are top notch."

"Well I have to say I agree with you on that. People at the club level can be pains in the ass at times, but they tend to be polite and even honorable. Look, when you have to call your opponent's balls in or out in most of your matches, you have to have integrity. The vast majority of tennis players do," Ray said. "Even at the pro level, most of the people in the game are solid. I don't think it's an accident that we haven't had any big doping scandals, if you know what I mean. But then, in all walks of life you get some guys who make their way playing the angles."

Miracle agreed.

Ray looked into Miracle's eyes, wanting his full attention. "You don't think much of me do you?"

"That's where you're wrong. We go back a long way. I know things about you that nobody else does. I can't say I approve of your lifestyle, but that's only because I can't help believing that you could have done more with your life."

"Maybe, but it's a little bit late to be worrying about me, isn't it?"

"You mean because I'm dying and should be worrying about myself?" Miracle asked.

"We're all dying paisan. Just a matter of when. I hate what's happening to you but my future isn't exactly bright either. I'm not trying to compare here. I'm just saying I'm looking down the barrel of old age without a pot to piss in and arthritis in every damn joint," Ray said.

"I understand, but you wouldn't want to trade places with me."

"No, and I wouldn't change a thing. Look, I'm not saying anyone should admire me for what I do or what I've done, far from it, but it's really all I know Miracle. Listen, most of my life, at least since my brief stay at Stanford, has been good. Over the years I got to meet some very interesting people. Did I ever tell you about playing against Jon Lovitz? And I played doubles once with Regis Philbin too. One time I took Donald Trump, yeah, The Donald for a bundle."

"I'll bet you did," Miracle said, a wide smile on his face. Ray was incorrigible.

One of the things about Ray that Miracle thought very few people understood was that he was a born storyteller. Most of his stories contained an element of truth, but Ray loved to add an outlandish detail or two for dramatic effect. He couldn't help himself. Miracle always remembered Ray telling a story at a party about how he and his girlfriend had spent a night in jail. The way he told the story, they had been stopped for speeding in Louisiana. The cop discovered marijuana in the car and put them in jail for the night. He went into some detail about their experience behind bars, saying they had both been made to strip for their mug shots. "It was unbelievable," he said. There were other questionable details as well. He said the judge was a rice farmer who sentenced them to a year without bothering to give them a trial, how they only got out because his girlfriend agreed to go out with the cop who arrested them the next night. Of course, the cop happened to be the judge's son. One of the guys in the crowd listening to Ray's story was a police officer. Irritated by all the exaggerations in Ray's story, he started to point out the discrepancies. That's when Ray's girlfriend, not wanting him to be embarrassed, broke in and said he should stop exaggerating.

Ray turned to her and said, "Don't worry about it. It's a good story. All they care about is that it's a good story."

It was an insight into Ray's personality that made Miracle like him even more. Ray wasn't working on the assumption that people weren't as bright as he was, Ray was merely trying to be entertaining. That he was doing so at his own expense didn't seem to bother Ray. Miracle assumed that as Ray matured, he probably toned down the dramatic license he took, but not completely.

The conversation wound down as the two men talked about Wendy, how she died and how Miracle's life seemed to spiral downward after she was gone. Ray apologized again for not being there. They were passing through Rocky Mount and headed toward Fayetteville. They found the trouble they were desperate to avoid when they reached the little town of Dunn, North Carolina.

Chapter 9

Tara was holding the van steady, doing the speed limit. A careful driver, she kept to the right lane. As Miracle and Ray chatted, she kept her mind busy thinking about what was next for her once Miracle's drama played out. Of course, she heard more of the conversation going on in the backseat than she let on. Ray's cavalier attitude about the women that had touched his life and more or less sustained him, was decidedly unattractive.

The time would come when they would have it out, but she wasn't ready for that yet. Miracle, on the other hand, was something of a mystery to Tara. He seemed so normal. He was courteous and, in spite of the difference in their ages, not condescending, at least not the way many older men were towards her. The fact that he was Ray's friend helped to redeem Ray a little bit in her eyes. She assumed there must be an aspect to Ray that he hadn't revealed to her. When he asked Miracle for the money for the tennis shop, she had been embarrassed even to be in the same room with them. Yet, when push came to shove, Miracle barely batted an eye. He even had the check for the Packard made out directly to Ray to avoid complications that might arise later. Maybe Miracle owed Ray more than either of them let on.

As she often did when on a long trip, she looked at the endless rows of trees, mostly pine, and marveled at the sky's deep blue texture. Tired, she did her best not to stare at the ubiquitous white lines dividing the lanes. They were hypnotic. She checked the van's gas gauge. That got her attention. It was showing about 1/8th of a tank. She would take the next exit and fill up. Just then they came to a hill not exactly steep, but noticeably different than the flat road she'd been driving on for the last twenty minutes.

Suddenly, the van wasn't responding. It seemed to be losing

power. She hit the accelerator and heard the engine roar but the van was losing speed. Tara turned her head toward the back seat. "Ray, the van isn't working right. I can't get any power."

"What are you talking about?" Ray asked.

"I'm losing speed. I'm down to 45 miles per hour. What's going on?"

"Pull over."

"No," Miracle said, "put your flashers on and let the van roll to a stop. Get on the shoulder now. I think the next exit is pretty close."

Tara did what Miracle told her to do. She rode the shoulder until the vehicle came to a stop. "What do I do now?" she asked.

"Are we out of gas?" Ray asked. "What does the gauge say?"

"We're at about 1/8th," Tara answered. She kept hitting the accelerator. She put the vehicle in neutral and then park. She put it back into drive and it started moving again. For a moment, she thought she had solved the problem. But right away, the power was gone again. They rolled to a stop again. The engine roared when she gunned it, but they were obviously in neutral. She repeated her maneuver, switching gears, even trying reverse but nothing happened.

"Is it the transmission?" Ray asked. Miracle nodded. "Probably."

"Now what?" Tara asked.

"We need to get help right away," Miracle answered. "It must be over ninety degrees out there."

The three of them sat in silence for a moment, no one sure of what to do next. Then Miracle remembered he was an AAA member. "Call AAA. Tell them it's an emergency," he said.

"We're low on gas. Maybe you should cut the engine," Ray said.

Tara turned around and looked at Ray. "We can't unless you want to kill your friend. We need to keep the van cool as long as we can."

Miracle gave Ray his AAA card and Ray called them. After being on hold for a while, the AAA representative told him a tow truck would be out to pick them up in 45 minutes to an hour. Ray pleaded with the guy to get someone out there faster and was told that 45 minutes was the best he could do, that they were, in his words, slammed. Under the circumstances he had already moved Mr. Morgan's request to the top of the list.

Miracle managed to get a hold of his cylinder. He would need a replacement soon. "How many cylinders do we have left?" he asked no one in particular. "Are we going to run out?"

Tara reassured him that they still had plenty of cylinders. "We're a hell of a lot more likely to run out of gas than oxygen, paisan," Ray added.

They sat and waited. Ray thought he should walk down the highway some, at least around the next curve, he said. Maybe there was an exit sign. If they were close, he might walk to a gas station and buy a five gallon can.

"It's too hot, Ray. Anyway, the van probably has a 35 gallon capacity. Even if we're low we can run a while," Miracle said.

Ray got out of the van anyway so he could smoke a cigarette. Tara moved into the back seat next to Miracle. "You want to take a nap Miracle?"

"Maybe later. I used to sell cars," Miracle said, just to make conversation.

"So you know something about them and what makes them work. You seem sure it's the transmission."

"I could be wrong, but yeah, that's a good bet." He looked out the window at the cars and trucks barreling down the highway. "I really liked selling cars."

"Why did you stop?"

"My first wife said it didn't fit our image, or the one she hoped to create when she was appointed to the United States Supreme Court."

"I guess the Senate confirmation hearings would have been

compromised with you handing out free oil change flyers to committee members," Tara said.

Miracle laughed. "You surprise me yet again, Tara."

"I know what you must think of me, first a star struck kid, who then became a gold digger in a nurse's uniform, trolling for doctors."

"Were you really in a movie when you lived in Los Angeles?" Miracle asked.

"Indeed I was. Want to know what it was called?"

"Sure."

"Killer Smog. It was a story about a new form of deadly air pollution that was killing people in LA County."

"Sounds interesting."

"It was, in a predictable sort of way. My little role took less than a day to shoot. After that, I went to Venice Beach."

"Is that where you lived?"

"No, not there, close by though," Tara said. "We should give you a breathing treatment now. Let me get your nebulizer set up."

It took 90 minutes for the tow truck to arrive. Miracle had gone through a full cylinder in that time and half-way through another one. Since they left the Baltimore area that morning, they had been on the road, or the side of it, for almost eight hours. All told, Miracle had used seven cylinders and was half way through his eighth. They were now down to 21 full cylinders, making Miracle increasingly agitated. "You have no idea what its like to need oxygen just to breathe. It's very scary. I should never have done this. I know that now."

"It's going to be all right, I promise you," Tara said, stroking his arm. Ray, back in the van, nodded in agreement, but he had his doubts.

The tow truck dropped them off at a transmission repair shop run by a guy named Benny G. Kays. Ray and Tara got out of the van as soon as the tow truck lowered it to the ground. The sign hanging over the garage doors said Big Boy's Transmission Repair. The doors were open, so they walked in. A short, good looking middle aged man was standing in front of a red Dodge Challenger, hood open and singing along with the radio. The song, turned up to near maximum volume, was I Feel Good, sung by James Brown. He was using a wrench for a microphone and doing a little dance a la The King of Soul himself. He saw them enter his garage out of the corner of his eye and stopped immediately. He walked over to the radio and turned it down. "Looks like you nice folks caught me in the middle of my act. Sorry about that."

"Not at all," Ray said. "I was thinking you were doing a fine imitation there. In fact, don't stop on our account."

Tara poked Ray hard in the ribs. "Pay no attention to him, please. The tow truck driver brought us here from I-95. Can you help us? We seem to have a problem with our transmission."

"Happens at least twice a month. I might could help you," Benny said. "Let's have a look at your vehicle."

Kays loved playing the roll of the stupid southerner for Yankees who stopped by, something a lot of southern men learned to do early in life when they discovered that northerners often made the mistake of equating a southern drawl with stupidity. More than a few Yankees got sucked in and hoodwinked, thanks to their own ignorance. The funny thing about it was that Benny himself was a Yankee from Buffalo. His wife Joanne was from Dunn though. Not long after he got out of school, Benny joined the New York National Guard based on the pitch a recruiting officer gave him. He did his basic training in Ft. Bragg, a stone's throw from Fayetteville, North Carolina. As luck, or fate, would have it, his bunkmate Bradley was from Dunn. Bradley took Benny to Dunn one weekend when they had 24 hour passes and introduced him to his sister Joanne. A romance quickly blossomed. Less than a year later, they were married and Benny happily learned to love grits.

They walked outside. "How y'all doing in this heat?"

"I'm used to it," Ray answered.

"Why is your truck still running?" Benny asked.

"Our friend is sitting in the van. He needs to stay cool, he has a medical condition," Tara said. "I hate to bother you sir, but do you have an air conditioned office where we could plug in his oxygen concentrator for a while?"

"What's wrong with him, if I may ask?"

"He has something called pulmonary fibrosis. It's a lung disease," Tara said.

"Never heard of it. Doesn't sound good though. Sorry to hear that. Do you need any help getting him to the office?"

Ray spoke up. "No, we're good. Just point us in the right direction."

"See that door on the right next to the air pump? Just go right on through there. That should do the trick."

Ray got Miracle out of the van and into a wheelchair. He rolled him as fast as he could to the office door and got him inside. Then he came back, opened the van's back doors and pulled out the concentrator. "This will calm him down some, maybe," he said to Tara, "just knowing he isn't using cylinders for a while."

Benny got in the vehicle and tried working the gearshift a few times, pressing lightly on the accelerator. He was pretty sure it was the transmission, most likely the torque converter. He turned the vehicle's engine off. Then he got out of the van and approached Tara and Ray who were standing and sweating in the heat waiting for the news. "Well, you do have a problem I'm afraid. Your torque converter is probably shot. I'll need to take a closer look, but I can tell you this won't be a quick turnaround. You folks on the way to Florida?"

Both of them nodded in assent. Benny smiled to himself, satisfied that he guessed right.   "How long will it take to fix it?" Ray asked.

"Depends on how long it takes for the parts to get here. I'm going to need your vehicle registration before I do anything else.

One other thing, I'll need a 50% deposit, cash or credit card."

"That's no problem," Ray said, "but can you give us an estimate on how long to fix it?"

"Well, if I get the parts I need by tomorrow afternoon, I'd say three, maybe four days."

"Really? That long?" Tara asked.

"That's about the size of it."

"Hey, please don't take this the wrong way, Benny, but is there another shop that could do the job faster?" Ray asked.

Benny laughed. He put his head down, pulled at his baseball cap and pushed a tiny stone around with his boot. "There's only two shops here in Dunn. There are some others down the road, but you ain't gonna do no better at one of them places."

"Why do you need the vehicle registration?" Ray asked.

"The VIN number will help me figure out what parts I need believe it or not," Benny said.

"It's in the glove compartment, I'll get it," Ray sighed. "Tara, maybe you should go and stay with Miracle."

"Miracle? Is that the dude in the chair's name?" Benny asked.

"Yeah, that's his name, why?" Ray asked. The situation combined with the incredible heat was making Ray irritable.

"Odd name is all I'm saying, bless his heart."

Ray got into the van which felt like an oven already and pulled the registration out of the glove compartment. He walked over to Benny and handed it to him.

"Let's join your friends in the office. Good to get out of this heat. That young lady your daughter?" Benny asked.

"No."

As soon as they got into the office, Tara said, "Ray, get the cooler out of the van please. I think Miracle could use a cool drink." Ray did as he was told.

Benny reached for a cigarette put it in his mouth and lit it. Miracle looked at him, but didn't say anything. He looked at Tara.

"Sir, I'm so sorry but you can't smoke that now. Our friend's lungs can't take the smoke."

Kays shook his head and walked over to the nearly full ashtray sitting on a desk and put out the cigarette. Then he took a look at the van's registration. "Whoa, Nellie! We got us a little problem here." Benny was staring at the registration form. "This van is a rental. Ma'am, I can't work on your van without authorization from your rental company."

"Why not?"

Benny launched into an explanation about the problems that might occur if he fixed the vehicle without permission from the rental car company. He could be sued, he said. He also pointed out that the rental car company, if they approved the repair, would be responsible for the bill. He explained that they could decide to pick up the vehicle and tow it to one of their own repair centers. In that case, they would replace the broken van with a new one. Might be faster, he said, since they seemed to be in such a hurry.

Ray walked back into the office, carrying the cooler. "There's another problem," Tara told him.

"Now what?"

She turned her eyes to Benny who was happy to explain again what he discovered. When he finished, Miracle said, "So where does that leave us?"

Ray stood there, absentmindedly pretending to hit forehands, considering their options. He noticed there was a Holiday Inn on the other side of the street. "Tell you what," he said, "let's see if that motel over there has rooms. If they do, we'll check in. I'll call the rental car company from there. Okay if we leave our van parked here for a while?"

"I guess so," Benny said. "Get back to me though as soon as you know what they want to do. I close up here around 5:30."

Ray walked across the street and went into the Holiday Inn. He booked two rooms for three nights. He went back over to the transmission shop to get Miracle and Tara. She had already switched Miracle back to a cylinder and unplugged the concentrator. She wheeled Miracle, while Ray pushed the concentrator. Ray made a couple of trips to the van to get their luggage and some medical items Miracle would need. By the time he was done, he was drenched, the salty sweat pouring into his eyes and stinging.

Once they got settled in the rooms, this time across the hall from each other, they talked over their options. "I don't think we can really wait for three or four days while that good ole boy, Bubba, fixes the van," Ray said, "as much as I'd like to see his entire floor show."

Tara just rolled her eyes. "I would say we should call the rental car company and ask them to send us a replacement, but we have all those cylinders and empties plus the racks attached to the wall of the truck."

"Yeah, I thought about that too," Ray said. He took the room in. Miracle was lying on his bed, trying to get some sleep. The room had that musty odor common to high humidity climates. The dark green, undistinguished wallpaper darkened the room, which made everything seem worse. The room was depressing; it made him feel confined. It was hard to think clearly.   "I'm going back across the street to talk to Benny for a minute. See if he has any ideas."

As it tuned out, Benny did have an idea. "I have a 1994 GMC Yukon I can sell you. Wouldn't work as well as your van as far as carrying everything, but if you leave your friend's easy chair, you might could get everything else in there."

Ray thought about that for a minute. "Tell you what Benny, we're going to be here overnight. Can I sleep on that?"

"I suppose that would be alright. What did the rental car folks say?"

"Haven't called them yet."

Back in the room, the three of them did their best to relax a bit. Tara made sure Miracle got a breathing treatment. Soon, he was in a sound sleep again. When Ray told Tara about Benny's proposition, she immediately whispered no. "Miracle needs that recliner. There is no way he can sit up in the car all that time. Have you taken a good look at him? He is showing signs of serious congestive heart failure. Look at how swollen his legs and feet are!"

"Does he need a doctor? If we do that won't they put him in the hospital?"

"He's a hospice patient so, no, they wouldn't, not normally, but we're in fucking Dunn, North Carolina, so maybe they would."

"Are you sure it's heart failure?"

"He isn't eating much and he seems weaker to me. We don't have a lot of time, Ray. Sorry about saying the F-word"

Ray smiled. "Don't worry about that. How much time?"

"Who knows? Could be days or it could be weeks. I just don't know. Why did I ever agree to do this thing? I must have been insane."

"Calm down Tara. I just got another idea. Let's rent another van. We'll use a different company and start over."

"What about the cylinder racks?" Tara asked.

"We're going to have to take that chance. Look it's only four o'clock. I'll call Avis and see if I can get another van. Then I'll call Hertz and tell them to pick up their broken down van. Maybe I can get Benny to give me a lift to the other rental car company. I'll give him a few bucks. We should be on the road by mid-morning."

"While you're at it, see if you can get him to switch the racks," Tara said.

Chapter 10

Melanie Morgan-Cox sat sipping her morning coffee, looking out her kitchen window at the birds. Her bird feeder was popular, not only with the birds, but with the squirrels. This morning the birds seemed to be in charge. Her husband Vincent, walked in with the mail, bagels and a gallon of milk he picked up at 7-Eleven.

"I love this time of year," she said.

"Me too, it's the whole point of teaching isn't it? We get the summer off, and just like when we were kids, by August we'll be bored as always," Vincent said.

"Speak for yourself, Vinnie boy. I could extend summer a full year and never miss the classroom."

Vincent poured himself a cup of coffee and picked out a blueberry bagel. He sliced the bagel, put a healthy portion of cream cheese on it and took a bite. Then he picked up the mail. There was a Toyota car payment and a post card from Bally's in Atlantic City offering a two-night special at the casino's Claridge Hotel for $59 a night. There was also a gas and electric bill. What came next really got Vincent's attention; a letter from Miracle.

"Hey, there's a letter here from your father."

"What? Let me see it!"

Melanie put her coffee down and carefully opened the envelope. She checked the postmark for the date, which was June 23rd. "What day is it?"

"It's Friday," Vincent said.

"The date, I mean the date, Vincent."

"The 25th."

Melanie started reading the letter. "I knew it!"

"What's going on?"

"Oh my God. My father went to Florida. Can you believe that? Ray, that asshole friend of his, took him to Florida."

"What are you talking about?"

"Listen to this." Melanie read the letter to her husband.

Dear Melanie and Brian,

I love you both very much! We all know I don't have a lot of time left. I'll be gone soon and happy to be relieved of my woes. I want you to know how much I appreciate all you've done to support me, especially as my condition got worse. Having thought about it, I agree with you that I shouldn't drive anymore and that living alone is no longer an option. I do however, have some unfinished business to attend to in Florida. I've asked Ray to drive me there so I can take care of it. At some point, I assume you will become aware of the details. Now, I must ask that you trust me and accept that what I am doing is the correct course of action. I have every confidence that you would and will do the same under the circumstances. I have a request of you both, a final wish if you will, that neither of you should take any steps to undo the actions taken in my 11th hour. I am not sure we will see each other again. Please know that is not how I wanted it, but it is very important to me to take care of a few things while I still can. This miserable disease robs a man of every shred of dignity and is extremely hard on loved ones. Please say a prayer, but do not grieve for me.

Love,
Dad

P.S. All of my affairs are in order.

"How did you know he was going to Florida?" Vincent asked.

"I didn't know. I just knew something was up, that he was going somewhere with his buddy Ray. Lord knows what Ray talked him into in the state my father's in."

"Your father sounds pretty lucid to me in that letter. I wonder what his pressing business is."

Melanie reached for a cigarette. Like most smokers, she was trying to quit and finding it was harder than she ever imagined it would be. Vincent hated her smoking. "Take it outside, Mel."

"Up yours. This is serious business. What if Ray kidnapped my father?"

Vincent shot her a challenging look. "Come on Mel, your father isn't that far gone. But what does he have going on in Florida?"

"I'll bet you it has something to do with his money and Ray has his hands in my father's pocket again. You know I think he has more money than he let on to me and Brian."

Vincent snatched the cigarette out of Melanie's hand and snuffed it out. He gave her another one of his looks.

"I hate you," she said.

"You wish you did, but you don't."

Melanie started to reach for another cigarette but thought better of it. The phone rang. "I'll bet that's Brian," she said.

It was Brian. He was sitting in his apartment he shared with two other students near the Rutgers University campus. One of them walked in with the mail while he was searching on line for a better summer job. "Did you get the letter?" he asked.

"Yeah, I got it. Just a few minutes ago. Did you know anything about this?"

Brian laughed. "Hell no, and I assume you didn't know anything either."

"You know his friend Ray, that jerk, was behind this, don't you?" Melanie asked.

"Cool it sis. We don't know that for sure. Has he ever said anything to you about business in Florida?"

"No way. The only time he ever mentioned Florida was when he talked about grandpa's real estate deal or going to the University of Miami."

"Right. So what the hell is this trip about? Think maybe Sandy would have an idea?" Brian asked.

Melanie thought that one over for a few seconds. In spite of the fact that her mother had been the one to file for divorce, she was always bitter about it. As Melanie grew into womanhood, her mother told her repeatedly how much of a disappointment her father had been. But Melanie could see that her mother had dark moods that could last for months. No matter what was going on between her parents, she had to admit that her father always treated her lovingly. It was rare for him to even reprimand her, another thing her mother criticized him for.

Getting her mother involved in this would only lead to another round of recriminations. After her father was finally diagnosed, Melanie put her foot down. There would be no more criticism from her mother about Miracle. Sandy tested it one time in a restaurant on her birthday, perhaps believing her daughter wouldn't make a scene in public. She was wrong. Melanie got up and left the table. Since they had driven to the restaurant separately, she simply said to Sandy, "I told you no more of that. I'm leaving; happy birthday." Sandy called out after her, but Melanie didn't even bother to turn around. After that, Sandy stopped making comments about her ex-husband. He still had a hold on her even after all these years, and she hated it.

"Brian, I'll ask her but you will owe me big time, baby brother," Melanie said.

Melanie decided to call her mother after she had her shower and did her hair and makeup. She and Vincent were planning to go to a farmers market in South Jersey that afternoon. While she was getting ready, she considered the letter's contents. What did her father mean by 'correct course of action?' If he knew they would eventually find out about his scheme, why didn't he just tell them what was up? And exactly what course of action was he contemplating? If he knew it was correct, why would he worry that she and Brian might try to undo it? The more she thought about it, the more she was convinced she had to confide in her mother. If they could locate him, there might be time to stop him from doing something foolish, most likely something that would benefit Ray Rosario.

She got her mother on the phone and read her the letter. Her mother laughed. "I'm not surprised," she said. Sandy had an alternative theory based on things Miracle had told her after they had fallen in love. "I suppose it could be Ray's doing. On the other hand, however, I seem to recall your father had a girlfriend down there when he was in school. Whenever her name came up, it was Marcy or Marcia, I can't remember which, it was obvious she had broken his heart. I swear he married me on the rebound."

"Come on mom, seriously? Why would he want to be in touch with her now after all these years? He's dying for goodness sake," Melanie said.

Sandy put her cell on speaker so she could finish applying her makeup. "All I'm saying is that your father had a meaningful relationship down there. For all I know he might have rekindled it while we were married. I wouldn't put it past him. Anyway, if he has another reason for going to Florida I have no idea what it is, unless Disney is planning to build another theme park. Maybe he plans to repeat his father's one moment of glory as his swan song."

"Mother, I have no idea why I bother with you sometimes," Melanie said.

"I still have money, which is more than your father can say."

"And how would you know that?"

"Your father made some horrible investments over the years. And he had a habit of giving money away to oddball charities, you know that," Sandy said.

"I don't know what I know anymore," Melanie said. "I get sick every time I think of him cooped up in that Packard of his. If anything happens to him, I'm suing Ray Rosario."

"Oh yeah, that should net you a tidy sum."

"I'll call you later mom."

Brian Morgan decided to drive over to his father's condo. He was willing to bet, given his father's mental state, that the old man left something useful there, some clue to his unfinished business in Florida. When he got there, he saw a man standing at his father's front door ringing his bell.

"Can I help you?" Brian asked.

"Who are you?"

"Brian Morgan, Miracle's son."

"Do you know where he might be?" The man asked

"Who're you?"

"Oh, right. I'm Mitch, the guy who bought your father's Packard."

"Wait, my father sold his Packard?"

"Yeah, a couple of days ago. I came over here to see if he had an extra set of keys," Mitch said.

Brian was momentarily stunned. "The hits keep right on coming," he said aloud, but really to himself.

"Something wrong?" Mitch asked.

"Not sure. Wait here; I'll see if I can find an extra set of keys for you. On second thought, sorry for asking, but how do I know he sold you the car?"

"Right kid, I stole it from him, and now I'm back here so I can ask him if he wouldn't mind giving me a second set of keys."

Brian held his hand up and made a face that was an apology of sorts. "Wait here." He walked into the condo and headed straight for his father's bedroom dresser. He opened the top middle drawer and found the extra set of keys. Twice a month, it seemed, his father would tell him where he kept those keys in case he locked them in the car when he was at the mall or grocery store.

Brian hurried outside to the landing where Mitch was standing. "Here you go. If you don't mind my asking, what did you pay for the car?"

Mitch hesitated. "I don't know if your father wants anyone to know that."

"I understand, but I was hoping I would be able to buy the Packard from him someday. I was saving up and I was just wondering how close I was," Brian lied.

Mitch smiled. "How much did you have saved up?"

"Like right now? I don't know for sure, man. About $15,000, maybe a little more than that."

"If it makes you feel any better, you're light seven grand kid," Mitch said, still smiling.

Brian watched him drive away, wondering why he didn't see the Packard when he pulled into the parking lot. Probably because he wasn't looking for it; he and Melanie assumed their father was in the car going somewhere with Ray. He knew Melanie would scream when she heard the car was sold. His sister was constantly calculating how much money they would inherit after their father was gone. It wasn't like Melanie to be mercenary before Miracle got sick. Either that, or she did a great job of hiding it. After Miracle told them his illness was terminal though, she suddenly seemed greedy. Then again, Vincent and Melanie had a lot of toys. Sea-Doos they hardly ever used sat in the garage parked next to ATV four wheelers they never used. Maybe they were in over their heads and needed the money, Brian thought. The professor in the finance class he took in the previous semester talked a lot about people and businesses being over leveraged.

He took a look around the complex. No one was outside. It was a hot day, close to 90 degrees. He walked back into his father's home. He went through the mail that was sitting on the coffee table. What he saw was routine; bills, one of those postcards from Bally's and a few grocery store circulars. There was nothing noteworthy in the kitchen or in his father's bedroom either. The dining room table was clear too, except for a high school yearbook which most likely was from his Dad's senior year. He and his friend Ray must have been reminiscing. It didn't take long for Brian to give up. He wasn't the type who would be comfortable going through closets and old shoeboxes with letters or strongboxes with stock certificates, for that matter. Melanie and her husband might sweep the condo like CIA operatives, but not him. He decided to go over to Mel's house and talk things over.

As he walked to his car, he spotted one of his father's neighbors walking her Scottish terrier. The dog was black, tail wagging constantly. "Hello Brian, is your father home already?" Brian was surprised she knew his name. He had seen her around the complex before, but he couldn't remember her name. Mrs. MacBrien was a thin, still attractive woman in her late 60s. She was petite and Brian towered over her. A widow who mostly kept to herself, Mrs. MacBrien wasn't exactly friendly, but anyone who approached would find her to be pleasant.

After accidentally bumping into her at the mailbox kiosk one day, Miracle learned she had been a social worker before she retired. He realized immediately that with her background she might be helpful. From then on, he would try to time his mailbox visits to coincide with the woman's trips. Occasionally, they would meet and Miracle always enjoyed their conversations. He knew he was failing quickly and he desperately needed someone he could rely on in emergencies. Neither Brian nor Melanie lived close enough to the condo to be there in a hurry. It would take at least 30 minutes to get to his place, too long to suit Miracle.

He told Mrs. MacBrien the story of his diagnosis, his reliance on oxygen and his fears about suffocating. Miracle was a shrewd judge of character. Mrs. MacBrien took the bait and offered her assistance. They exchanged phone numbers. And Miracle was careful not to become a pest. Only once did he call her and ask if she might pick up a few items for him if she was going to the supermarket that day. Some days, he really didn't have the energy to do anything. The woman was happy to help, she said.

When Miracle decided to drive to Florida he asked Mrs. MacBrien to keep an eye on his condo while he was gone. He was aware that Mrs. MacBrien was a confirmed people watcher. She could sit for hours staring out her window watching her neighbors come and go, take trash out, wash their cars. Naturally, she noticed all the activity going on when Miracle, Ray and Tara were making their preparations for the trip. Not that she recognized it as such, but she witnessed Ray's theft of the oxygen cylinders. She also saw the haggling over the Packard. When she asked Brian if his father was home already, she saw the concern in the young man's face.

"No, he isn't home yet. Did he mention to you that he was going to Florida?" Brian asked. The terrier jumped up and began sniffing Brian's jeans.

"Quit, Marcy!" Mrs. MacBrien said. "No, he didn't say that. All he said was he was going away for a few days. He asked me to keep an eye on his condo."

"I see."

"Is there a problem?"

"Might be. We haven't heard from him since the day he left. Frankly, we don't know where he's going, or how he's getting there."

"Well, I probably shouldn't tell you this but I think he left with his friends, a man about his age and a much younger woman. They left in a white van, which I assume was rented."

"They rented a van? I wonder why they did that." Brian said.

Mrs. MacBrien bent over to scoop up what her dog dropped while they were talking, taking a moment to think about what she was about to say. She didn't want any trouble. She had a strict policy of not meddling in the affairs of others. This situation was different though. Her neighbor clearly wasn't well. There was no telling what kind of predicament he might be in now. "I believe they needed the van to carry the oxygen cylinders. There were a lot of them. Oh, yes, they took a recliner chair with them too," she said.

"Is that so?"

"You seem worried," Mrs. MacBrien said.

"Yeah, a little I guess. He didn't mention going to Florida?"

"No, he didn't but when I was walking Marcy, I overheard an exchange between the young lady and the man with the ponytail."

Brian waited for her to continue but she didn't seem to know whether to say anything more than she had already said. "And?" he prompted her.

"Well, the young lady asked the man how long he thought it would take to get to Bonita Springs. I couldn't hear his answer."

"Anything else?"

"No, sorry that was all I could hear. I wasn't trying to listen, honestly. My dog was trying to go after a squirrel. I was pulling on her leash and walking a bit fast. By the time he answered her, I was out of earshot I'm afraid."

"No problem. You've been very helpful. What did you say your name was?"

"Karen MacBrien."

Brian thanked the woman and headed as fast as he could without running to his car.

As he pulled up to his sister's house, he was trying to recall everything he heard and trying to make sense of it. He rang the bell and waited, not sure what to think about everything he just learned. Vincent answered. Brian wasn't crazy about Vincent and the feeling was mutual. He took a good look at his brother-in-law and again wondered what his sister saw in him. He was a handsome guy, but he was at least an inch shorter than Melanie and he was clearly showing signs of an emerging pot belly. Brian thought Vincent was lazy, that he married Melanie because he believed her family had money. As far as Brian could tell, the guy was in for a surprise.

"What are you doing here?" Melanie said as she walked into the living room from the kitchen.

"Did you talk to your mother?" Brian asked.

Melanie rolled her eyes. "Oh yes I did. Do you remember dad

or Wendy ever mentioning an old girlfriend dad had in Florida?"

"What do you mean old girlfriend? Like, how old?"

"Don't worry, little brother. I'm not about to tell you he cheated on your mom," Melanie said, "I'm talking about when he went to the University of Miami."

"Nope."

"Does the name Marcia or Marcy ring a bell?"

"Let me see, I just met a Scottish terrier named Marcy, does that help?"

"I'm serious."

You know who Karen MacBrien is?" Brian asked.

Melanie nodded. She knew who Mrs. MacBrien was. She ushered her brother into the kitchen and got him a beer out of the refrigerator. It was just before noon. Vincent followed them in. "Got one for me too, Mel?" he asked.

Melanie gave him a look that said go find something to do in the yard. His face got visibly red, but he complied after he snatched a beer.

"Thanks for sending Vinnie Vampire outside for a while," Brian said.

"Why do you insist on calling him that? His fangs don't even show," Melanie said, smiling.

"You know why. He's a blood sucker when it comes to money."

"Stop, he is not. I am though, and I'm going to find a way to cut you out of dad's will."

They looked at each other. Over the years they used humor to deflect a lot of problems that might have kept them from being close. Brian had grown up living with his father and mother. Melanie was always the visitor who got to spend weekends or part of her summer vacation with her father. Fortunately, Wendy was a good stepmom who didn't treat Melanie like an intruder. She actively encouraged the half-siblings to support each other.

"So, what's Mrs. MacBrien's story?"

Brian filled her in on what he learned from the neighbor, including the reference to Bonita Springs.

"Where is Bonita Springs?" Melanie asked.

"Must be somewhere in Florida," Brian said. "Got a map?"

Melanie went into the living room and found an old road atlas on one of the book shelves and turned to the page with Florida on it. Brian spotted it right away on the west coast between Ft. Myers and Naples.

Then Brian told Melanie about the Packard. That really bothered her. "I just know he gave the money to that scumbag Ray," she said.

"So what if he did, Melanie? It's his money isn't it?"

"That is not the point Brian. Dad is in no condition to make decisions like that. Do I need to remind you that a brain deprived of oxygen isn't fully engaged? Not to mention, I have power of attorney. He can't sell the car without my signature."

"Can't? Really? He did it." Brian shook his head. He took a long swallow, put the bottle down and started picking at the label. "Right, power of attorney. What can we do about it?"

"I think we should put out an APB on him before Ray does more damage."

Brian laughed. "Seriously? An all points bulletin on dad? Why would we do that? He'll kill us. That might really put you out of the will, sis."

Melanie asked her brother if he wanted something to eat. He asked for a sandwich and she got up to make it for him. She looked out the kitchen window. The grass needed to be cut but Vincent had a golf club in his hands, hitting chip shots. She would have to make it up to him for sending him outside, but she knew her brother wasn't going to be completely forthcoming as long as Vincent was around.

"Think about it, Brian," she said. "We have a dying man trying to get to Florida to take care of what he calls unfinished business. He has Ray and some woman, probably Ray's latest conquest, which means she isn't Mensa material, escorting him to his rendezvous in Bonita Springs. Doesn't that worry you?"

"When you put it like that, yeah, maybe."

"I'm calling the cops. If there isn't a good reason to look for him, they will tell us. Fair enough?"

"Do it."

Chapter 11

Ray's talk with Benny went well. He said he couldn't drive Ray to Avis until the next morning because he had to get home and get ready for a rehearsal dinner. His good friend and brother-in-law Bradley was getting married again Friday evening. When Ray asked him if he would remove the cylinder racks from the Hertz van and put them into the Avis van, Benny hesitated.

"I'll make it worth your while Benny," Ray said.

"I'm a businessman. Talk to me," Benny answered.

"What's it worth to you?"

"I am losing out on a lucrative transmission job here, and I already invested some time on checking your vehicle out. Plus I'm going to drive you to Avis. Then there's always a risk you might tell somebody who doctored the new van. Plus, when the Hertz people get here, they might notice the holes left from the racks I took out."

Ray smiled to himself. Here was his counterpart, doing in his métier what Ray did so well on the tennis court. He had to respect Benny's style. "Just tell me what you want and let's see if we can make it work," Ray said.

"I'll tell you what my friend, $1,500 should do it."

That surprised Ray. For a moment he thought he chose the wrong profession. He didn't have time to bargain though. And, he knew from experience they would all be better off if Benny was happy with the deal. He also knew not to leave Benny with the impression that he was leaving money on the table and that he could have asked for more.

Ray let out a low whistle. "Wow, that's a hefty sum. Let me call my friend and make sure we can cover it, okay?"

Benny nodded. "Sure."

Ray stepped away and dialed Tara on his cell. They spoke briefly. Ray told her to just listen. He would explain later. He made a few gestures that seemed to suggest they had no choice. He shook his head no and then he raised his voice so Benny could hear. "Do we have enough or not?" Then he said, "Okay, good. Yeah, if we're careful we should still have enough to get where we're going." Tara had no idea of what he was talking about, but it didn't matter. He had made his point with Benny.

The three of them settled in for the night at the Holiday Inn. Ray managed to rent another van. He would call Hertz about their van after they were safely on the road again. They were all too tired to go down to the restaurant to eat. Instead, they ordered room service. Ray had a steak, Tara a chef's salad and Miracle ate most of his hamburger. At least his appetite was good. Tara wouldn't let him put salt on his fries. She let him have a little catsup. "You have to be really careful about salt intake now," she said.

After dinner, Tara and Miracle chatted, Tara was eager to learn more about him. "Miracle is such an interesting name," she said. "Is it a family name?"

Miracle was used to this question. Over the years, he had developed a variety of answers, mostly to amuse himself since he grew tired of answering the question long before his 25th birthday.

"I was born on Christmas Day. The night before I was born, my mother and father were home watching the movie, Miracle on 34th Street, when my mother's water broke. She had no idea what to name me so when they got to the hospital the name Miracle seemed like a natural." The joke was that in 1950, the year Miracle was born, which was actually in July, Miracle on 34th Street was only three years old. His parents didn't even own a TV set at the time. Remarkably, few people caught on.

Tara smiled and said, "What an interesting story. Reminds me of how I got my name."

Miracle, suspecting she was on to him, was eager to hear her story. "Tell me about it." Ray was not paying any attention to them. The Wimbledon Tournament was well into its first week and he was engrossed in a replay of one of the matches.

"My mother was in the movie, Gone with the Wind. She was one of the Tarleton Twins. She couldn't very well name me Twelve Oaks, so she called me Tara."

Miracle really laughed. He started coughing and had a nervous moment when he had to gasp for breath. Tara jumped up to assist him, but he waved her off. "I'm sorry Miracle."

But once he regained his breath, Miracle asked her another question, just to keep the game going. "Weren't the Tarleton twins men?"

"Yes, they were. My mother was made up to look like a man though. It ruined her career."

"Ray, are you listening to any of this?" Miracle asked.

Ray turned away from the television and said, "Not really. I've heard all the stories about how you got your name, except for maybe the real one."

"You heard the real one enough times. In fact, wasn't it your idea that I make up stories about it?"

"I don't know. Was it? I don't think I even remember the true story anymore."

"I would like to hear it," Tara said.

Over the years, Miracle had told very few people the true story of how he got his name. As a younger man, he would have been too embarrassed to tell it. "Miracle is actually a girl's name," he said. "My mother had her heart set on having a girl. When I was born, she was very disappointed. She and my father decided to call me Miracle anyway."

"Was that painful for you?" Tara asked.

"Not really. My mother got over her disappointment eventually, and I never doubted that she loved me. There was never any doubt about that. And nobody in our neighborhood ever heard of the name Miracle to begin with. I wasn't teased about it, at least as far as it being a girl's name."

"It's a great name," Ray said. "Oh man, will you look at that!" One of the players made an incredible shot, managing to return a ball as he was falling to the turf.

They turned their attention to the tennis match. Two of the game's lesser known players were battling it out on the grass in London. Ray stared intently at the set. Miracle found it disconcerting. It only reminded him of how much he missed playing the game. He always thought he would play well into his seventies, if not his eighties. Now he would be gone long before his 70th birthday. Ray turned to him to make a point about a shot one of the players just made, but he saw something in Miracle's face that made him think twice. He turned the set off. The three of them played cards until it was time to turn in. Tara went across the hall to her room. Ray and Miracle each had a double bed to sleep in.

The next morning, a Friday, it was raining hard. "Listen to those rain drops," Tara said. "It sounds like everyone in heaven is tapping their fingers on the hotel roof." Promptly at 8:00 a.m., Ray ran across the street to the Big Boy Transmission shop. But, Benny was no where to be found. The place was locked up. Ray hurried back to the motel, his clothing completely soaked. Neither room's windows looked out on the transmission shop, so Ray sent Tara downstairs to wait in the lobby to look for signs of Benny's arrival. In the meantime, he helped Miracle shave and get cleaned up. He was having a difficult morning. Ray was worried, but tried not to show it. Miracle sensed this and said, "Listen Ray, if for some reason I don't get there, promise me you'll see Marcia and Jagger for me and take care of things."

"That won't be necessary, paisan. You just need to rally a little. You can make it."

"Promise me, Ray."

"I'll take care of it, promise."

"One more thing; make sure you find a priest to give me my last rites."

The better part of the morning went by with no sign of Benny. Ray called Avis to reconfirm the rental for an afternoon pickup, hoping for the best. Finally, at 11:30 Benny pulled into his parking lot. Tara went up to the room and informed Ray.

When Ray walked into Benny's office, the guy looked terrible. His eyes were puffy and red. Obviously his face never got anywhere near a razor that morning.

"Big, bad night last night," Benny said.

"Are you in shape to do what we agreed to do?" Ray asked.

"I am now. Took a lot of coffee though."

"Can we go over to pick up the new van now?"

"Whoa, keep your britches on. I got a few things I need to do here. One of my mechanics called in sick. I have to finish up a job he started. Then we can go."

"How long will that take?"

"Not sure. Give me your cell number and I'll call you," Benny said.

Ray was irritated, but knew better than to show it. He went back to the motel to wait. Miracle was watching the History Channel. Tara was cleaning Miracle's nebulizer kit after his treatment. It wasn't raining as hard as it did earlier, so Tara decided to walk over to a convenience store near the hotel, the kind with gas pumps outside and an impressive array of products, from milk to motor oil, on the many rows of shelves. She said she needed something for a headache. When she got back she wanted to use the bathroom but Miracle was already using it. "How long is this going to take?" she asked. It was a rare sign of annoyance, but the bathroom in her room was out of order and the hotel's maintenance staff was behind schedule.

They had another room service lunch brought in. They ate in silence, listening to the rain. Tara, who skipped breakfast, made up for it by ordering a large Cobb salad. She quit after just a few bites.

"What's up with that?" Ray asked.

"Are you going to take an inventory of everything I eat now?" She stood up and gathered the remnants of everyone's lunch and placed them outside the door. "I'm going stir crazy in this room," she said. It was an apology of sorts.

A couple of hours passed before the phone finally rang. Benny told Ray he would be ready to go in about 30 minutes. Ray saw that Miracle was napping. He picked up the TV remote and started switching channels looking for Wimbledon. Tara was sitting on the edge of the bed, watching him run through the channels when she saw something that sent a chill down her spine.

"Stop! Go back to CNN," she said.

"What's wrong?" He switched to CNN.

There was a photo of a white van identical to the one they rented. The reporter was saying, "A 60 year old man traveling in a white van with New Jersey license plates and believed to be heading to Bonita Springs, Florida, may be making the trip against his will." The shot switched to a video of Melanie and Brian, standing side by side outside Miracle's condo. The reporter continued. "According to the man's daughter, Melanie Morgan-Cox, her father, Miracle Morgan, may be traveling with a long time friend named Ray Rosario and a companion of Mr. Rosario's."

This was followed by Melanie talking to the reporter. "My father is very sick. He is in the advanced stages of pulmonary fibrosis and he may not be thinking clearly. I am very worried about him because he needs medication and a constant supply of oxygen."

The voice over again: "The three travelers have been on the road for three days now and have likely reached their destination. However, authorities and medical facilities along the I-95 corridor have been notified to be on the lookout for three people traveling in a white van. Morgan's daughter has made numerous attempts to reach him on his cell phone, but there has been no response. CNN has learned that Morgan rented the van from Hertz, using a credit card on Tuesday at Newark's Liberty International Airport. A representative from Hertz told us that the vehicle was not equipped with a GPS unit."

The report went on to talk briefly about pulmonary fibrosis and the risks of exertion during travel. The screen showed a head shot of Miracle taken a few years ago and a toll free number for viewers with helpful information to call. The contrast between Miracle's appearance now and just a few years ago was indeed stark.

Tara stared at the television in disbelief. "We are in so much trouble," she said.

"If you want to get off the bus here, I would understand, but I'm going to do what I can to grant him his last dying wish," Ray said.

"You're really willing to stick your neck out that far for him?" she asked.

Ray sighed and nodded his head. "If that's what he wants. After everything he's done for me, how could I say no? Let's wake him up and bring him up to speed. It's his decision now."

They woke Miracle up slowly and let him get acclimated before saying anything. Since the trip began, probably because he wasn't used to waking up in any place other than his condo, he was usually in a confused state for a few minutes before he came around. "Baltimore, right?" he said, looking around the room. He was putting them on a little.

"No, we're in North Carolina now, Miracle. How are you doing?" Ray asked.

Miracle yawned and stretched a little. His vision cleared and he said, "What time is it?"

"About two o'clock." Ray again.

He sat up in bed and said to no one in particular, "I need to use the bathroom." He shuffled over to the bathroom with Ray following him from behind. While he was taking care of business, out of the corner of his eye he noticed something in the wastebasket. He picked it up and gazed at it, not wanting to comprehend what he saw. His suspicion was confirmed, but he didn't see any reason to congratulate himself for his powers of observation. That done he managed to get himself back to the chair that sat near the bed. "When are we getting out of here?"

"There's a problem," Ray said. He told him what he and Tara just saw.

Miracle nodded and asked, "Did Melanie say anything else? Damn those kids."

"No, that was all," Tara said. "What do you want to do Miracle?"

"I don't want to go home. They'll put me on some 24 hour watch, or have one of those people from that ridiculous Friendly Visitors outfit monitoring my every move."

"We can try to get to Florida, but it is going to be harder now," Ray said.

"Are you in or not?" Miracle asked, fixing Ray with a hard stare.

"If you're up for it, I'm in."

He turned to Tara. "How about you?"

"I'm in."

"You sure?"

Tara nodded. "Good to go."

Miracle nodded and took a deep breath. "I know this doesn't seem to make a lot of sense, what we're doing I mean. I get that. But can I tell you something?"

Ray and Tara nodded.

"All these years I've felt, I don't know, guilty? When Marcia broke things off between us, I thought she was hiding something from me. As it turned out, I was right. She was pregnant."

"Okay but why should that make you feel guilty? You didn't know she was knocked up for a fact and, let's not forget she dumped you," Ray said.

"That's right, but when Sandy got pregnant with Melanie

and she had all the usual symptoms, it dawned on me that maybe Marcia was pregnant and I was just too dumb to see that. I remember the last week we were together, she woke up every morning feeling nauseous, morning sickness, I guess. I thought it was those crazy health foods she was eating and said so. "

Tara walked over to the window. She pushed back the curtains and looked out at the parking lot and the nearly full dumpster. "And then she asked you to leave?"

"Right, she was very definite about it. I loved her so much, tried to talk her out of it, cried, and screamed, the whole works."

"So that's why you're putting yourself through all this now?" Ray asked.

Miracle looked at his friend and smiled; a sad smile. "Ray, you read her letter. She's had a tough life. Her son, our son, must have been a difficult challenge to handle on her own all those years. Maybe if I had the brains back then to figure out what was going on instead of bolting for New Jersey, things would have been different."

"Maybe," Ray said, "but you painted a picture in your mind of this defenseless woman and child all these years, when you can't know what their lives were really like. Do you think maybe she lived with a few different guys who helped out during all those years? Seriously paisan, she was outrageously good looking, remember?"

Miracle smiled. He struggled out of the wheel chair he was sitting in and dragged the tubing tied to the concentrator behind him, heading toward the tiny dresser. He stood there, hunched over and breathing hard. He turned to Tara and said, "Would you like to see a picture?"

"I would love to see Marcia's picture. Is that what you're going to show me?"

Miracle shuffled back to his chair. Ray helped him get back into it. He stuck his fingers into one of the pockets of his wallet but couldn't get the photo out. He handed the wallet to Ray, who quickly pulled it out and handed it to Miracle. Tara walked over to the wheelchair. Miracle was looking at a photo of Marcia. She was standing in front of the ocean on Haulover Beach in Miami. He handed it to Tara.

"Oh Miracle, she is beautiful. I can see why you fell in love with her," Tara said, fighting back tears.

Ray took the photo from Tara and gave it a long appraising look. "Yeah, that's exactly how I remember her," he said. "The picture doesn't do justice to her red hair. Man, she had a beautiful complexion."

"Then you will help me try to reach her?"

"Didn't I say that already?"

"Good, because one thing really worries me; if I don't get there to see Marcia and Jagger, I'm afraid my kids will deny him the help he needs."

"Are you sure about that Miracle? Your daughter seems very concerned about you," Tara said.

"No, no, I'm not sure, just worried I guess. Anyway, I don't want to take that chance and I really don't want to go home."

"I wonder if Gomer Pyle down at the transmission shop saw the report," Ray said.

"If he did, we're probably done for," Tara said.

"Maybe, but I have a feeling that a few more bucks in his pocket might help him see things our way. One thing for sure, we can't rent a van. We are going to need Benny's Yukon, I think."

Chapter 12

"Where are we going to stay tonight?" Tara asked.

"Good question. Do you have a credit card?" Ray asked. "Nobody seems to know your name."

The rain had finally stopped and the evening sun was peaking through. They were riding in their faded, red GMC Yukon XL, with well worn, black cloth seats, bought from Benny for $2,500. The price included a vow of silence. As Ray had predicted, Benny was more than willing to comply for a few extra bucks. Benny even towed the Hertz van to a rest area off the Interstate in the next town over. Benny assured Ray the vehicle wouldn't be found for at least 24 hours, maybe 48. That would buy them some time.

The Yukon XL drove like a dream. Benny promised them they would be satisfied, that it wouldn't give them any trouble. They would make it to Florida and back, if necessary, he said. It had North Carolina plates on it, registered to Benny's wife Joanne's late father who died only a few months ago. Before they left the transmission shop, Tara drove it to a nearby Wal-Mart and picked up an air mattress that just fit in the back of the SUV, if the back seats were down. Benny had a couple of long wooden boxes that were perfect for holding the cylinders. Miracle's recliner, leather and only a year old, was part of the transaction with Benny. As soon as the mattress was put in place, along with a couple of blankets and a pillow Tara bought, they loaded up and left the motel, headed for Columbia, South Carolina.

"I have a credit card, yes." Tara answered.

"When we get to Columbia, you go into one of the smaller independent motels and see what you can do."

"We'll have to do it after dark and try to get me in a side

entrance," Miracle said.

"I wouldn't worry too much about it. If Benny the trans-man didn't figure it out, maybe we won't have any problems," Ray said.

"Please! Is that why you gave him an extra $500 and said, 'mum's the word?' I got a good look at Benny's face when we went over there to get the car. He knew. He just didn't care," Tara said. "Well, I guess we don't have a choice, but the idea of staying in a motel worries me."

"Me too, so what happens once we get to Columbia?" Miracle asked.

"Not sure, but you know what? I used to know a guy on one of the tours who I think settled down in Columbia," Ray said.

"Is he a friend of yours?" Miracle asked.

"We were pretty close once, yeah. I wonder if he would let us stay with him for the night."

"Probably safer than staying in a motel with the cops looking for us," Tara said.

"Do you owe this guy any money? Did you bamboozle him out of a small fortune, anything like that?" Miracle asked, laughing. Tara was giggling too.

"You know, you both like to get on me for the way I earn my living, but I never sandbagged anybody, not really. Every guy I ever took knew I was a pro before he made the bet."

"You never acted like you were playing with a painfully bad shoulder or bum knee to lull your opponent into complacency?" Miracle asked.

"No, when money's involved that's a dangerous game. You like to stick that needle in me though. Listen my friend, I have a lot of fans, you know. I'm serious, pick a city and I'll name at least three people who would want lessons."

"Amelia Island," Miracle said.

"Put that nebulizer thing in his mouth, Tara," Ray said.

They continued on I-95 to Florence. After a quick stop to get gas, they jumped onto I-20 toward Columbia. They weren't planning to stop for anything but fuel, but Ray caught a whiff of smoked barbecue at a rib joint that was attached to the convenience store next to the gas station. He walked in and saw a middle aged couple who actually seemed to resemble each other, dressed in identical denim overalls, standing behind the counter. The woman eyed Ray suspiciously which made him nervous. Then she said to her husband, loud enough for Ray to hear, "Lee, I didn't know there was any hippies left. Got us one right here."

Ray smiled, decided he wasn't that hungry and turned to leave. He shook his pony tail in the woman's direction as he was leaving.

By 8:30 that night, they were approaching the outskirts of Columbia. There had been some showers and the streets were wet and shiny. They had only ten and a half hours more of driving to do. But, considering what happened in North Carolina, Tara was beginning to worry. And she couldn't be sure that Miracle wouldn't need a higher flow setting than ten liters per minute. What if he needed twelve or even fifteen? All bets would be off then. Miracle had blown through another 4 cylinders since they left Dunn. They had just over 17 full cylinders left, still enough to get them to Florida by Ray's calculation.

While Ray was thinking about whether his friend who would put them up for the night, Tara was thinking about who she could reach out to who might give them some cylinders.

"Listen," Ray said. "The guy I'm thinking of used to live in Lexington, just south of Columbia. If he's still there, he would probably put us up."

"Will he keep quiet about it?" Tara asked. Miracle was snoring in the back, his breathing labored.

"I can't guarantee it, but I think so. I'll get off at the next exit and find a pay phone."

After seeing the news report on CNN, Ray and Tara turned off their cell phones just to play it safe. Ray found a pay phone on the edge of a Waffle House parking lot and called information. He was in luck, his old friend, tennis pro, Brooks Riley's number was listed. He hadn't spoken to Brooks in maybe ten years but they had once been close. Brooks was a good enough player to have played briefly for the Charlotte Heat in the World Team Tennis league. They met playing in a regional tournament, and quickly discovered they had similar interests and a similar outlook. Then Brooks met a woman and, uncharacteristically, fell in love and got married. Understandably, the woman, whose name Ray couldn't remember, wanted nothing to do with Ray. She wouldn't even allow him to attend the wedding.

Ray picked up the phone and called. A young woman answered. "Hi, I'm looking for Brooks."

"Dad! It's for you."

Brooks got on the phone and Ray gave him his pitch. He could tell that Brooks was happy to hear from him which was a good start. He asked what Brooks was doing now and Brooks was eager to tell him he owned a tennis shop with three locations where he sold racquets, sneakers and clothing and even golf equipment. This was music to Ray's ears, considering his new venture. Brooks said he was happily married. He had two daughters, both in college.

Ray congratulated him and then got to the point. "I'm on the way to Florida with a sick childhood friend. He needs to get there soon, but for a variety of reasons a hotel isn't a good idea. Can we stay with you just for tonight?"

"Let me ask my wife. Shouldn't be a problem," Brooks said.

"Sorry paisan, but I don't remember her name," Ray said.

"Angelina," Brooks answered. "I'll be right back. Don't go away."

The name didn't ring a bell, but he was pretty sure the woman who wouldn't let him attend his friend's wedding wasn't Angelina. It took less than fifteen seconds for Brooks to give Ray the green light. He gave him directions to his home and told him it should only take twenty minutes, tops.

When they got to the Riley residence, Ray said he would

go in first just to be sure it would be okay. The house was huge, a beautiful two-story, brick southern colonial sitting on an acre, filled with trees. The interior was also upscale.

"Looks like you've been living right my man, cleaned up your act," Ray said when Brooks ushered him into the living room.

"Long story with lots of twists and turns including a second marriage," Brooks said.

"What ever happened to what's her name?" Ray asked.

"That was Tammy Jane. As it turned out, she didn't like me much more than she liked you."

Angelina walked in to join them. She was a short but trim woman with black hair and brown eyes. It was obvious from the first second Ray saw her that she was not a woman to be trifled with. Ray wondered how Brooks could ever have found contentment with such a powerful woman. She was shaking Ray's hand and welcoming him to their home, but her smile made it clear that one wrong move by Ray, and they would need a hotel room. Obviously, Brooks had told her stories about him.

He got right to the point with Angelina, describing what they were trying to do and how Miracle's kids had the authorities looking for them. He said he would understand completely if they couldn't help. He acknowledged that he and Brooks hadn't been in touch in years. He was playing every note to perfection, a con man practicing his art at its best.

Angelina listened without saying a word. When Ray stopped talking she said, "Please bring your friends in so we can meet them. We've already had dinner of course, but you're in luck, we have plenty of leftovers. Honey, go out and help your friend Ray get Mr. Miracle."

Luckily, Tara was dressed a bit more conservatively than she had been the first couple of days on the road. She had a pair of cutoff jeans and a short sleeve blouse, buttoned up. Ray had asked her why. She told him, "If we get arrested, I don't want to look like a slut." Regardless, she looked beautiful. Brooks noticed.

When he and Ray went back out to the car to get the concentrator and remaining bags, Brooks said, "Well, time hasn't slowed you down any. Is she as good as she looks?"

"I wouldn't know," Ray said.

Brooks wasn't buying that for a second. "Come on, the great Ray Rosario hasn't been jumping that twice a day?"

"No, I haven't. Listen Brooks, we've been having a hell of a time on this trip. Miracle and I go way back so I owe him, but I gotta tell you if I had any idea how tough this was gonna be, I would have told him no."

Brooks shrugged his shoulders. "It's cool."

They went into the house and immediately got Miracle set up in a guest room on the first floor with his concentrator and 50 feet of tubing. He thanked the Riley's profusely but it was obvious he was worn out and would soon need to get some rest. Lying on the air mattress was certainly better than sitting upright in a car for hours at a time would have been but not much better. He missed his recliner.

The Riley girls, pretty 19 year old identical twins, were home from college. They introduced themselves and quickly left for a party at a friend's house. Tara wheeled Miracle into the dining room, which was elegantly decorated. Well done prints, copies of European and South American art hung on the walls. The furniture was mahogany and obviously expensive. Miracle hadn't seen anything like this since his marriage to Sandy. The funny thing was that dinner was served on inexpensive plates with ornate floral designs around the edges of the plates. And the food itself was pedestrian; meatloaf, mashed potatoes and green beans, all warmed up in the microwave and served with iced tea.

Most of the conversation during dinner was about the good times Ray and Brooks had during their heyday on mini tennis tours, much of it sanitized for the benefit of Angelina. Brooks had met Angelina when he was rehabilitating one of his knees. She was a physical therapist assigned to his case. They hit it off immediately, and Brooks, recently divorced from Tammy Jane, was ready for a change. Angelina's parents had emigrated from Argentina. They built a business cleaning offices. Eventually, they took a chance and purchased one of the buildings they cleaned, a more profitable venture. Now they owned ten buildings in office parks in and around Columbia. They were well heeled.

When Angelina's father saw his daughter was serious about Brooks and more importantly, that Brooks was serious about Angelina, he set them up, providing the seed money Brooks needed to start his tennis shop. With Angelina's help, he worked hard and made a go of it, eventually adding golf clubs and golf accessories.

And Angelina still worked as a physical therapist. She was delighted to discover that Tara was a nurse. Like any good clinician, she took a sincere interest in Miracle's disease. She didn't know much about pulmonary fibrosis, but she could plainly see that the poor man was near the end. When she got up to clear the dishes, Tara pitched in. When they got to the kitchen, Angelina asked, "Do you think he can make it to Florida?"

Tara didn't answer immediately. Instead, she took in the exquisite features of the Riley's gourmet kitchen with its beautifully tiled floors, gleaming cabinetry and beautiful mosaic art on the walls. The countertops were made from rich looking granite. Everything about the kitchen screamed these people had money, which made Tara a bit skittish. Having just met the woman, she was wary. In spite of having heard Miracle's love story, the woman might have her doubts. Who knew what she might do? She seemed the type that might call the authorities. "I know he is determined to make it."

"Yes, I can see that," Angelina said, "the spirit seems willing enough, but am I right that he is suffering tremendously from congestive heart failure?"

"I'm afraid so," Tara said. "I'm worried about that. In fact, I don't think his lungs are as much of an immediate threat as his heart. I think we can get to Bonita Springs by early afternoon

Sunday at the latest, as long as nothing else goes wrong."

"A doctor should have a look at him, don't you think?"

Now alarm bells started ringing in Tara's head, her mind racing as she contemplated whether they could make a quick getaway when everyone supposedly retired for the night. But Angelina saw the concern in Tara's eyes. She smiled. "Don't worry," she said, "We're not going to try to stop you. It's just that my brother is a doctor. He lives near here. I'm sure he would take a look at him. Maybe he could help make things a bit easier for Miracle for the rest of the trip."

Tara relaxed. Now she could see the deep warmth in the woman's eyes. "That would be great. Let me ask Ray about it, okay?"

"Of course."

The two woman chatted a while as they finished cleaning up the kitchen. They talked about their careers. They laughed together when they discovered that they both had an unrequited love for writing. Neither of them wrote much, but they agreed that someday they would find the time.

As they were getting ready to join the men, Angelina asked, "May I ask what your relationship is with Ray?"

Tara looked at Angelina, trying to decide how much she could trust her. Like Ray, she saw as soon as she met her, that Angelina was a very intelligent woman, completely in control of her life. Right now she really needed to trust someone. Miracle wasn't well enough. His long friendship with Ray might be a problem. She wasn't sure she could trust him. She decided to trust Angelina. "Ray? Well, only one way to say this I guess, he's my father. He doesn't know that yet. I wouldn't be too surprised if blood work would have to be done to convince him."

"I see. Why haven't you told him yet?"

"I'm not sure he deserves to know."

Chapter 13

Ray and Tara were sitting in the upstairs guest bedroom Brooks assigned them. The room was large enough for a king size bed, a dresser and a bureau plus a sitting area. Brooks had no idea what Tara had said to his wife, so he was still working under the impression that for some reason, Ray was just being coy. Tara was too good looking. Something had to be going on. To test the theory, he made a bit of a show of escorting them to their room with its king size bed. "You two should be comfortable here," he said. Ray was about to say something, but thought better of it. It occurred to him that maybe Brooks wasn't totally reformed.

As soon as they were alone, Tara pointed to the spacious cushioned window box and said, "One of us is sleeping there tonight." Again, Ray wanted to say something, but he felt off balance, an unusual state of affairs for him. He didn't know where things were headed with Tara, but he realized that under the circumstances, this wasn't time to find out. He didn't want to say or do anything that might cause a problem.

Alone in the room, Tara told Ray about Angelina's brother, how letting a doctor get a look at Miracle might be a good idea. He agreed. If nothing else, the doctor could confirm that Miracle was still of sound mind, something that might come in handy should the situation with Miracle's kids get dicey. Obviously, if the doctor suggested otherwise, the deal was off. Miracle would probably die in a nursing facility in Columbia, South Carolina. It was a chance they would all have to take.

"Before we get the doctor over here," Ray said, "we need to get Miracle's permission. I want Brooks and Angelina in the room with us when we ask him."

"Good idea."

There was a gentle knock on their door. It was Angelina. "Tara," she said, "you mentioned keeping an eye on your friend during the night. I just asked Brooks to put a cot from our camper in Miracle's room. Would that be sufficient for you?"

Tara felt enormous gratitude toward Angelina. She congratulated herself on her judgment about the woman. "That would be lovely, so thoughtful of you. Angelina, we have decided that we would like your brother to see Miracle, as long as Miracle agrees."

"What kind of doctor is he?" Ray asked.

"You're in luck. He's a cardiologist," Angelina said.

"When can he see him?" Ray again.

"Since tomorrow is Saturday, anytime. How about the first thing in the morning?"

"I would like to ask a favor of you and Brooks. I'm going downstairs to ask Miracle if he wants to see the doctor. I would very much appreciate it if you both would listen to his answer," Ray said.

"We can do that, but aren't you concerned that with four of us in the room he might feel intimidated? Perhaps that's the point. You want to force his hand and make him see the doctor?"

"No, that's not it. We'll abide by whatever Miracle wants to do," Ray said.

"In that case, am I correct in assuming you want a witness in case he refuses to see the doctor?"

"Right," Ray said.

"May I suggest that just you and I ask him? I have just met the man and I have just met you as well."

"That is a great idea," Tara said before Ray could answer.

Miracle was feeling weak. At the same time he was restless, trying to get used to new surroundings again. Just a few days ago he had control of his life. He was free to be up and down at will. He still had his car. He was getting his mail. He could still count his cylinders whenever he wanted. Now, he was completely out of his element and dependent on Ray and Tara. Regardless of how sick he was, he hated that he had given up his freedom. He hadn't counted on that when he decided to make the trip. He thought they would be in Florida by now, not some stranger's house in the middle of nowhere.

When Ray and Angelina approached him about seeing a doctor, he flatly refused. Just someone else to tell him what to do, he said. "If I die before I get to Florida, so be it. But I don't think I'm going to die, at least not yet. I'm going to keep breathing for a while."

"If that's the way you want it, paisan, that's what we'll do, but I was hoping maybe Angelina's brother would write you a prescription for more oxygen cylinders."

Miracle's eyes got wide. His whole body seemed to come to attention. "You manipulative son of a bitch. I thought you said we have enough cylinders to get to Florida. Why would we need more?"

Ray saw that he had miscalculated. He suspected Miracle would refuse to see the doctor at first but he had been sure he could convince Miracle to see him if he brought up the cylinders. The one constant in Miracle's conversation from New Jersey to South Carolina was his worry about running out of cylinders. "Okay, Miracle, no doctor. But I'm worried about the possibility that your kids are going to claim you were kidnapped. I thought having a doctor say you were completely with it might help."

"What kind of doctor is your brother, a psychiatrist?" Miracle asked Angelina, a note of sarcasm in his voice.

Ray and Angelina laughed. "There is nothing wrong with this man. I will testify to that in court, if it comes to that," Angelina said.

"Listen, write something up that says I refused medical advice, that I'm not crazy, just short of breath, okay?"

"Won't be necessary. Get some rest, paisan," Ray said.

"I want to leave first thing in the morning," Miracle said.

Miracle had a decent night. He slept through most of it, at least until somewhere near 4:00 a.m. when he got tangled up in his tubing again and woke in a terror. He started cursing, something he rarely ever did and that woke Tara. She quickly got the situation under control, but Miracle was done sleeping. They talked quietly in the dark for a while.

"Do you think we're going to make it to Florida?" he whispered.

"I hope so," Tara said.

"But you have your doubts."

Tara wasn't sure what to say. In the short time she knew Miracle, she had grown fond of him. She was impressed with his will to live in spite of how miserable he felt. That he was so determined to help his son was both heartwarming and heartbreaking under the circumstances.

"I would never bet against you. We'll make it."

"Thanks for saying that," he said.

"Miracle, can I ask you a question?"

"Will it be a hard one? Is it multiple choice at least?"

"Seriously, why are you and Ray friends? I mean as far as I can tell, he pretty much flew in and out of your life all these years. It doesn't take a lot of reading between the lines to see that when he did show up, he wanted something, usually money," She said.

"You have to understand that Ray had a tough life as a kid. Did he tell you his father went to prison?"

"No, he never mentioned that."

"It was pretty bad. People thought Mr. Rosario was in the mafia, being Italian I guess they would think that, but he wasn't. He was just a tough guy. Before he went to prison, he used to smack Ray and his brother around a lot."

"So sad," Tara said.

"It was. And Mrs. Rosario was what people used to call a loose woman."

"Oh my, I guess he didn't have anyone in his life to set an example."

"Ray is very bright. In spite of all that happened to him, he did pretty well in high school, and he had a lot of friends. My parents used to let him sleep over a lot but then his mother put a stop to it when Ray said he wanted to live with us. We were maybe in the ninth grade at the time. After that, he couldn't stay over except weekends for a while."

"You were more like brothers then."

"Yeah, we were. Now let me ask you something." Miracle said. "Really now, what are you doing with Ray? You don't really fit his usual profile. In all the years I've known him, he's been with a lot of different women, but never with someone so much younger."

"It's not what you think."

"What do I think?"

"I don't know, maybe the same thing his buddy Brooks thinks, that I'm just another tennis groupie."

"I know that's not it, but there is more to this than a casual pickup in a bar, isn't there?"

"Did Angelina say something to you?" Tara asked.

"No, she didn't. What would she say though if she did say something to me?"

Tara felt she had been maneuvered into an admission, or maybe she maneuvered herself. She knew what Miracle would say once he learned the truth, that she should tell Ray who she was. That certainly had been her intention when she found Ray, but after meeting him, watching how he interacted with people, she had her doubts. She cleverly used her femininity to get Ray's attention initially, not realizing what a dangerous game she was playing. But Ray turned out to be easy to handle. He was a womanizer, but he wasn't a brute.

When she saw that he seemed a bit uncomfortable about the huge difference in their ages, she used that to her advantage. Of course, she still had her doubts when he asked her to go to New Jersey with him. They didn't know each other that well, but she wanted to learn more about him. And she didn't want to lose track of him now that she finally worked up the courage to find him. If for some reason he became amorous, she had her hole card, being his long lost daughter.

When Miracle asked them to take him to Florida, she immediately saw her chance to see Ray under what were sure to be challenging circumstances. She had learned early in life that people revealed who they really were when they were forced to deal with misery. This trip was the perfect opportunity for her to find out what Ray was made of.

"If I tell you, will you promise not to tell Ray?" she whispered.

"Tara, I can't do that. Ray is my friend. If it's something he needs to know, how could I not tell him?"

"I know that, Miracle. Please trust me on this okay?"

"Will you give me a breathing treatment if I say yes?"

"Of course." She got off her cot, put on a robe Angelina loaned her and found the nebulizer and the medication. She put the meds in a cup, turned on the device and walked over to Miracle's bed where he was now sitting, his swollen feet dangling off the edge of the bed.

"You ready to tell me?" he asked.

"Okay, let's get you started first." She handed him the mouthpiece attached to the tubing. "Here's the thing. Remember I told you about my mother, Dana? How we lived in southern California?"

"Uh, huh."

"Well, my mother and Ray were together for a while."

"And you're his daughter?" Miracle couldn't help it, he was laughing.

"Why is that funny? Don't you believe me?"

"Oh I believe you. It's just that I always knew this would

happen one day. And by the way, I was on to you in North Carolina."

"You were not. You tell stories just like he does," Tara said.

"Are you certain you're his daughter?"

"Are you sure Jagger is your son? Some things you just know. My mother was really sure. You know, she didn't tell me about him until she was dying. She loved him, but it didn't matter. He broke her heart."

"Very sad, but my generation specialized in that."

"You won't tell him will you?"

"No, I won't tell him but you should and soon. Don't let him make a fool of himself. He might feel pressured to make a move on you to impress his asshole friend Brooks."

"Angelina is nice."

"Yes, very nice. Now I have another question for you."

"What's that?"

Miracle took a deep breath, inhaling a final dose of his medication. "Who's the father?"

Tara looked at him in shock. She tried for a humorous tone, but she was trembling now and her voice betrayed her. "Whatever are you talking about?"

"I saw your home pregnancy test in the bathroom at the hotel in Dunn, sorry."

Tara quickly wiped a tear from her eyes. "I don't want to talk about it."

His treatment finished, Miracle got himself back into bed and quickly drifted off to sleep.

Tara tried to sleep, but it was hopeless. Tired of tossing and turning on her tiny cot, she got up and went into the kitchen. Daylight was beginning to creep through the shutters and she needed a cup of coffee. Angelina told her the night before to simply turn on the switch to the coffee maker if she got up early. Everything was set. Just as she was pouring a cup, she felt a presence behind her and then something else. She knew exactly who it was. He bent down to kiss her neck, but she moved away and turned on him.

"I don't know what you think you're doing, but you are making a huge mistake. I'll call Angelina and Ray. Don't test me. "

Brooks backed off. He was grinning. "I had to try. It's in my DNA, I guess."

"Go back upstairs to your wife now and maybe I won't say anything." Tara was shaking in fear and anger.

Then they heard the shuffling of another man's feet. Miracle was on his way to the kitchen. "Please leave," she said to Brooks.

Brooks made his getaway, taking the hall on the opposite side of the kitchen so he wouldn't bump into Miracle. For the second time in the space of one hour, Tara quickly wiped the tears from her eyes so Miracle wouldn't see them. When he got there, he asked, "Everything alright?"

"It's fine. Get some sleep. We have a long day ahead of us."

By eight o'clock that morning everyone was up. The Riley twins were not home, having slept at their friend's house. Angelina was making a pancake breakfast while Tara showered. Ray, having showered the night before, was helping Miracle get ready for the day.

Brooks, who never ate breakfast, was in the sunroom watching the morning news while he walked on his treadmill. When a Fox News reporter said, "We have an update on the search for a 60 year old man suffering from a fatal lung disease, and possibly dementia," he jumped off the treadmill. He had to catch himself on a nearby chair to keep from falling.

He stood in front of the TV transfixed by what he was seeing and hearing. Authorities had found the abandoned van near Dunn, North Carolina. They had also found the AAA tow truck driver who led them to Benny Kays. At first, Benny denied knowing who they were. When the authorities informed him of the AAA records that led them to his shop, Benny got nervous. Still wanting to live up to his promise to Ray, he told the troopers he didn't recall seeing a wheelchair, or oxygen equipment. But Benny panicked when they kept asking the same questions repeatedly, obviously not satisfied with this answers. Finally, he told the troopers about the Yukon XL he sold them. He also identified the young woman as a young, attractive blonde but he got her name wrong, identifying her as Teri. Obviously, it would only be a matter of time now until the cops tracked Miracle and Ray down.

"Ray, I've got some bad news for y'all," Brooks said. Everyone was sitting around the kitchen table eating the pancakes and sausage Angelina prepared.

"What's up, Brooks?" Ray asked.

Brooks told them what he had just seen on the news. They all sat in stunned silence. Finally, Miracle realized it was his move. "We tried," he said.

Brooks looked at Angelina, then at Miracle. "Don't give up just yet. We could lend you our van. We have one we could do without for a few days, don't we honey?" He looked at Angelina for confirmation.

Angelina gave him a look in return as if to say, are we getting into something we might regret? She picked up her coffee and took a sip.

"It would mean the world to Miracle if we could get him to Florida," Tara said.

"I know that. I'm just not sure the van is in good enough condition to make the trip." She took another sip and was about to say something else but, not sure what that should be, she remained silent.

Brooks looked at Ray who was still holding a forkful of pancakes, seemingly suspended in mid-air. His eyes met Tara's next. She was staring intently at him. It was his move. Then he surprised everyone, including himself. "Angelina, they're taking the van. I'm going to get it ready for them. Let's go, Ray."

Ray looked at Angelina. She nodded and said, "Go."

Miracle stood when Ray did and started walking with him. "Where are you going?" Ray asked.

"I want to help you guys," Miracle said.

"Forget that. Just go get your things together."

"I'm not an invalid, Ray. I'm just going to hook up a cylinder, okay? I'll come out and help."

Ray started to protest, but Tara said, "I'll help you get hooked up, Miracle. I think these two can use all the help they can get."

Brooks was already on his way out the door. Ray shook his head no. "Shut up, Ray. He can be a huge help. Give him a chance," Tara said.

Brooks pulled the van out of the garage. The van was dark green with white lines drawn to give it the look of a tennis court with bold white lettering that said, A&B Tennis. Just below that were the words, Match Point. Ray opened all the doors and beckoned Miracle over to have a look. He inspected it and said, "That should work." The van was a lot like the one they had rented in New Jersey only smaller.

Ray and Brooks worked quickly to get the van outfitted. Ray asked Miracle where he thought they should put the mattress, suitcases and concentrator. Miracle tried to move one of the suitcases, but he was out of breath just from standing. Even though it was barely 9:00 a.m., the sun felt hot standing in the driveway. Tara appeared and said, "Miracle, I brought your wheelchair. Why don't you sit down for a bit?"

Miracle was happy to comply. He was sweating and his breathing was labored. "Maybe we should go back inside now until it's time to leave," Tara said. "You can save that cylinder for later, okay?"

Miracle nodded. He had tried to help and that was important to him in that moment. About 20 minutes later, they were ready to go. Brooks pulled the Yukon into his garage. He and Angelina would remove the plates and leave it in an abandoned warehouse area on the other side of town that night.

Tara wheeled Miracle back outside so he could get into the van. They all took turns saying goodbye to each other. When Brooks approached Miracle and stuck his hand out, Miracle just stared at him. But then, out of the corner of his eye he noticed Angelina saying goodbye to Ray, but looking in their direction, a quizzical look on her face. Miracle relented and shook hands with Brooks. "Thank you for everything you've done. Take good care of your family, Brooks, there's never as much time as we think there is."

"I'll do that," Brooks said, a look of relief running across his face.

Tara got behind the wheel first and pointed the van back to I-20, which would take them into Georgia and then Atlanta where they would pick up I-75. Today would be their big push. They were determined to make it to Bonita Springs that night. Any more delays would be too risky. And both Ray and Tara saw reason to worry almost as soon as they hit the Interstate. The van had a noticeable shimmy at speeds over 65 miles per hour.

They had been made twice now and while the tennis van probably offered a decent bit of camouflage, it by no means offered perfect cover. Brooks told them that the news report mentioned Ray again, this time adding that he was a former tennis pro who had played Wimbledon.

Miracle had started with a nearly full cylinder to work on. Two hours later, he was nearing the end of his second cylinder when they stopped for a bathroom break. Ray waited for him to finish, then wheeled him back to the van. They were nervous about being seen. It was obvious that anyone who had seen the news coverage would recognize them. As they were making their way back to the van, Tara said, "we have a man in a wheelchair, an old guy with a ponytail and a young chick with blonde hair. Even a detective school dropout could spot us."

"Maybe you should dye your hair," Ray said, only half in jest.

"And you should cut your ponytail," Miracle said.

"Right, and you should rise and walk, my friend," Ray added.

But Ray's heart rate jumped when he went into the back of the van to get another cylinder for Miracle. He found one box that Benny had given them still nearly full, 8 cylinders. The other box was missing. He remembered they had decided to leave the empties in the Yukon to give them more space in Brooks' smaller van. He had left the job of transferring the tanks to Brooks while he went back into the house to get his shaving kit which he forgot to pack.

He pulled one of the cylinders out of the box and connected Miracle. His hands were actually shaking, but Miracle was too groggy to notice. "Tara, come outside and have a smoke with me," he said.

Tara was about to yell at him, tell him they didn't have time, that they shouldn't stay in one spot any longer than necessary, but she caught the hitch in Ray's voice. Ray told Tara what he found out. She blanched. "What else could possibly go wrong? Will you tell me Ray?"

Chapter 14

"I was going through a few old letters and I found this one."

"What does it say, mother?"

Miracle would have howled with laughter had he heard that; a few old letters. His ex wife saved everything, every scrap of correspondence between them. She successfully coerced Miracle into a better divorce settlement because of some notes that passed between them after a brief separation where he made promises to provide for her, in his words, beyond his means, if necessary.

"I think I found the full name of that woman in Florida your father was so crazy about," Sandy said.

"Let me see the letter," Melanie said. Melanie had just arrived at her mother's townhouse. They were planning on going to the mall later that afternoon.

"No, a lot of it is private. Your father may not have loved me the way he loved this Marcia Lacy woman, but he could be romantic, in writing at least."

"Fine, just read me the part involving that Lacy chick."

"No need, really. He just said he was deeply in love once, but that it was over a long time ago. He must have mentioned her a couple of times. I probably got pissed off, so he wrote to explain."

"Probably? What else did he say?"

"They were just college kids. It was his first meaningful relationship. He said he didn't want to hide anything from me because we should have no secrets. So he told me her name and where she lived at the time, which was Coral Gables," Sandy said.

"I wonder if she's there now, but that wouldn't make any sense, would it? Why would he be going to Bonita Springs if Marcia wasn't there?

"You are assuming that he is going to Florida to see her, but that may not be the case. His buddy Ray is really all the motive he needs."

"Mom, what is the deal with Ray? Why are they so close?"

"All I know is something happened between them when they were kids. In spite of your father's promise not to keep secrets, that is one thing he never wanted to discuss, at least not with me."

"I haven't heard much about Ray in the last few years. Daddy used to mention him at least once in a while. After he got sick, he just stopped talking about him."

"When we were married, once a year, your father used to go to one of Ray's tennis clinics. As I recall, every time he went, it was somewhere different than the last time. Your father loved the game," Sandy said. "He was a good tennis player in his time."

Melanie nodded her head in agreement. "Where the hell is he?"

"Have you heard anything from the police?"

"No. I get more information watching the news than I do from them. Did you see the news this morning?"

"No, I had an early yoga class."

"On Saturday morning? Since when do you get up so early on weekends?"

"Mind your own business," Sandy said, a sly smile on her face.

"No wait, you have a boyfriend?"

"Did you watch the news?" Sandy asked.

"No, Vincent and I slept in. That's probably what you were doing. Yoga my ass. Let's put CNN on before we go to the mall, see if there's an update." Sandy got up to look for the remote. Melanie's cell phone rang. It was Brian.

"Heard the latest? They found the second car, the red Yukon. It was just on the news."

"You're kidding, where was it?"

"Wait till you hear this. Some guy named Brooks Riley got stopped in South Carolina around nine o'clock this morning driving the car. He said a friend of his, which was Ray of course, asked him to keep the car for him until he got back from a trip he was on."

"Unbelievable! Did the report say anything else?" Melanie motioned to Sandy to hurry up and get the television on.

"The report said the guy got stopped for running through a stop sign. He claimed he only saw Ray, and that Ray wasn't traveling with anyone. Then he said all he knew was Ray was headed to Florida, but decided to fly rather than drive."

"What else?"

"Not much. This guy, Riley supposedly took Ray to the airport. Claims he doesn't know anything beyond that. He said they were tennis buddies."

Melanie put her brother on hold while she brought Sandy up to date.

"Obviously, this Riley character is lying," Sandy said. "Tennis buddies; another bum in on the scam if you ask me. Wait until they find out how little money your father really has left."

"What does that mean?" Melanie asked.

"Don't worry, Melanie. They probably won't touch your father's insurance. You're protected at least that much."

"I was concerned about dad being taken advantage of."

"I'm sure you were. This is just an impossible situation. It will all be straightened out once they find him."

Melanie got back on the phone with her brother and suggested that Brian meet them at the mall to discuss what, if anything, to do next. An hour later, they were together in the mall's food court. The mall was busy; mostly people who wanted to get out of the heat and into the air conditioned confines where they could browse the shops. By now, Melanie's appearance on the news had run enough times for her to be recognizable. Walking through the mall to find Brian, she was stopped several times by well meaning people who wanted to offer her an encouraging word. Of course, as is often the case, they wanted to share their tale of woe about an elderly parent or grandparent.

Melanie bit into a slice of pepperoni pizza. "I'm going to need a disguise to go out now," she said.

"Come on, you love it, sis," Brian said, "I'll bet Vincent is way envious."

Sandy smiled. There was a good bit of truth in Brian's words.

"Do you believe that guy Riley's story? You don't think Ray would abandon dad do you?" Melanie asked.

"No, no. I'm sure he wouldn't do that," Sandy said.

"Unless he's dead already," Brian said.

"Even Ray wouldn't be that stupid. What would he do, leave him dead or dying in a motel room? The man is selfish, not stupid," Sandy said.

"So they probably switched cars again. I think we should try to get this Riley guy on the phone. He's probably covering for Ray. Maybe if a family member talks to him he might tell us something," Melanie said. "It just kills me to think of Daddy suffering so much cooped up in yet another car."

"You're the last person this guy is going to say anything to, Mel. You gotta figure he knows why Dad and Ray are being so secretive, and why Dad isn't making this crazy trip with us instead of Ray," Brian said.

They sat in silence for a few minutes.

"I wonder how they knew enough to switch vehicles so quickly," Melanie asked.

"They're probably watching the news too, just like us. When they found out the cops knew about the Yukon, they ditched it," Brian said.

"I'm sure you're right, Brian, but what I am now wondering is how are they supplying him with enough oxygen? How many of those cylinders can they be carrying and where did they get them?" Sandy asked.

"Yeah right. Maybe they paid off a delivery guy," Melanie said.

It was a good question, though. In the rush to find Miracle, the authorities apparently overlooked Miracle's constant need for oxygen. Certainly the driver of the oxygen delivery van noticed something wrong on his first stop after Miracle's. He soon discovered he was short 28 cylinders. He counted and recounted. He knew he would be fired if his manager ever found out he left his truck unlocked, something that was strictly against policy and FDA regulations. So, he didn't say a word to anyone about it. The facility he worked for was large, with more than 1,000 oxygen patients. He decided to cover the loss with paperwork, and figure out what to do about it later.

When Miracle's story hit the news, he didn't panic. He put a story together in case he was asked, but so far no one said anything about it. His plan was to deny losing any cylinders. It would be hard to prove otherwise. His only worry was the chance that the cylinders would be found. Stickers with the company's name and logo were attached to them. Had he known that Tara had the foresight to remove the stickers, he would have rested easier.

"Vincent said maybe we should think about going to Florida, to see what we could find out," Melanie said.

Brian was about to say something unkind about Melanie's husband. He looked in Sandy's direction and thought better of it, but Sandy smiled. She understood perfectly. "How would you know where to look or where to even start?" Brian asked, biting into an Italian sub.

"That's what I said. But now we know about this Lacy woman. For all we know Dad is already there, planning a deathbed wedding to the unforgettable Marcia Lacy. It might be worth a shot."

Brian couldn't help laughing. "You're priceless Mel. But, what if he is there, then what?" Brian asked.

"Good question," Sandy added. "And if he isn't there, which

is more likely, then what are you going to do? Do you want more air time? Is that it? Maybe Piers Morgan will have you on. You can discuss the coincidence of having the same surname."

"Suppose you're right, mom, and the whole thing is about Ray and whatever happened between them in the past? I hate to say this but Daddy is dying anyway. We could lose everything if Ray takes the money and runs to some tropical island."

"I think you will be made to look foolish if you run down there," Sandy said.

"Why? Tell me why you think that?"

"There is nothing you can do for your father now. His life is over. What could possibly be your motive for harassing that poor woman if you find her? Maybe that's where your father is headed and maybe it isn't. Either way, your only real concern seems to be about the money. Very unseemly, Melanie."

"You should talk, Mom."

Sandy got up. "I'm glad we've taken to driving everywhere separately. It seems that we can't be civil to each other long enough to make it through a simple meal," Sandy said. "If you are determined to go to Florida, take your brother. Your husband is likely to make an even bigger mess of things."

Chapter 15

As they were approaching the outskirts of Atlanta, Tara and Ray agreed not to tell Miracle what they discovered yet. There was no point in upsetting him. No doubt he would quickly go into a full blown panic if he knew they were running low on cylinders. His breath rate would increase and make the problem bigger than it already was.

"Time for plan B," Tara said.

"What's that?" Ray asked. They were speaking softly so Miracle wouldn't hear, but it wasn't necessary. He was listening to music on an iPod. Tara actually did a double take when she saw him with the ear phones. It was the first indication she had that he had any interest in music. Miracle was listening to Beethoven's Symphony No. 5 in C minor. His interest in classical music was recent. A social worker he met when he was still doing pulmonary rehabilitation recommended it to him as a way to relax.

"Remember, I told you I used to work for a homecare company?"

"Vaguely."

"Well, I did. I was a sales rep for Perfect Respiratory. They're the largest provider of home oxygen services in the country," Tara said. "Don't you remember? I told you about it a couple of days ago when we were in Virginia, I think."

"Yeah, that's right. Was that in California?"

"San Diego. I did it for 5 years. Made president's club three of those years. You probably won't believe this, but I was named best sales rep for the whole company one year."

"Wow, one question: How does that help us now? We're not in San Diego. We're on the way to Atlanta."

"I got to know a lot of people, pretty much all over the

country," Tara said. "The Big P, that's what they call it, has a huge location in Atlanta."

"You know anybody at the Big P in Atlanta?"

"I do if he still works for the company. Turnover's always been high, so I can't be sure. Anyway, we dated a while when we were both sales reps"

"In San Diego?"

"Yes, Ray, pay attention. Last time I spoke with him, at least a couple of years ago, he told me he was transferring to Atlanta, which is where he's from actually."

"What's your plan? You gonna call him?" Ray asked.

"I think I have to. We can't get to Bonita Springs if we don't get more cylinders."

Tara explained her plan to Ray. She would call her old boyfriend, David Sasso and see if he would meet her for a drink. She would ask him to help, hoping he hadn't heard about the missing pulmonary fibrosis patient. "We shouldn't get our hopes up on that though. Considering what he does for a living, it's like hoping somebody from Pepsi wouldn't hear about a Coke recall," she said.

"Well if he's heard about us, then what?" Ray asked.

"Like I said, he probably has. David was always a news junkie. I'll ask him to do us a favor; maybe let us sneak into the warehouse at night and get some cylinders or something like that. We could give him a few bucks for his trouble. I would like to get 15 more cylinders. Even if we could get ten, I think we'd be alright."

"Do you really think this guy will go for it?"

"I don't know. First things first, he has to be still working there," Tara said.

"I'm not sure that does us a lot of good anyway, Tara. Not unless these people work on Saturday," Ray said.

"That's right! It's Saturday. Somebody has to be on call for emergencies though. That's standard procedure."

"I hate to be so far behind the curve, but how does that help?"

"Whoever is on call will know him if he works there. He might even be on call himself."

She picked up her cell phone and turned it on. Ray gave her a worried look. "I know, they might be monitoring us for calls, but we're already vulnerable, Ray. Maybe my cell isn't being checked. None of the news reports have mentioned my name. It's a chance we'll have to take. Anyway, getting off the Interstate and trying to find a pay phone is risky too. And, in case you haven't noticed, there aren't a lot of pay phones around."

Directory assistance provided her with the number she wanted, and connected her to the company's answering service.

"Perfect Respiratory, help is on the way, how may I help you?"

"Hello, can you tell me who's on call today?"

"Let me see, yes, it's Jillian Crockett."

"Would you put me through to her please?"

"Is there an emergency?"

"Yes, please hurry."

"Transferring you now."

"This is Jill Crockett, how may I help you?"

"Hello Jill, I'm very sorry to bother you, especially on a weekend, but I am looking for a former colleague by the name of David Sasso."

"Wait, you called this number on a Saturday to look up a friend of yours?"

"Yes, and I'm so sorry but it's very important that I reach him. Does he still work for Perfect Respiratory?"

"As a matter of fact, he doesn't work for us anymore."

"Do you know where I can find him?"

"Who is this calling?"

"Jackie Brown."

"Well Jackie, he works for one of our competitors now, here in Atlanta. He's a friend of mine too."

"I would be ever so grateful for his number," Tara said as sweetly as she could.

The woman gave Sasso's cell phone number to Tara. "Please tell him I said hello."

When she got off the phone Ray was waiting for her. "Jackie Brown, like the Tarantino movie?"

"Pretty slick, huh? I was watching that movie in my room when I couldn't sleep while we were cooped up in that miserable motel in North Carolina. Anyway, I didn't dare give her my real name."

She called the number Jillian gave them and quickly got Dennis Sasso. "Hot damn, I remember you, girl. How could I forget? Are you in town?" Sasso was sitting in a Starbucks a few miles from his home, drinking a mocha latte and fiddling with a spreadsheet on his laptop.

"I am. I was hoping maybe we could meet for a drink, maybe tonight," Tara said.

"Cool, Being Saturday and all, I might have to move a few things around, but yeah, I can do it."

They played catch up for a few minutes and agreed that Tara would call Dennis as soon as she saw how her day was going. She made sure to find out the name of the company where he worked now and where it was located. She promised to call or text him so they could decide where to meet.

They got to Atlanta at eleven that morning. They desperately needed a place where they could hook up Miracle's concentrator and get him off the cylinders. They worried about their chances of being caught even if they checked into a seedy roadside motel, but what choice did they have? "Probably not much to worry about," Ray said. "The people who work in these dumps are probably too busy watching The Jerry Springer Show to keep up with the news."

"You are an enlightened man, aren't you?" Tara said.

When Miracle questioned why they were checking into a motel so early in the day, Ray told him the van was giving them some trouble. He would have to get it checked out. By now they knew Miracle would ask questions if he suspected something was off. They rented just one room, hoping he wouldn't think anything was amiss. It didn't work. Miracle asked Ray about it. "We just need a place to hang out and plug you in while they work on the van. We should be on the road again by this afternoon."

Not that Miracle was entirely convinced. He listened to Ray's explanation for the delay and said, "You wouldn't kid me would you, Ray?"

Ray assured him the problem was probably minor, but he didn't want to take another chance of being stranded on the highway especially in this heat. They found a small roadside motel and quickly got Miracle situated. Tara switched his oxygen hookup from a cylinder to a concentrator. The poor guy looked awful. His feet and legs up to his knees were really swollen now. He could barely stand or walk without being hunched over. Still, to avoid any chance they might be spotted by a nosy motel resident or a guest who rented by the hour, they pushed and cajoled Miracle to walk to his room rather than sit in his wheelchair.

It was shaping up to be another hot, muggy day. Ray and Tara stepped outside to talk. "What am I supposed to do now, go out and drive the van around for a few hours?" Ray asked.

"That's about the size of it, Ray. I don't think we should tell him any more than we have to. Just so you know, if we don't get this mess taken care of so we can be on the road by morning, I'm pulling the plug on this operation."

"That's not your decision."

"It is Ray. Did you forget I am in charge here? Maybe you would prefer that I leave now. Care to drop me off at the Atlanta airport?"

Ray looked Tara over as if he was really seeing her clearly for the first time. She was indeed a force to be reckoned with. She had a way of opening her blue eyes very wide and staring you down to reinforce her point, when necessary. He wondered how he missed that before. "Okay, you're probably right anyway. I'm going to get going."

"When you get back, park the van on the other side of the building."

Tara went back into the motel room, which was easily the worst room she had ever set foot in. It was dirty and had an odor that made the room in Dunn seem like fresh flowers in comparison. Miracle was waiting for her.

"What's really going on?" he said.

"What do you mean? Ray just took the van to find a mechanic," Tara said.

"Tara, we haven't known each other very long. A few days, right? But I know enough about you to know you are a terrible liar. Now, what's up?"

Tara looked at Miracle's face. He looked exhausted and worse, defeated. "You have a right to know. We're running short of cylinders. We think we accidentally left some at the Riley's home. But we do have a plan."

"What's that? Miracle asked. He reached for a tissue and blew his nose. "I hope we're not running out of tissues."

Tara explained her plan. She had an old friend who she was sure would help them out. She told him that they dated for a while when they lived in San Diego.

"Why did you break up?" Miracle asked.

"He really wasn't my type of guy, I guess," Tara said.

"Why?" Miracle wasn't satisfied.

"I guess we weren't on the same page. He wanted to have fun. He was kind of wild I guess; lots of drinking and partying, if you know what I mean. I was looking for someone a bit more serious."

"You seem nervous talking about him," Miracle said.

"I'll be alright, really."

Miracle nodded. He maneuvered his wheelchair so he could look out the window, wondering if Ray would be back soon. Tara had to go to the bathroom again. When she came out Miracle was waiting for her.

"I know this is none of my business, Tara but on the matter of your pregnancy, I assume you know who the father is."

"Of course I do. I can't believe you just said that."

"Easy, I'm on my last legs here. When I said I assumed it, I meant exactly that. Have you told him yet?"

"No, I haven't had time."

"But you will tell him."

"I haven't decided, Miracle. I'm sure under the circumstances, considering what you're going through to meet your son, you think I should."

"My circumstances are mine, not yours. But yes, Marcia's decision not to tell me about Jagger was unfortunate, for me at least. I'm just saying if he's someone you care about and respect, in my opinion, you should tell him.

Tara held up her hand. "Sorry, I can't discuss this right now. I try not to even think about it."

Miracle was about to ask another question, but he had to blow his nose yet again. "Time for a breathing treatment?" he asked. He forgot what his question was.

Ray was gone for about three hours. He came back, soaked with sweat. He had taken his tennis bag with him. To kill the time, he found a private club where he had played several years ago. He had no trouble finding a game. No money changed hands; he just needed a good workout. Somebody at the club recognized him, most likely because Wimbledon was going on. The guy gave him a touch of the celebrity treatment, which he always enjoyed. In the moment, it didn't occur to him that he was also a celebrity for a different reason now. Fortunately, no one asked him anything about his involvement with Miracle and the search that was going on, but one guy, the player he trounced in straight sets, commented on his van with the A&B Tennis logo.

When Tara heard where he had been, she had a fit. "How

could you be so, I don't know, stupid?"

"Nobody said anything to me. We're fine. I just needed a workout." He didn't mention the comment about his van. "The auto mechanic's shop was right across the street from the club, I couldn't resist." Ray winked at Tara. "I got a ride from the mechanic. He thinks we should be good to go by tonight or tomorrow morning."

"He knows," Tara said.

"Who knows?"

Tara pointed at Miracle.

"Oh, sorry paisan, we thought it might be better not to say anything."

"I understand. Listen, Tara and I have been talking. If we can't get the cylinders, just get me to a decent hotel and call a local hospice. I've had enough, I think. As much as I want to see Marcia and meet my son, this is more than I bargained for."

"You ready to quit now? We can do that if you want to," Ray said.

"I don't know. You think I can make it?"

"Doesn't matter what I think Miracle. It's what you think that matters. But to answer your question, I believe you can make it."

"I know I don't have to say this, Ray, but even if this ends here, you should keep the money," Miracle said.

"We'll make it, Miracle. Have faith." With that, Ray went to take a shower. After a match he always followed the same routine, alternating hot and cold water. It helped to relieve his aches and pains. For his part, it never occurred to Ray he might have to give the money back. As soon as they crossed the New Jersey line into Delaware, the money was his.

His tennis shop deal was real. Of course, it was a more complicated transaction than he let on to Miracle and Tara. He was, in a sense, going to be gambling with Miracle's money, but this time he would also be gambling with whatever was left of his life. As he saw it, he had no choice. He had a chance to win enough money to get a backer to take him seriously so he could open his shop. Tennis was all he knew. Playing the game for a living though, was simply becoming too hard to do.

Tara placed her call to Dennis just before five o'clock. They agreed to meet at an upscale tavern called Horizons in Buckhead at 6:30. Ray would drive her to the place early so Dennis wouldn't see the van, at least not right away. They would have to leave Miracle alone for a while. He was fine with that. "Just get the cylinders," he said, "I want to leave tonight."

The plan was to convince Dennis to help and tell him that Ray would meet them at the facility to pick up the tanks. If all went well, they could be on the road by 8:30, nine o'clock at the latest. Tara decided to take a shower. They had only rented one room. The idea of taking her clothes off and actually using the bathroom made her ill. While she was showering, Miracle waved Ray over to the bed where he was lying and said, "I want to talk to you."

"What's up?"

Miracle struggled to sit up. Ray gave him a hand, placing a couple of the motel's flimsy pillows behind his back for support. "Listen, I am not too keen on Tara's plan. That ex- boyfriend of hers might be a problem."

"How in the hell would you know that?" Ray asked.

"We talked earlier while you were hitting passing shots down the line. It wasn't so much what she said as the way she said it."

"Tara can handle herself. She's done a great job of keeping me at bay."

"As far as I can see, you haven't really tried. Why is that?"

"I don't know why. Good question, I guess."

"Is there something about her that's maybe different?" Miracle asked.

"There is, but I can't put my finger on it. Maybe it's me, slowing down, as much as I hate to admit it," Ray said.

Miracle was once very good at this type of conversation. He

could lead people down the path he wanted them to take almost at will. It was the reason he was successful selling cars and real estate. He wasn't a manipulator; he really believed it was the right path for his customer. But he didn't have the energy or the patience anymore. His mind, oxygen deprived now, would wander. His judgment wasn't what it used to be either.

"Ray, she asked me not to tell you this. Maybe I shouldn't, but it might be important now. I wouldn't want her doing something she will regret just to get me oxygen tanks. I won't have that."

"Okay, fine, but what exactly are you trying to tell me then?"

"That girl thinks you're her father."

"Oh no, fuck me, that can't be true."

"Hand me that little notepad next to my wallet," Miracle said. "I have to write almost everything down now. The last few months I can't remember much of anything." He leafed through some pages in his notepad. When he stopped he took a quick look at the bathroom. Tara had just turned the water off. "We don't have much time. Do you remember a woman named Dana who lived somewhere near Malibu?"

Ray's face turned a very pale shade of white. He nodded. "Damn it! My God Miracle, I think I just put my finger on it. She looks just like her. I have to say Doodles –that was her nickname, was great. She was an actress, I think. Sure, I remember her. But that doesn't make Tara my daughter."

Miracle shook his head. "Who would ever imagine that in the span of less than a week you and I would both discover we might have a kid we didn't know about? She could be yours right?"

"Yeah, it's possible, but like your deal, how do you know for sure?"

"What do your instincts tell you about her?"

"Don't even want to think about it paisan, not even a little bit."

"I hope I did the right thing. Keep an eye on her tonight. One more thing, let her tell you, okay?"

"Okay."

They got to Horizon's early, as planned. Before she got out of the van, Ray said, "Don't wait too long before springing the favor on this guy. "People get annoyed when you don't level with them."

Tara who was looking directly at Ray, turned her head and looked at the car parked in front of them. She turned toward him. "Seriously? You think you have the credibility to offer that kind of advice?"

Ray ignored her. "Listen to me. You can be sure he's built up your reunion with something specific in mind. The longer you wait to tell him what you really want, the more pissed off he's gonna be." Tara nodded, still looking straight ahead. "One more thing. Don't do anything stupid."

"Wouldn't think of it."

Dennis Sasso was married but not entirely happy about it. He never wore a wedding ring and he wasn't about to tell Tara he was married. He had some trouble getting free, it being a Saturday night. In fact, he picked a fight with his wife so he could storm out of the house. He was clever enough to suggest earlier that they get dressed up and go out to dinner. About fifteen minutes before it was time to leave, he started in on his wife. It didn't take much. He knew which buttons to push. Now, he was out of the house and dressed for dinner. He was pleased with himself.

Now, sitting with Tara, enjoying a margarita at one of the most popular watering holes in Atlanta, he was glad he made the effort. He had teased her when she ordered a non-alcoholic drink but she told him drinking made her sleepy and she had a long night ahead. He laughed and said, "Me too."

She looked incredible, better than he remembered. She was always sexy no matter what she was wearing and time had changed her a little. Her approach was a bit more subtle now, rather than in your face. She was wearing denim designer, tapered leg jeans and a silk short sleeve peach colored blouse. He liked that.

Tara wasn't so enthralled. She had indeed changed. She could now clearly see in Dennis what she wasn't able to see years ago. Her intuition told her that once Dennis knew what she wanted, he would use it as a bargaining chip to get what he wanted. She gripped the stem of her virgin margarita glass hard. She would give this jerk what he wanted to help Miracle. She knew that. It made her feel good and sick to her stomach at the same time.

She decided to take Ray's advice and not waste time. As soon as they dispensed with a few pleasantries, she got to the point. "Dennis, I need to ask a huge favor of you. I'll understand if you can't do it but I have to ask, okay?"

"Shoot."

"I need about fifteen full E cylinders. Please don't ask why."

"I don't guess I'll have to." He picked up his drink to make a mock toast. "Let's see if I get this right. To the mystery woman on the news. The fair lady on the run with the pulmonary fibrosis patient. Am I right?"

"I'm afraid so."

"I don't believe this. Tara Ridgley scamming an old man out of his fortune."

"You don't know what you're talking about Dennis. I am just doing a favor for a friend."

"Do you know what they're calling the story now?"

"No."

"The Miracle Mystery."

"Sounds lovely." Tara gave Sasso a brave smile. "Will you help us?"

"You're one hot chick in more ways than one. What you're asking me to do isn't exactly legal and it's very risky. I don't know how you got this far, but you should know as well as I do how foolish it is to carry oxygen around like that. I wouldn't be able to forgive myself if you got blown up."

"We have them secured; at least we did most of the way. I

know I'm asking a lot, but won't you help me get this poor man where he wants to go? It's his dying wish."

"You want to know my dying wish?" Dennis reached under the table and squeezed Tara's knee.

"Please Dennis. We were close once. I really need this."

"Where are you going" Sasso asked.

"Trust me, the less you know the better. Anyway, you won't have to get in trouble. You can make it look like they were stolen, or maybe even cover the lost cylinders with paperwork. By the time anybody knows anything, this whole mess will be over with."

"How did you ever get mixed up in this? I mean this doesn't sound at all like the Tara I knew back in the day."

Tara reached into her bag for a tissue. She was crying a little. "It's been a nightmare Dennis. It's much too long a story to go into now. I'll have to tell you about it sometime." She took a sip of her drink and got her tears under control. She had not expected that.

Sasso gave her an appraising look. He grinned and said, "you know me right? What's in it for me?"

There it was. He wasn't wasting any time either. "What do you want?"

"Spend the night with me."

Tara took a deep breath. "You haven't changed a bit. Even if I wanted to do that, I don't have the time. We have to get out of here tonight."

"What's your hurry? You look like a girl that needs to loosen up, unwind a little," Sasso said.

"I can't spend the night with you. Is there some other way you might be willing to help me?"

"Not really. Tell you what though; let's go over to my office. I guess I can settle for a quickie," Sasso said a leering at her. "How did you get here?"

Tara took another sip of her drink. The place was beginning to get crowded. She wished she could disappear into the crowd and forget everything that happened during the last few days.

"Yo, Tara, how did you get here?" Sasso asked, deliberately elongating each word.

"The guy, Miracle you referred to has a friend." Tara said.

"Oh yeah, the tennis pro. Where is he now?"

"He's waiting outside in our van."

"Ditch him. Tell him to come to the office a couple of hours from now. We'll get you loaded up after you and I get fully reacquainted."

"If I do this, will you promise not to say anything to anyone, ever?"

"Promise. Anyway, once I give you the cylinders, it's my ass too if I tell. I'll be satisfied with your ass," Sasso said, an even wider grin on his face. This was working out better than he expected. Although Tara had been kind enough not to mention it, he had gained about 35 pounds, all of it around his middle, since the last time he saw her. In spite of his swagger, he lacked the confidence he once had.

"Ray, it's Tara. My friend is going to help us. Meet me at his office in two hours. You remember where it is?

"What do you mean two hours?" Ray asked. Miracle's concern was front and center now.

"Don't ask questions. Just do it," Tara said. She disconnected the phone and told Sasso to finish his drink, which he did in one quick gulp. She could feel tears welling up in her eyes, but she fought them off. This was the last time anyone would ever take advantage of her she told herself. Sasso paid the waitress. Then, his arm tightly around Tara, they headed for his 300 Series BMW.

They drove to an industrial park area in the southern part of the city near Hartsfield International Airport. Sasso turned his CD player on to listen to Kanye West. He was in good spirits. "Tell you what I'll do, Tara. I have a couple of old freestanding cylinder racks. I'll let you have them. That will give you something to hold the cylinders. By the way, if you have any empties, I want them."

"No problem. Do we really have to do this, Dennis? We were

close once. Doesn't it bother you to have me this way?"

"A little, I guess."

"But you're still willing to make me do it anyway?"

"Come on Tara. We used to do it three times a day; in the office, the car. I think one time at the movies. You're just making a trade for something you want; although I have to admit, I can't figure out why. You owe this guy something?"

"Like I said before, it's complicated."

"Okay, but in my opinion, if you're willing to do it for something like this, I'm guessing this isn't your first time. So don't get all holier than thou with me."

Tara didn't respond. She sat looking at her hands. She noticed a chip in her nail polish on her right index finger. She wanted nothing more than to distract herself at that moment. Dennis was dead wrong. She had never traded any part of her body for anything or anyone.

But was Dennis right that if she did it for him now, gave into him, she would do it again, and maybe again after that? Was that what happened to her mother? Was she, Tara, born because Ray extorted her? What could she have wanted or needed from him? She had no proof of course, but hadn't Ray more or less extorted Miracle, taken the money in exchange for taking him to Florida? Maybe when it got right down to it, she was just like Ray, a born hustler, maybe like Ray's father, a convicted criminal, her grandfather. Was she the latest in a long line? The thought frightened her. Yet, she knew what was at stake for Miracle. What choice did she have?

When they got to the facility, Sasso again put his arm around Tara, but he let his hand slide down around her buttocks and gave her a squeeze. He opened the door and deactivated the alarm. He ushered Tara in and walked her down a long corridor that was filled with cardboard file boxes stacked on both sides of the wall. At the end of the corridor, there was an open space filled with desks. Tara noticed more boxes stacked in front of cubicles which partially hid otherwise recognizable posters meant to motivate worker productivity. Sasso hurried her along to his office, which wasn't as cluttered as the other areas. It had a small maroon couch against the wall, opposite from where his desk sat, perfect for a moment such as this. Sasso was so excited about his good fortune that he neglected to lock the entrance door.

"Let's get naked," he said.

Tara was crying softly. She couldn't help it. She had been a bit wild, perhaps even a bit easy a few times when she was younger, but around the time she learned her mother was dying, she made a conscious decision to change her ways. Not long after that, she started thinking about finding her father. It took months to find the courage to look for him, and almost as many months to work up the nerve to approach him once she found him.

Well, now that she found him, he was as unavailable as ever. In the moment, it didn't matter that she still hadn't revealed herself to Ray or that she had instructed him to wait two hours before picking her up. She needed him now.

And suddenly, he was there. Just like that, he was standing in the doorway. Sasso already had his shirt off and was unbuckling his belt. Just as he started to urge Tara to get her clothes off, he looked up and saw Ray standing there.

"Who are you?" Sasso asked. But he knew.

"Ray, get out of here," Tara said.

"Excuse me," Ray said, calmly looking directly at Sasso. "I don't want to interrupt, but it looks to me, my friend, like the lady is crying. What's up?" His words were casual. His demeanor though, left no doubt that a wrong answer by Sasso, who was trying to re-buckle his belt, would mean trouble.

Sasso quickly assessed the situation. "Why don't you both get the hell out of here," Sasso said.

"Ray, he was going to help," Tara said.

"I can see that. Know what? I'll bet he's still willing to help us."

"Listen dude, what I'm going to do is call the cops," Sasso said.

Ray held up his right hand. "Nobody is going to make you do anything. We need some cylinders. I'm sure Tara explained all that. How much do you want for them? Name your price."

Sasso quickly thought things over. It occurred to him the night didn't have to be a total loss. "She said she wants fifteen tanks," he said, pointing to Tara. "You can have them for $100 each."

"You got a deal, but I don't have that much cash on me. Tell you what I'm gonna do. I'll give you $300 now and I'll send you the rest later, okay?"

"Get serious dude. You expect me to believe I'll get another dime from you? What the fuck do you take me for? Forget it."

Ray's eyes scanned the office for a minute. He was looking for something that would give him an edge, something more to bargain with. There was a Bose radio on the credenza behind Sasso's desk, A San Diego Chargers poster on the wall and a football sitting on the edge of his desk. Then he saw it. He took a few steps closer to it to get a better look. "That picture there on your desk; it looks like you and maybe your wife."

"So?" Sasso was too nervous to think.

"I'm just saying that fifteen hundred bucks is a pretty good deal. You can buy her something nice maybe. What's her name?"

"That's none of your business, dude."

"None of your business; long name, don't you think, Tara?"

Tara looked at Sasso. "Whatever."

"How about it, do we have a deal my friend?" Ray asked.

Sasso, hands on hips now surprised Ray. "No deal chump. It's my word against yours,"

Now Ray was beginning to lose his patience. He took a couple of steps toward Sasso. The expression on his face changed. Tara had never seen him look like that. She was frightened. "You're running out of time kid. We need the oxygen," Ray said, his tone now threatening.

"Everything was set until you walked in here," Sasso said, a worried look on his face.

"Well, that party has been cancelled. But I'll tell you what will happen if you don't get wise fast. My friend dies here in Atlanta? I'm going to make you pay. Your wife is going to know all about what you were planning to do tonight. Tara and I will visit her personally. And I'll make sure your employer knows what happened too. Remember, you set the price, you're going to look like maybe the worst jerk in the world by the time we're done with you. By the way, did you know we're all over the news?"

"Yeah, so what?"

"We're going to make you famous too, pal. I'll make sure you get in on the story. When I tell them what you wanted in exchange for helping a dying man, you'll be on the front page of the New York Post. Listen, how about you take my deal? Put some extra money in your pocket and let's all be on our way."

Sasso didn't have to think it over. He was beaten. He was still standing there in his office bare chested, his belly shaking. He felt like a fool. "You'll send me the other $1,200?"

"In cash," Ray said.

"Alright, I'll do it."

"Don't forget the cylinder racks you promised me," Tara said.

Chapter 16

As soon as the van was loaded Tara and Ray pulled away and headed for the motel. It turned out that Sasso only had 12 full cylinders available. As he handed him the $300, Ray promised him he would still send him the $1,200 as long as he kept his mouth shut.

"Will you really send him the rest of the money"? Tara asked.

"Sure, the money and a nice Confederate flag," Ray said, laughing. "I really wanted to smack him."

"We need to talk, Ray."

"I know."

After they were a few miles away from the facility, Ray pulled the van into a parking lot surrounding a complex of offices. They sat in silence for a while each one waiting for the other to break the ice. Finally, just to say something, Ray said, "So guys like Sasso, were there a lot of them when you worked for Perfect Respiratory?"

"Are there a lot of guys like you who play tennis?"

Ray started to say something, but he was tired of defending himself. Miracle and Tara would never get it.

"No, he isn't typical," Tara continued. "I'm afraid the home care industry is the best kept secret in healthcare. Most of the people love the business because they get to help people like Miracle."

"That's nice to know," Ray said, a hint of laughter in his voice.

"I'm serious. Every business has its rogues, you know that. Hardly anyone gives these people credit for the good work they do. That's why I stayed at Perfect so long. These people are truly dedicated to their work and their patients. And the government is always harassing them."

"Harassing them? For what?"

"Well for starters, they keep adding crazy regulations just to slow down how and when they get paid."

"Any regulations on extortion?" Ray was enjoying the chance to turn the tables a bit.

"Look, Dennis Sasso is a jerk, but even he was always a stickler for good patient care."

"Well, so far I've met two people from your homecare industry, not including you. The first guy let us steal a couple of dozen oxygen cylinders. What's up with all that?"

Yeah, I really feel bad about that," Tara said.

"Why?"

Tara let out a long, sad sigh. "You don't get it. The guy is probably a decent employee. He just got careless," she said. "And guess what, Ray? He'll probably get fired because eventually his company will realize they lost some full cylinders they can't account for."

"Seriously? One mistake and he gets canned?"

"Yes, one mistake like that can get you fired, Ray. The FDA is very serious about things like that."

"Okay, I believe you. Maybe Sasso will get fired too. He deserves it," Ray said. Then, "I still think I should have knocked his teeth out."

Tara shook her head. She knew it was pointless to discuss this with a man who never had a real job. "I understand, Ray. And thanks for what you did back there. That was sweet of you."

"It was Miracle really. The guy has always had an amazing ability to read between the lines. Something you told him raised a red flag about your friend Sasso. When you said to wait a couple of hours, I decided to follow you. It didn't take long to figure out where you were going. I pulled in, lights out, just as you were going through the back door."

"Miracle tell you about me?"

Ray wasn't expecting that. And he didn't have Miracle's way with words. Miracle could play a conversational point out, using patience and judgment the way Ray played a point in tennis.

"You mean like you think I might be your father?"

"I know you're my father. I'm just sorry you found out the way you did. That wasn't how I wanted it."

Again, Ray was surprised. He was seeing Tara with very different eyes now. Whether or not she was his daughter, she was special. She had hung in there with him and with Miracle when many young women would have run long ago. Regardless, he wasn't quite ready to accept the fact that this young woman was really his daughter. "Okay, but how do you know I'm your father?"

"My mother told me. She was very sure of it. I don't know it for sure, but I think she was in love with you. Anyway, she knew you were my father."

"When did she tell you this?"

"A few days before she died. Until then, she always said she didn't know who my father was. She would apologize and say, 'It's a sad but true fact Tara Marie.'"

"That's your middle name? Marie?"

"Yes, why?"

"Wait a second. Sorry I have to ask, but what was your mother's last name?"

"Quigley. Do you remember her?"

Ray hesitated for a second. "Yeah, I do. One last question, did your mother have a nickname?"

"You quizzing me Ray?" Tara was getting annoyed now. "Think I'm trying to play you?"

"Slow down kid. Just answer my question. Did your mother have a nickname?"

"She had several as I recall. Doodles was her favorite."

"Unreal, totally unbelievable. Your mother and I were together for only about five months, maybe even less. We actually lived together for a while and even talked about marriage once, if you can believe that. I brought it up one night. I was drunk at the time, sorry about that. The next day. she asked me if I remembered our conversation. I lied and said I didn't. Must have had a scared look on my face because your mother laughed and said, 'I love you dearly Raymond, but you're a tennis junkie. You'll never marry me or anyone else. I know that.'

"Anyway, one thing I always avoided with women was the whole life story thing that people go through. Those stories are like super glue or maybe spider webs. They bind people together. Everybody's having so much fun telling their stories they don't even see what's happening. Then bang, just like that you're tangled up in each other's webs."

"When you say things like that, I start thinking, or maybe hoping, my mother lied to me about you," Tara said.

"You're mother didn't have a sharp tongue like yours, I'll tell you that. How did you get like this?"

"I guess I got it from your DNA. So why did my middle name weird you out?"

"I was getting to that. I remember that night after we started drinking, your mom started asking me about my life. We were having such a good time I figured what the hell, so I told her a few things. My mother's name was Marie."

"Wow! So you are my Dad. Should I call you Daddy now?"

"Not until the DNA test is back," Ray said, but he was laughing.

Tara smiled. "Thanks for what you did back there, really."

"I would have done that even if you weren't my daughter. I hope you know that."

"Did Miracle tell you the other thing about me?"

"No, but maybe you should tell me. Are you a fugitive from justice or something?"

"Maybe later. You've had enough excitement for one night."

Ray started the van and pointed it toward the motel again. "Do we have enough cylinders now to make it?" he asked.

"We should be fine. I'm not worried about that. But I am worried about this van now. Obviously, Dennis got a good look at the van. My guess is he would report us if he could get something out of it."

"You really think he would take the chance, knowing that we might say something to his wife?"

"One thing I know about that man is he cares about himself first and last. And, I still can't believe you took the van to a tennis club. What were you thinking Ray?"

"We're leaving tonight. Chances are we're good to go; nobody knows for sure where we're headed. I think we'll be all right."

When they got back to the motel room, Miracle was sitting in his wheelchair. He had tried to make himself a peanut butter and jelly sandwich earlier, but the jars were on the floor along with the bread. He wasn't entirely coherent. While Ray picked up the items, including the plastic knife, Tara checked his concentrator. It was down to 5 liters per minute instead of the ten she had set it on. He wasn't getting nearly enough oxygen to sustain him. She quickly turned up the concentrator flow meter to ten. There was no way they could move him in the state he was in. They would have to wait until morning.

They got him into bed right about the time the extra oxygen was beginning to have the desired effect. He was still exhausted, but he managed to say, "The news, check the news." Tara turned the TV on to the news channel. About fifteen minutes later, she saw what Miracle must have seen. There was an update from Atlanta. A tennis pro from the club where Ray played recognized him. Since Ray was alone, he said, he just wasn't sure he was the guy the cops were looking for. The tennis pro figured a guy who was the subject of a nationwide manhunt wouldn't be foolish enough to be out on a tennis court in the middle of the morning. Or, maybe the sick guy they were looking for was found, so he let it go. But his wife urged him to contact the authorities. That's why he was coming forward now. He identified the green tennis van.

"Ray, take a look at this." Tara said.

Ray stared at the TV. He looked over at Miracle who was sound asleep already. "I'm fresh out of ideas. Where in the hell are we going to get another van? We don't have enough cash left for that. That's why I didn't hand over the money your boyfriend wanted."

Tara squinted at him. "He isn't my boyfriend, but I do have a boyfriend."

"Whoa? When did that happen?"

"I know. You thought I was hopelessly devoted to you."

"Not the guy I took for $500 the day I met you!"

"The very same."

"You said he was a casual acquaintance," Ray said.

"I said and did a lot of things. I wanted to spend time with you, get to know you before I decided whether to tell you who I am."

"Were you ever going to tell me? I mean if Miracle didn't tell me, would you have said anything?"

"I think so. You aren't as much of a jerk as you seem to be… maybe."

"We'll have plenty of time to decide whether we like each other later. We have to figure out what to do now. I'm thinking maybe we take him to a decent hotel in the morning and call a hospice, just like he asked."

"Maybe we should, but one thing we haven't really considered here is Jagger. His mother is dying. For all we know she could be dead already. I know Miracle didn't get in touch with her because he thought we would be there by now. Anyway, if we don't take Miracle to Bonita Springs, what happens to his son?"

"In the condition Miracle is in, does it matter?"

"Good question, but we'll never know unless we try. Miracle was obviously worried about how his kids will react. He hasn't said it in so many words, but I think he's afraid they might try to screw Jagger out of everything. If he makes it to Florida, maybe he can see to it that things work out."

"Maybe you're right," Ray said. "Let's see what kind of shape Miracle is in tomorrow morning. But even if we decide to go, we still have a huge problem. The cops are probably pissed that they haven't picked us up yet. The green tennis van won't be hard to spot."

"I have another idea," Tara said. "I need to make a phone call."

It was almost 100 degrees in Bonita Springs that Sunday morning. The dilapidated mobile home's air conditioner wasn't up to the task. Marcia Lacy and her son Jagger were in for a miserable afternoon. Marcia's hospice nurse Destiny, was changing a dressing on one of her bed sores while Jagger watched cartoons.

Although there were periodic updates on the missing pulmonary fibrosis patient on the news, Marcia wasn't aware of them. She rarely watched the news, even when she was healthy, and now, she spent a lot of time sleeping. When she was awake and alert she spent time looking for alternatives for Jagger. She wasn't having much luck beyond the state run services.

Jagger had been diagnosed as mildly retarded when he was six years old. He was put into special education classes when other kids his age were going into the seventh grade. Jagger grew into a tall, slim young man whose face showed only minor traces of his retardation. His forehead was only slightly sloped and his ears were a bit larger than what might be considered normal. Marcia had him tested numerous times and every IQ score fell somewhere between 59 and 65.

It wasn't that the state agency charged with handling cases like Jagger's were terrible. They provided funding services, primarily arranging for the mentally challenged to live in small groups of 1-3 people with similar situations, somewhat independently, in a house staffed with 24 hour workers. Advisors explained to Marcia that one alternative would be to allow Jagger to live in her mobile home alone while the state provided support. Unfortunately, the waiting list for this type of support was long. Of course, Marcia's condition was considered a crisis that might move Jagger up on the waiting list.

What bothered Marcia most about having her son live with strangers was her decision, made long ago, to shelter him and protect him from the world and the evil people in it. She never foresaw the problems it might cause him later in life when she was no longer able to protect him. Now she felt if Miracle would step in and take care of Jagger, the problem would be solved. That Jagger might struggle mightily with suddenly having a father he never heard of certainly crossed her mind, but she felt it was well worth the risk in the long run.

They were lucky in one respect. Jagger could hold a job. He worked four days a week at a local supermarket as a checker, earning minimum wage. He liked his job, he said, because he could help people. He knew how much to put in a bag so it wouldn't be too heavy to carry. He was helpful around the house too, especially when Marcia told him she had cancer.

"Ever hear from that old boyfriend of yours?" Destiny asked. Marcia just shook her head no.

"Maybe you will honey, bad as they be, men can still surprise us."

"I was really harsh to him when we broke things off. He wanted to work it out, but I wasn't willing," Marcia said.

"You knew you were having a baby at the time?" Destiny asked.

"Yes, but I never told him."

"I know that. You read me the letter before you sent it. I dropped it in the mail for you, remember?"

"Not really. Anyway, he was my last hope." Marcia looked over to her son who was engrossed in a Simpson's rerun. She let a few tears run down her cheeks.

"What was his name again?" Destiny asked.

"Miracle. Miracle Morgan."

"Funny name, Miracle. Maybe he will turn out to be just that."

Marcia tried to smile. She had entered hospice care less than three months after she had been diagnosed with pancreatic cancer. Marcia felt lucky that Destiny had been assigned to her case. Destiny was such a big help and relentlessly upbeat. "Did I ever tell you how I met Miracle?"

"No honey. How did you meet?"

"We were undergrad students at Miami. We met at a peace rally, you know that damn Vietnam War. I was one of the organizers. I was a real hippie back then."

"I'll bet you were. All tie-dyed and high on marijuana," Destiny said.

"Uh-huh, just like that. Anyway, Miracle was there. A mutual friend introduced us. I could see he was smitten right away, not that we would have used that term back then. Anyway, he was."

"How about you?" Destiny asked. She could see that Marcia was enjoying the reminiscence. It was the first time she had really smiled in weeks. "Was it love at first sight for you?"

"Oh no. I was a bit turned off. He came on kind of strong. I could tell by the way he was dressed he was anything but a hippie. We were all wearing bell bottoms and sandals, you know, the long hair and the whole trip. They were wonderful, carefree times. But Miracle was a buttoned down kind of guy, definitely not my type back then. The very next day, a friend of his who happened to be in my sociology class, approached me, wanting to know if I liked Miracle. Would I go out with him?"

"And you said no, I'll bet."

"I said yes. Want to know why?"

"I'm probably not going to like this but do tell me girl."

"Destiny, I've never told this to a single soul, but his friend told me Miracle was rich. So I said I would go out with him,"

Marcia said.

"Ooh, life is full of surprises. A sweet little flower child having her head turned by the Benjamins. I love it."

"Well, what I told myself was that he might give me a few bucks to help the cause. But, deep down I liked the idea of being with someone for once in my life who had money."

Destiny finished applying the dressing. She asked Marcia to turn over so she could check her other side. She saw a new sore that needed tending. She would need to keep Marcia talking. "Were you ever in love with him?"

"After we dated a while, I was moved by his intensity. No one ever reacted to me the way he did. He was very kind and he treated me like a queen. I will say, to his credit, he made no attempt to buy my affection. He just had a gentle, even considerate, way about him."

"Uh huh. And?"

"I did love him but those were times when young women were experiencing a new found freedom. I wasn't ready to get serious the way he wanted to. He asked me to marry him."

"Well honey, if he shows up here, you tell him he was your one and only true love and you never got over him even for a Nano-second. That is if you want him to help you out with our Mr. Jagger," Destiny said.

"If he shows up, I won't have to say anything. He'll take care of everything."

Tara made her call to her boyfriend. Elian Lopez was a second generation Cuban American, who was being groomed to take over his father's business, the largest maker and installer of pool and patio enclosures on Florida's gold coast. He and Tara had only been dating for about six months, but he was crazy about her. They met while waiting for their luggage at Miami International Airport. They were on the same flight from Los Angeles. She was moving into town and he was returning from a visit with an old friend. They didn't start dating right away but they did exchange cell numbers. It didn't take long for him to call her.

Tara was reluctant to go out with Elian because he was seven years younger than she was. Elian insisted that it wasn't an issue for him and shouldn't be one for her. He told he felt an immediate chemistry between them, that just standing next to her gave him chills. When she actually spoke to him, joking about the color of his luggage when he pulled it off the baggage carousel, he was thrilled by the sound of her voice. She wanted to know why on earth, as she put it, he would own a turquoise blue colored suitcase. He explained that he had the suitcase specially made in that color because it was the true color of the blue in the Cuban flag.

Tara was charmed by Elian's attentiveness and his self confidence. Yet, he hadn't introduced her to his family because, in spite of his dismissal about the difference in their ages, he worried about how his parents would react. And, she wasn't a Cubana.

A very good tennis player, he took the bait with Ray just to impress Tara. She had tried to persuade him not to do it because, by then, after just a few days hanging around the tennis resort, she knew what Ray's game was. She watched him go into his act a few times while Elian was on the court playing one of his friends. She never mentioned to Elian that Ray might be her father.

When Elian heard Tara's voice, he was thrilled, then angry because she hadn't returned any of his text messages or calls for days. She quickly explained what was happening, leaving out the part about who Ray really was. But Elian had already connected most of the dots. He had seen the news reports. He was shocked to learn that Tara was involved in the Miracle Morgan mystery.

"You and that hustler Rosario, are you getting it on? You getting to know each other? Elian asked.

"It's isn't what you think, Elian. Not even close, trust me. I need you to come to Atlanta, please. Come tonight. I can explain everything, I promise," Tara said.

"You're asking me to drive to Atlanta tonight to help you

transport a fugitive. Why would I do that?"

"He's not a fugitive. He is a man on a very important mission. He asked us to take him to Florida," Tara said. "Do you have a plain white van you can take?"

"I have at least 20 vans, you know that. They all say Paradise Screen Company on them."

"That will work. Oh, Elian, please I need your help. I love you." She wasn't sure she loved him, not yet anyway, but she was desperate and, certain that Elian was in love with her, she said the words. It was easier that way, at least for now.

"You have a lot of explaining to do, Tara. I won't be made a fool of."

You have no idea how much explaining needs to be done, Tara thought. Elian was about to become a father. Since her pregnancy test, she had been wrestling with what to do about that. She really had no time or energy to focus on it. She was struck by the parallel of her situation with Marcia's.

The more she heard Miracle's story, the more she felt that Marcia had been a terrible person for hiding her pregnancy from him. Yet, from the moment she learned she was pregnant, she began to understand why Marcia might have chosen the path she took.

"You won't be, I swear. I can't stay on the phone too long." She gave him the motel's address. "I'll be waiting for you."

Elian Lopez wanted to say no. But his heart wouldn't let him. He wrote down the address and promised to get to Atlanta as fast as he could. Then he went to the closest Paradise Screen location to pick up a van. He also went to Starbucks and downed two double espressos. It was going to be a long night.

Chapter 17

When Miracle finished his nebulizer treatment early Sunday morning, he was feeling better than he had since the day they left for Florida four days ago. Like many terminal diseases, pulmonary fibrosis didn't progress in a straight line from diagnosis to final destination. Miracle knew he would die, and soon, but that morning his final breath seemed more distant than it had the night before. Maybe he would see Marcia after all, he thought

He was completely up to speed now on everything that happened. When Tara told him how Ray handled Dennis Sasso, he stuck his hand out for Ray to shake and said, "Way to go. I'm proud of you."

Just before nine o'clock that Sunday morning, Elian walked into the motel room. Miracle was immediately impressed by the young man. Not yet 30, he was a short, muscled, good looking guy, dark hair with a carefully trimmed beard. The kid looked tired but he was clear eyed and confident. Tara, a bit taller than he was, kissed him as soon as he walked in the door, but circumstances being awkward, they embraced only briefly. Miracle saw immediately that Elian was crazy about Tara.

"I can't thank you enough for coming all this way. I hope it doesn't turn out to be a waste of your time," Miracle said.

Elian quickly took in the scene. Here was a guy in a wheelchair, tethered to some breathing device. He looked like death was imminent. When Elian saw Ray with his ponytail, he let go of Tara and said, "You owe me $500 amigo."

"Whatever you say, paisan. You want it in tens or twenties?"

"Elian, I want you to meet someone," Tara said. "Ray is my father."

"You serious? Your father? Did you know that when he was

hustling me on the tennis court?"

Tara smiled. "Uh, huh, I knew he was my father but he didn't know it," she said, pointing to Ray.

"So I was being set up by you and him both?" Elian said, also pointing at Ray.

"Wait, I tried to talk you out of playing him," Tara said. She couldn't help it, she was laughing.

"Take it down girl," Elian said. "Nothing funny here, you know? You and your friends, your daddy, can go to hell. I'm outta here."

"Slow down kid," Ray said, "Tara's being straight with you. For the record, she had nothing to do with how you wound up on that tennis court with me. But if you really want that $500 back, it's yours."

Elian looked at Ray, and then at Tara, not as sure of himself now. Tara took his hand in hers, made eye contact with him and held it. "I swear, I wasn't in on anything."

Elian relaxed his shoulders. His face softened. He wanted to be strong, walk out of the motel room, and head home but Tara's touch reverberated throughout his body. The chemistry he felt with her was unyielding. Ray reached into his wallet and started pulling out twenty dollar bills.

"Forget it, man." Elian grasped the situation immediately. Taking the money would make him look small. He believed Tara all the way. He had to.

"Cool, now let me see your van. We need to get loaded up and out of here pronto," Ray said.

"Ray?" it was Miracle. "This young man just drove all night. He probably needs some rest before we go."

Elian took another look around the sorry motel room. "Thanks man, but I'm not sleeping in this excuse for a room. I'd rather sleep in the van." He stretched his tired muscles and said, "Okay if I take a shower and change before we get started?"

That done, Elian and Ray went out to the parking lot. The

van was large with plenty of room in the back. It was in fact, the same model as the vehicle they rented in New Jersey from Hertz, except it had only two seats. With four of them now, that would be a problem. At least Elian had followed Tara's instructions to empty the van of all contents.

The two men went back into the room. "Only two seats," Ray said.

Tara looked at her watch. "Stores should open around noon. Ray, go to Wal-Mart and pick up another recliner. Better yet, get two."

"Wal-Mart's probably open now, but I don't remember seeing one," Ray said.

"Yeah, there is one about a mile from here. I saw it when I was driving over here," Elian said.

"Great. You go with him Elian. You can help him load them," Tara said.

Elian turned to Tara. "When did you start giving orders? I don't see you for two weeks, which you still haven't explained, and now you're telling me what to do?"

"Didn't she tell you? She's in charge of this project," Ray laughed.

"Thank God for that," Miracle said. That broke the tension. "By the way, that ponytail has to go, Ray."

"Whoa, what are you talking about?" Ray said, but he knew. He looked over at Tara. "Care to cut your old man's hair?"

"Are you kidding? I can't wait. Let me get a pair of scissors out of my suitcase."

By eleven o'clock, they were on the road again. Elian took one of the new recliners pushed it back and was soon asleep. While they were loading the van, Tara gave him the shortest version she could manage of what had happened to them and where they were heading. Elian didn't ask any questions. It wasn't the time or place for that. In any case, he desperately needed to sleep a while. He was out on his feet.

179

They rode in silence for more than three hours, right through Valdosta. Elian finally woke up when they stopped for gas. Miracle had been napping too. When Tara told him they would reach the Florida line in just twenty minutes, he had a big smile on his face. He even asked if they could stop for a hamburger somewhere and some ice cream. It was a real shot in the arm for him to know that finally they would be almost within reach. Another six hours and they would hit Bonita Springs. Even if he didn't make it all the way, he would at least make it to Florida. That meant something to him.

"Do we have enough cash to get a room near Bonita Springs? A decent room."

"What do you need that for?" Ray asked.

"I want to get cleaned up before we go over to Marcia's place. Don't want to look like a bum after all these years. It's bad enough I've got these tubes, tissues in every pocket and snot running down my nose."

"We'll take care of you, promise," Tara said.

The crossover into Florida was almost anticlimactic after everything they had been through. The big sign along the road saying 'Welcome to Florida,' with its colorful picture of orange groves and palm trees, made them all feel good. But a few minutes later, Miracle started to cough. It started slowly but kept getting worse. Tara gave him a breathing treatment. It helped a little, but he kept complaining about his nose being stuffed. He was having trouble breathing.

Tara adjusted the regulator on the cylinder to increase his liter flow to 12 liters per minute. That seemed to help too, but he was more agitated than they had ever seen him before. He started repeating himself, asking for more oxygen, at one point insisting they had turned it down on him not up. He was confused now. He kept asking the same questions about Elian.

"Who's the kid with the beard?"

"That's Elian, Tara's boyfriend," Ray said.

"Oh, okay, but who is he? Why is he here?"

"He's my boyfriend and he's helping us get to Marcia's house," Tara said.

"I understand that. What I'm asking you is, who is he?"

"Who do you think he is?" Ray asked

"That's what I'm asking you. If I knew who he was, I wouldn't be asking, right?"

This went on for a while longer until Tara managed to change the subject. "It looks like we have plenty of cylinders now, Miracle." That subject always got Miracle's attention.

Elian, who was driving now, whispered to Ray, "Hey, this guy isn't going to make it man. Sorry, but I don't want the guy dying in my van."

"He isn't going to die in your van," Ray said, but he was worried. Miracle appeared to be completely with it in the morning. Now he looked and sounded like a man on his last legs. Miracle was, in fact, failing. Something was different now. His breathing seemed more labored and he was getting confused frequently. Ray looked back at Tara. "How's he doing?"

Tara picked up a white vinyl bag that held Miracle's medication and handed it to Ray. "Get me one of his anxiety pills."

Ray reached around to the back. He grabbed the carry bag with all the meds in it. He found the bottle Tara was looking for and handed it to her. She gave Miracle the pill and waited anxiously to see what would happen. The medication worked. His breathing improved and he wasn't agitated anymore. He dozed off again.

"You think now that we're getting close to Marcia's place, he's getting nervous?" Ray asked Tara.

"Maybe, she said, "but I think he is really failing now. I've seen this before. I'll bet he only has a few days left, if that."

"But he will make it to Bonita Springs right?" Ray asked.

"I hope so."

"To tell you the truth, I'm a little nervous about seeing

Marcia myself," Ray said.

"Why is that?" Tara asked.

"Why? I don't know. I'm just saying maybe she wasn't the saint Miracle thinks she was."

"What is that supposed to mean?"

"I don't know. What difference does it make now? They're both dying, he said. He sat there for a moment massaging his temples, seemingly lost in thought. He picked an orange out of the bag and started peeling it. "Oh man, I just had a bad thought. What if she died already?"

Tara looked out the window, thinking about what was happening, and how little she had considered all the implications of making this trip. She still wasn't sure about Ray. She couldn't tell yet when he was being straight with her and when he was hiding behind a façade of faded and worn machismo. Certainly, she would have preferred to have more time with Ray under circumstances more favorable to her purposes before she told him who she was. Then there was her other secret, literally growing within her.

Ray reached around and tapped her on the knee. "Tell your boyfriend to pick up the pace."

Elian pushed the accelerator. He got the van up to 85 miles per hour. "We need to make better time," Ray said. Tara looked hard at the back of Ray's head, as if she was trying to read his thoughts. She didn't say anything, but she was worried about getting stopped for speeding.

Ray wasn't worried about that. He was now beginning to get concerned about his big deal. It might slip away if he didn't get back to Miami soon. His check for twenty-two grand would be put to good use, if he got the chance. Whatever was waiting for them at Marcia's, he just wanted this to be over. He was ready to move on.

For once on this trip, they caught a break. It was smooth sailing all the way into Tampa. It was five o'clock in the afternoon. They decided to take a dinner break and then drive the last three hours to Bonita Springs.

Miracle Morgan was having a dream unlike any dream he had ever had. He was completely healthy. His lungs were clear and his breathing was normal. It was a perfect day, sunny, not too warm. He was standing on a tennis court in a magnificent stadium. For some reason, even though he wasn't dressed for tennis, there was a huge crowd watching him and cheering him on, but he didn't know why.

A man on the other end of the court, dressed in a spotless Wimbledon-white suit, was beckoning Miracle to follow him. Miracle hesitated, but the crowd urged him on. He took a few tentative steps toward the man and then, walking a bit faster, he approached the net, which magically disappeared making it possible for him to get closer to the man in the white suit. The crowd's cheers became more distant now, as if he was hearing them through a speaker with the volume turned way down. He reached the man in white, who took hold of his hand. And then, at long last, peace.

Chapter 18

Southwest Airlines Flight 102 from Newark to Ft. Myers, Florida arrived on time at 1:30 on Sunday afternoon. "Okay Mel, we're here, now what?" Brian asked.

"Now what? Now we can see for ourselves what's going on. If Dad really isn't with that Lacy chick, we'll drive over to Miami and look for the creep."

"That would be Ray?"

"Please. Let's go, brother."

They walked quickly through the terminal in Ft. Myers. It wasn't very busy at this time of year. By the end of June, the snowbirds had long since left for their homes, mostly in the Midwest. Brian wanted to stop at the food court but quickly saw there wasn't much to choose from. Melanie hurried him along to the rental car agency that sat in the building adjacent to the terminal. The sight of palm trees enchanted them. The blast of hot air they got when they stepped outside, tempered their excitement about being in Florida.

The decision to go to Florida wasn't an easy one for Melanie. In spite of her mother's ideas about what was really driving Melanie, she was genuinely concerned about her father's well being. Sure, she didn't want to lose out on her inheritance, but she was thoroughly disgusted with the hapless way the law enforcement authorities were handling the case of her missing father. When Vincent suggested they contact the police about the Marcia Lacy lead, she rolled her eyes and said, "No way. They will only screw things up even more."

But that wasn't the only reason for her reluctance to involve them. As much as she hated to admit it, her mother had a point. She, Melanie, would be made to look foolish if she needlessly involved an unsuspecting woman in the case.

Not that her worry about looking foolish or causing an innocent woman grief (if she was innocent) didn't stop her from going to Google to find Marcia Lacy's address and phone number. or giving the woman a call the day before they left for Florida. She made up her mind before she placed the call that she would only make the trip if the so-called lead that was Marcia, seemed promising. On the way to Newark Airport, she had related the brief conversation to Vincent and Brian. "My God, the woman sounded like she was 80 years old, not 60.

"I asked her, is this Marcia Lacy? She says, 'Yes, it is. May I ask whose calling?' So I say, I'm a friend of a friend."

Vincent, annoyed because Melanie was steadfast in her refusal to let him go to Florida with her and Brian, said, "That was a clever response."

To calm him down, Melanie had to promise they would go to Florida for the holidays. She gave him a gentle punch in the arm and went on with her story. "She says, 'how may I help you?' Do you know a man by the name of Miracle Morgan? Then there's this like really long pause before she answered."

"What did she say?" Vincent asked.

"She said, 'why do you want to know that?' Well, now I'm thinking he's definitely there or he was there. So I said, just tell me this; have you seen him recently? The next thing I know, some other chick is on the phone. She says, 'this is Destiny. Who's calling please?'"

"Then what?" It was Brian this time.

"I hung up."

But Melanie felt sure the woman knew exactly who Miracle was. Most likely he was either there when she called, or had been there recently. That pushed Melanie over the edge. She had to find out what was going on, whatever the cost. That's when she called Brian. She convinced him to go to Florida with her the next day. He resisted at first. He thought it was a stupid idea. He said he didn't have the money. Then Melanie offered to buy his ticket. When that didn't work, she told him if he didn't go, Vincent would go with her. That worked.

What Melanie didn't know of course, was that Marcia had given up hope of hearing from Miracle, let alone seeing him. The mysterious call from out of the blue actually gave Marcia renewed hope that Miracle might show up after all. As for her refusal to say whether she knew Miracle, force of habit made her cautious. For years she had found it necessary to be careful dealing with callers, many of whom were bill collectors demanding payments she was in no position to make.

Some instinct, or maybe it was simply that she was weak and tired, kept her from admitting she knew Miracle. When Destiny saw the worried look on her face she grabbed the phone to see what was going on. After Melanie hung up, Destiny asked Marcia what had happened.

"Some woman wanted to know if I knew Miracle. Asked me if I saw him. Do you think it means Miracle is on his way here?"

"It's possible, honey. You did the right thing not telling that dame anything. Why couldn't she tell you her name? What was that about?"

Marcia shook her head. She looked over at Jagger who was in their tiny kitchen making a ham sandwich. "Destiny, what if he is on his way here? I look terrible. I hate for him to see me this way," Marcia said.

"Don't worry Miss Marcia, we won't let him in here until you're ready to see him. You still a pretty lady. We'll fix your hair and put a little makeup on you."

Melanie and Brian had no trouble finding Marcia's place. Their rental car was equipped with a GPS. As they were pulling into the entrance to her trailer park, they looked at each other in disbelief. The sign over the arch they drove through said, Garden Estate Park.

"Somehow the word estate doesn't exactly fit here," Brian said. He was looking out the window of their rented Chevy Impala as they slowly made their way to Marcia's trailer on Indian Trail. The mobile homes were all at least twenty-five years old. Most of them were weather beaten with dull, peeling paint and rust spots surrounded by the remnants of landscaping gone fallow years before.

"Here it is, 4444," Melanie said. "I don't see any signs of a van. Maybe they switched to a car."

"You're grasping at straws, sis."

Marcia's home had a single vehicle parked in the driveway, a dirty, beat up, green Toyota Corolla.

"You sure we should be doing this? There's no sign of Dad," Brian said. "Actually, there's no sign of life."

"We came this far. Let's just check Marcia Lacy off our list. Then we can go find the creep."

"Melanie, that guy never did anything to you. Didn't he give you a tennis racquet, some balls and lessons when you were a kid?"

They walked to the door, climbed the steps and knocked. "It was one lesson and he yelled at me for not paying attention. Not to mention that I hated him calling me Melanie Sweet all the time."

When nobody came to the door, Brian said, "Let's go." Melanie knocked again. This time, the door opened. A man in is late thirties answered.

"Hello. Are you here to take care of me when my mama dies?"

Melanie started to laugh, but then she saw the guy was completely serious. She could see now he wasn't quite right. "No, we're here to see Marcia Lacy. Is she home?"

"Who is it, Jagger?"

Jagger turned toward his mother and said. "Two people, a girl and a boy, want to see you mama. Can I let them come in? It's hot outside."

"Okay, let them in," Marcia said. She assumed they were representatives of the state assistance program, possibly making a preliminary visit to check up on them. Marcia had lost track of the days of the week. She didn't even realize it was a Sunday. A hospice worker was on call, but Destiny had the day off. It was just Marcia and Jagger.

Melanie and Brian walked into the trailer. Like the outside, it was well worn, but it was uncluttered and reasonably clean. There was an old portable television seated on a dresser. Jagger had already returned to his recliner to watch TV again. A woman, obviously Marcia, was lying in a bed that for some reason, sat in the tiny living room area. There was also a ratty purple couch pushed up against the wall to make room for the bed. The kitchen wasn't as neat as the rest of the place. There were dishes piled high in the sink. The trash can was piled high, just short of overflowing. There were a couple of empty pizza boxes on the counter next to a very old rotary dial phone with a long cord on it. The air in the tiny space had a hint of mold.

"Hello, my name is Brian. This is my sister, Melanie. Are you Marcia Lacy?"

"I am. What can I do for you?"

"We're Miracle Morgan's children," Brian said.

"Yes, and we're trying to find him," Melanie added. "Has he been here?"

"You're the woman who called yesterday, aren't you?"

"Right, that was me."

"Why did you hang up on me?"

"Mama, should they sit down here next to you?" Jagger asked, pointing to the purple couch.

"In a minute, honey."

"Mama's very sick. She is going to die from a cancer she got."

"I'm very sorry to hear that," Melanie said.

Marcia looked at both of them. They didn't look like they

were related. Brian had red hair and Melanie was blonde, although that might have been a dye job, she thought. "I haven't seen your daddy in 40 years. Why would you think he was here?"

"Our father is very sick. He's dying too I'm afraid," Melanie said.

Marcia's eyes immediately filled with tears. Melanie and Brian both assumed Marcia was reacting to the news about her former lover's illness. Neither of them could know that Marcia's tears were really for her son. Hearing that Miracle was dying too made Marcia sad of course, but if that was true, how could he possibly help Jagger?

She also saw that neither of them had shown any interest in Jagger. It was obvious Miracle hadn't said anything to them. They were unaware of who he was. Since that was the case, she saw no reason to bring them up to speed. The possibility of meeting Miracle's kids hadn't entered her mind when she wrote the letter to him. She was hoping to see or at least hear from Miracle, not his kids. This was a complication she hadn't considered.

"What's wrong with your father?" she asked.

"He has a lung disease," Brian said.

"Oh, was he a heavy smoker? I don't remember him smoking. He wouldn't even try marijuana, as I recall."

"He doesn't have emphysema. It's something called pulmonary fibrosis. It's a horrible disease," Melanie said. "What kind of cancer do you have, if I may ask?"

Marcia fiddled with her bed sheet. "I have pancreatic cancer. Now tell me please, why did you think your father might be here?"

Melanie explained her father's disappearance; that he left only a cryptic note and took off for Florida with his friend, Ray. How her mother, Sandy, Miracle's first wife, had found a letter from Miracle written years ago explaining who Marcia was. She also told Marcia about how Mrs. MacBrien overheard the words Bonita Springs. "It just seemed to add up, is all. I'm really sorry we bothered you," Melanie said.

"Well, he hasn't been here. I'm sorry you can't find him. If you do find him and he is here in Florida, I would very much like to see him. Would you like something to drink? Jagger, honey would you get some iced tea for Brian and Melanie?"

Melanie looked over at Jagger. She had the strange, and to her mind, silly sensation of having seen him somewhere before. "Oh no, that's not necessary. We have to go over to Miami. That's where his friend Ray lives. He might be there. Ever meet Ray?"

Marcia hesitated. "I did. They were close friends, your father and Ray. It's nice to know they're still close."

"Right, it's wonderful." Now Melanie wanted nothing more than to get out of the trailer, which felt almost as warm as being out in the sun.

"Do say hello to your father for me. I hope he's all right. Ask him to call me, if he can."

In spite of the news about Miracle's situation, Marcia couldn't help but hold out one last hope for Jagger. She so wanted to ask whether Miracle was well off financially. She resisted the temptation but not because the thought shamed her. She simply couldn't come up with the right words to ask the question. There was something about the demeanor of her visitors that concerned her. Might they be cold and calculating? That's why she decided not to reveal Jagger's identity to them. And, in spite of all the morphine she was taking for pain, her mind was just clear enough for her to realize that Jagger listened to everything she said.

He would understand that he might have a brother and sister, something he always wanted. The news, offered so suddenly, might well upset him. And no doubt, he would be crushed if they denied him. Given what Marcia knew and had kept to herself for so many years, it was too risky to spring something like a long lost brother on Brian and Melanie. They seemed nice enough, but their indifference to Jagger, the way they ignored him, bothered her.

She had seen it before of course. As a younger woman, she dated many men. Eventually, she learned to make certain the men met Jagger when they picked her up to go to dinner or a movie. Men who actually paid attention to Jagger were scarce. A man who wasn't thrown by Jagger's special needs almost always got a second date with her. And very few of those men demonstrated the sensitivity, the staying power it would take to make a commitment.

Melanie and Brian said goodbye, asked again if Marcia needed anything and made a hasty exit to the car. "Did you get a good look at that lady's red hair? She's dying and still her hair is so thick. It looks great," Melanie said.

"I spent $596 for a flight plus the cost of a rental car to see a dying old lady?" Brian asked.

"Stop whining, Brian. I paid for your ticket, remember? Dad is probably in Miami with Ray. Take out that stupid little map we got and figure out the fastest way to Miami."

"We're stopping for something to eat. I need a very large Coke or something," Brian said. "That place had a terrible odor."

"Whatever. Get that AC cranked up. I'm dying in here."

They drove back to I-75, planning to take it across the state to Florida's gold coast. "Do we even have a clue about where Ray lives? Miami is a big city. Lot's of tennis courts sis."

"Vincent is working on it. Stop worrying."

"Oh yeah, I'm very relieved now."

An hour-and-a half later, Melanie got a phone call. Brian didn't have to worry about where Ray lived anymore. He was on the phone with Melanie.

"Dad, is that you?" The caller ID on her cell plainly said it was her father calling.

"No, it's not your dad. It's me, Ray Rosario."

"Where's my father?" Brian steered the car toward the exit. They were almost in Ft. Lauderdale. He looked for a place to pull over. He had a feeling their plans were about to change.

"Tampa. Listen, kid, I got some bad news for you. Your father died late this afternoon. I'm very sorry, Melanie Sweet. I'm sure you and your brother have a lot of questions. If you can fly down to Tampa, I'll pick you up at the airport and tell you what happened."

Melanie was stunned. It wasn't that she wasn't expecting her father's death. She knew that was inevitable. But she always assumed that she would be with him when it happened. She turned to Brian and said, "Daddy died. He's in Tampa."

Miracle's two children sat and cried. Ray, who was still on the phone, listened, not sure what to say or do. "You still there?" he asked.

Melanie handed the phone to Brian. "Hello, Ray?"

"Is that you Brian? I'm glad you're with your sister. When can you fly down here?"

Brian gathered his composure and explained they were in Florida looking for their father. That news shook Ray. For the first time, he really grasped what Miracle's kids must have been going through. Ray told Brian that Miracle died in the van while trying to reach south Florida. He assured him he hadn't suffered, that he died in his sleep. The body was now in a funeral home near the Tampa Airport. They could claim the body anytime and have it shipped back to New Jersey.

"Can you tell me why my father left home to go to Florida?" Brian asked.

"It's a long and complicated story, Brian. Where in Florida are you?"

"We're near Ft. Lauderdale," Brian said.

"That's about a four hour drive. It's about six o'clock now. You can be here by ten o'clock, maybe sooner if you leave now. I'll tell you whatever you want to know when you get here."

Brian got the funeral home address and said goodbye. He turned the car around and headed west where they came from. It would be a very long four hour drive.

Chapter 19

It wasn't until they stopped for dinner that they realized that Miracle was gone. Ray had been enjoying a much needed nap in the recliner next to Miracle. He woke up when Elian raised his voice to Tara. He kept his eyes closed and listened to her explain her reasons for leaving Miami to go to New Jersey with Ray. Elian was upset that Tara left without letting him know where she was going or why.

"I thought we had something bigger going on than that," Elian said. "I can't believe you couldn't call me first. Not even a text, no email, not a damn thing, girl."

Tara apologized, but Ray could tell she was saying she was sorry mostly to get Elian off her back. Ray wondered if Tara was as invested in the relationship as Elian was. When they pulled over at one of the low cost steakhouse chains for dinner, Ray was happy to have a break from Elian's harping over the status of their relationship. He had to admit though, the kid really cared about her. He was obviously hurt by the way Tara disappeared without a word. Still, the kid was overplaying his hand to Ray's way of thinking.

As Elian and Tara exited the van, Ray turned to Miracle to wake him so they could get him out of the vehicle and into the restaurant. When he didn't respond, Ray froze. "Tara, you better get in here," he said. Miracle's body was still warm, giving Ray the impression that Miracle might be having some kind of episode. He wasn't prepared for the alternative. In the moment, it didn't even occur to him.

It was left to Tara to make the call. She said he must have died less than an hour ago. The minute Tara confirmed that Miracle was dead, Elian became very upset. The three of them were standing outside the van unsure of what to do next. Elian spoke rapidly to himself in Spanish for a minute or so, then turned to Tara and said, "We are in deep shit, girl. There's a dead guy in one of my father's vans. We could get arrested for this. My father is not going to understand. He's old school, you know? Believes reputation is everything, Tara."

"Slow down, Elian, "Ray said. "Nobody is going to be arrested. We didn't break any laws. We just granted a man his dying wish. At least we tried."

"Is that all? You think the cops are going to see it that way man? You've been evading them since you left New Jersey. They've been searching all over for you. What do you think is going to happen? Maybe a parade down Biscayne Boulevard?"

"Take it easy, Elian," Tara said. She took hold of his arm. "Here's what we're going to do. We'll take him to a funeral parlor and let them take it from there. You can take off as soon as they take him out of the van. You won't have to be involved, okay?"

"That's bullshit Tara. The name of my father's company is all over the damn truck. Somebody at the funeral home is going to say something about it to somebody. It's going to be all over the news."

That's when Tara started to cry. Elian's selfish concerns surprised her. For someone who said he was so much in love with her, he was quick to run for cover. The fact that Miracle was gone hit her hard too. She had grown fond of him. Now he wouldn't even get the chance he so desperately wanted to meet his son and see Marcia one last time. And here was her boyfriend, worrying about his reputation.

Her tears softened Elian's anger, at least toward her, but he needed an outlet for his frustration and Ray was there, the perfect foil. The old man should have known better than to get Tara involved in such a foolish venture, Elian thought.

Ray didn't help matters any. When he saw Tara was crying and Elian standing there making no effort to console her, he said, "if you had any class at all, Lopez, you would be holding your girlfriend and telling her everything was going to be alright."

Elian, seething now, stepped up to Ray and took a wild swing at him, missing his jaw by a foot or more. Ray, ever the athlete, was still quick on his feet. "You son-of-a-bitch!" Elian said.

"Stop it, both of you!" Tara screamed. "A man is dead, don't you get that?" Two couples were walking to the door of the restaurant. When they heard Tara's screeching they turned and stopped. One of the women in the group pointed at them and said something. The two men started to walk over to them.

"Get in the van, everybody. Now!" Ray said. They moved quickly and were on the road before anyone could buckle a seatbelt.

Using Elian's GPS, they found the Palmetto Funeral Home. It was about two miles from the Tampa airport. Ray went inside and asked for the funeral home's manager. A young man ushered him into the manager's plush, tastefully decorated office.

"Why hello, my name is Natalie Roselli. How may I help you?

Ray gave her his name and explained that they were traveling from the north and that a man died in his sleep.

"I'm so sorry for your loss. Is he in the morgue? Which hospital?"

"No, he's in our van parked outside," Ray said.

"Oh my! Has the deceased been declared dead by a physician?" Mrs Roselli asked.

"No, we didn't know what to do so we came here. I figured you would know what to do."

The woman was growing concerned. She had heard about the search for Miracle, but it didn't occur to her yet who the man standing in front of her was talking about. She was wary though because, in her many years as a mortician, she had heard stories of gangsters and desperate people who would bring a body to a funeral home, offering lots of money to make the problem go away. "Is the deceased a relative of yours?" she asked.

"No, he isn't. He was a very close friend." Ray hadn't had time yet to process what had happened to Miracle. Grieving would have to wait. He was operating on instinct now.

"I see. Were the two of you traveling alone or were others in the car with you? Perhaps a family member I could speak with?" Mrs. Roselli asked.

As much as Ray thought Elian was being a jerk, for Tara's sake, he didn't want to get him into trouble. He really didn't think the authorities would give them a bad time once they knew the whole story, but it was always possible they would. Regardless, what choice did he have? Mrs. Roselli and one of her workers were going to see Miracle's body lying in the van with the Lopez family's company logo and phone number written in large letters. "My daughter and I were driving him here from New Jersey. A friend of hers was helping out. It's a long story."

Now the woman was beginning to catch on. "Is that so? What was the man's name?"

"Morgan. Miracle Morgan."

"Oh dear, I'm going to have to call the authorities. You understand, I'm sure," she said. "Do you know how I can contact his family? I'll need to do that as well."

"I understand. I'll call the family, if you don't mind," Ray said.

"That's fine, but I will need their names and contact information, or the police will in any case."

"I think they have it," Ray said.

It wasn't ten minutes before a police car rolled up to the funeral home's driveway, an unmarked car right behind it. "I can't believe this. If you had told me how sick that old man was, I would never have come to Atlanta," Elian said.

Three men and a woman got out and conferred with Mrs. Roselli, while Ray, Tara and Elian waited. Tara had placed a sheet over Miracle's body. The cops looked inside the van and removed the sheet. One of them started taking photos. Once that was done, they told Mrs. Roselli she could remove the body from the van, which was still running to keep it cool.

A detective Palmer approached the threesome and asked a few questions. She confirmed that they were indeed the people everyone was searching for and asked each one to make a statement. While they were waiting for the cops, Ray had Tara remove Miracle's updated will and the letter he received from Marcia from his personal effects. Tara stuck them in her suitcase.

The way Ray saw it, there was no reason to tell anyone the real reason why Miracle wanted to go to Florida, at least not yet. After speaking with Brian and Melanie, he didn't think it was the time to introduce a 38 year old, mentally challenged sibling into their lives. And, involving Marcia and Jagger at this point, making them the subject of unrelenting media scrutiny, seemed cruel to him. Jagger would still get the proceeds from the condo, according to Miracle's will. Unwanted publicity wasn't necessary.

By now, the media had word that Miracle had been found. Just then, one of the many summertime thundershowers that Florida is famous for arrived. The three of them quickly walked back to the funeral home before it started to pour. The sweet smell of the rain drops gave Tara some comfort, as if the rain might wash away her sadness. As they stood looking out at the parking lot, they saw several reporters pull up, camera crews in tow. They got to work quickly, trying to set up their gear in spite of the rain. Reporters would soon descend on them and ask for interviews.

"Don't even think of talking to the media," Elian said to Tara and Ray. "You know they can't be trusted."

Ray pushed right past him and went over to one of the cable news network's reporter's and introduced himself. He had, of course, done interviews before, so he wasn't intimidated by the cameras.

"I have former tennis pro, Ray Rosario here with me. Mr. Rosario, can you confirm that Mr. Morgan has died?"

"Yes, he died late this afternoon en route to Tampa."

"Were you aware that there was a nationwide search for you and Mr. Morgan?"

"Vaguely; Mr. Morgan was a lifelong friend of mine. He knew he was dying and didn't want to die in his condo. He was very insistent that we make a trip to Tampa. He was hoping he could persuade the transplant center here in Tampa to give him a new lung. I just complied with his wishes," Ray said.

"Was the transplant hospital aware that Mr. Morgan was planning to seek admission to the program?"

"I don't think so. He knew it was a long shot. I think he felt he would have a better chance if he made the journey and asked in person."

"Authorities say you may be arrested for kidnapping and carrying someone across state lines. Are you concerned?"

"Not at all," Ray said. "I was just granting a man, my best friend, his dying wish. We didn't make it to the hospital, but we got close. He was not unhappy. He was hopeful until the very end actually. No way would I have taken him anywhere, not even around the block, if he didn't want to go."

The questioning went on for a while. When they became repetitive, Ray abruptly ended the interview. He refused to talk with any of the other reporters, which drove them crazy. They tried to speak with Tara and Elian, but they refused to talk to any of them. The best they could do was Mrs. Roselli and the detective who had taken their statements. For her part, the detective was forced to confirm that there were no outward signs of foul play. An autopsy would be performed of course.

Elian would not be able to get his van back until the vehicle had been fully processed and the autopsy results were available. He was inconsolable. He wasn't angry anymore. He was simply resigned to the fact that his father would probably disown him.

Ray called Melanie as soon as he, Tara and Elian settled in

at their hotel near the airport. Not hiding from anyone anymore they decided to stay in one of the area's better hotels overlooking Tampa Bay. The hotel was large, with a conference center and a huge lobby, decorated in a modern, business-like fashion, complete with floor tiles and furniture all in muted earth tones. Only the occasional palm tree paid homage to the hotel's main drawing card, Southwest Florida.

When it was time to check in, Ray asked for three rooms. Elian stepped forward and interrupted him. Only two rooms would be necessary. Ray couldn't believe his ears. He looked at Tara, whose only response was to shrug her shoulders and blush. Her eyes begged Ray not to make a scene. He changed the reservation to two rooms. Elian insisted on paying for the room he and Tara would share.

That settled, Ray said he needed to speak with Tara privately. "Why don't you take the bags and go up to your room. You can give Tara one of your room keys."

"What's up, Ray? Please don't give me a lecture about Elian, okay?"

"This isn't about Elian. If he's really your guy, there's no point in talking about it right now. What I do want to talk to you about are Miracle's kids. They'll be here in a couple of hours. Do you want to meet them?"

"I wouldn't mind. What do you think?" she asked.

Ray had been thinking about it. He doubted that Miracle's kids would believe the story about the transplant center. He knew from his conversations with Miracle, that Miracle's letter to his kids said nothing about looking for another chance to beat his disease. And, soon enough, Melanie and Brian would see their father's amended will and learn that their father had left his condo to Jagger. When questioned about it, Tommy Price, Miracle's long time lawyer would no doubt explain the situation.

The reason for Miracle's trip would become obvious immediately. Still, he worried about telling Miracle's kids anything before it became absolutely necessary. Miracle must have had his reasons for withholding such an important thing from them. The fact that Brian and Melanie were in Florida didn't help matters. What if they decided to run down to Bonita Springs to meet Marcia and Jagger? Ray had no idea of course that they had already made a visit. Better to let Tommy handle Miracle's kids. He felt he owed it to his friend to do whatever he could to see that his wishes were granted, even if Miracle's other children objected.

"Here's the thing. I don't think this is the right time to tell Miracle's kids their father had a son they know nothing about. They're already dealing with his death and the fact that he slipped out of town on them and wouldn't take their calls."

"Alright, what do you plan to tell them?" Tara asked.

"If it was just Brian, it would be easy but Melanie is a tough nut. She isn't going to be easy to satisfy, and I gotta tell you, I am way too tired for a long, drawn out battle over this."

"Can't you just tell them what you told the media about the lung transplant?

"They don't think much of me now. Telling them a lie like that isn't going to help. Miracle sent a farewell letter to his kids, remember? He didn't even think of the transplant explanation until we were in North Carolina." During their long conversations on the road, Miracle essentially forecasted the idea that he wouldn't make it to Bonita Springs. It was Miracle who came up with the story about the transplant center in Florida. He wanted to protect Marcia. "Anyway, in a day or so, Melanie and Brian will know about Jagger. Telling them the transplant story will only make them angrier than they already are."

"Good point. Now what?"

"One thing I'm worried about is these kids trying to make a case that Miracle was incompetent and I took advantage of him. My whole deal would be shot if I got arrested or something," Ray said.

"Well, first Miracle's lawyer, what's his name, should be able to handle something like that. He saw Miracle the night before he left. And your friend Brooks and his wife Angelina met Miracle too. Assuming they're not too pissed about you leaving their van in the parking lot of that fleabag motel, they would vouch for you, and so would I. I took care of him remember?" Tara started to tear up again at the thought of Miracle's death.

Ray put his arms around her. He shuddered for the first time, finally fighting back his own tears. Neither of them spoke for a while.

"Why don't you just tell them that their father's lawyer can explain everything? Say you were asked not to say anything about the trip. Tell them Miracle swore you to secrecy or some story like that?"

"That's not bad kid. We could tell them he was on a mission; that he didn't spell it out for us. We say he was very brave and in good spirits which is true, he was."

"Good, the less we say the better it will be for all concerned. Elian's waiting. Call me when they get here," Tara said.

Ray was about to say something vulgar, but then he remembered. Tara was his daughter.

Chapter 20

On the way to Tampa, Melanie and Brian discussed what to say to Ray. They had a lot of questions about their father's disappearance. Why did he suddenly leave town? Why didn't he tell them where he was going or what his plans were? When Melanie last spoke to him, the day he left, he was obviously already on the road. Why did Miracle lie to her about his whereabouts? Then too, when the media was reporting the search for their father, how could Ray have so callously disregarded their worry and concern for their father?

"I mean, once he was on his way, what harm would it cause to tell us he was all right, even if they wouldn't tell us where they were going?" Melanie asked.

"Who knows? Maybe he told Ray not to talk to us. I've been wondering if this whole thing might have happened because we told him he couldn't drive anymore. He really wasn't happy about that," Brian said.

"Well, we were obviously right. He died less than a week later. We should have stopped him sooner."

"If he didn't run off to Florida, would he have died so soon? He was at least comfortable in his condo and we were there to help when he needed us," Brian said.

"Ray Rosario has a lot to answer for. I wonder how much money Dad gave him this time," Melanie said.

Melanie's cell rang. It was Sandy. "Melanie it's me, Mom. Are you with your father? This is so terrible; oh that asshole Ray. I'm going to kill him."

"I guess you heard. Sorry I didn't call you, Mom. This is just unbelievable. How did you hear about it?"

"It was all over the news. Ray actually had the nerve to speak with a reporter" Sandy said.

"Really, what did he say?"

Sandy gave her daughter a brief description of the report.

"A transplant? Really? What bullshit. Dad never said anything about a transplant after he was turned down the first time."

"I know that. I'm just telling you what Ray said to the media. Where are you now?"

"Brian and I are in the car, on the way to Tampa."

"How did you find out he died? Did Ray at least have the decency to call you or did you find out the way I did, on the evening news?"

"No, he called me."

"Call me after you talk to Ray. In fact, do you have his cell number? I want to speak with him," Sandy said.

"No I don't, Mom, Anyway, I'm not giving him any opportunity to work on his story. I'll call you later, promise."

Melanie and Brian arrived at the hotel just after 9:30 Sunday night. Brian had driven like they were on the Autobahn. They agreed that Brian would call Ray when they got in. Ray picked up right away and told them he would meet them in the lobby.

Melanie and Brian were standing a few feet from the hotel's check in counter when they saw Ray get off the elevator. A young woman was with him.

"Hey kids, I'm very sorry about your father. He was a great man, right to the end," Ray said.

"Is there a place where we can sit?" Brian asked. Melanie was strangely subdued for the moment. Seeing Ray made her think about her father. She had not counted on crying in front of Ray. She wanted to scratch his eyes out, but Ray's face looked sad, and he was, at the moment, the closest contemporary of her Dad's available.

"Let's go to the bar. Looks quiet tonight. You kids hungry?"

Ray asked. "Oh, excuse me, this is Tara Ridgley."

Melanie looked her over. "Who are you?"

Ray answered before Tara could speak. "She's a nurse. Tara took care of your Dad on our trip down here."

"I see. Obviously you did a great job Tara," Melanie said.

"Slow down Melanie Sweet. You have no idea what you're talking about here," Ray said.

"My name is Melanie, Ray, just Melanie, got it? And I have a very good idea of what I'm talking about." Over her initial shock, Melanie was in high gear now. "You led my father on some wild goose chase and your nurse bimbo here helped. What did you tell my father? Did you promise him a stake in one of your famous tennis comebacks?"

Growing up, Melanie had overheard the story plenty of times from Sandy about how Ray would tell Miracle he had a plan that would get him back on the tour if only he could get a sponsor. In truth, that was one story Ray never told when he asked for money. Miracle knew too much about the game and Ray's shoulder for that to fly. Sandy knew it too, but she enjoyed the sarcasm at the heart of her stories about Ray and Miracle. As a child, Melanie didn't understand that.

"First of all, Tara is my daughter. Second, let me straighten you out right now about your father. The trip was his idea. He asked us to take him to Florida," Ray said.

"Really? Like my Dad was competent to make a decision like that? You'll say anything to cover your tracks, you excuse for a human being."

"Brian, can you help here? Your sister is obviously under a lot of strain. I can't talk to her. Maybe I can talk to you," Ray said.

"I need a cigarette," Melanie said. She pulled a pack out of her bag, and tried to get her lighter to work.

The waitress, who just arrived to take drink orders said, "I'm sorry but this is a non-smoking hotel. You'll have to go outside if you want to smoke."

Melanie was annoyed, but she put the cigarette away. Brian spoke up for the first time. "Ray, let's say we believe you; that my Dad really wanted to come to Florida. Why? You said you would tell us when we got together. We all know the transplant story you floated to the media was a lie. We're here now so…"

Ray decided to ignore Brian's challenge. The kid had no way of knowing for sure whether his father might be seeking a transplant. "You're probably not going to like this, Brian. All I can tell you is your Dad was on a personal mission that was very important to him."

Melanie jumped in. "That's it? That's all you have to say? Are you for real or what? Did the sun down here fry what was left of your brain? I'm going to sue your ass when this is over, you can count on that."

Tara had been quiet, content to let Ray handle it. After all, she never met Melanie or Brian. It wasn't her place to say anything. But now she was angry. "Sue him for what? You have no idea what you're talking about. As soon as your father's body is released, take him back to New Jersey. See if you can show a tiny bit of respect for the man. If you really want to know what this trip was about, speak with your Dad's attorney. Ray, what's the lawyer's name?"

"I know what his name is, sister. But why should we have to wait to find out why our Dad died in a strange vehicle twelve hundred miles from home?" Turning to Ray, Melanie added, "After all we've been through, why can't you show a little respect?"

"That's how your father wanted it, kid. If he wanted you to know, he would have told you." That shut Melanie down. Ray's response was cruel but effective.

"Let's get out of here, Brian."

"You have the location of the coroner's office?" Ray asked.

Melanie was already walking toward the hotel lobby. She never looked back at him. She gave him the finger, which was how Ray knew she heard his question.

Miracle's body wouldn't be released until the coroner could complete the autopsy, which would take a couple of days. The toxicology report wouldn't be ready for another two weeks after that. Brian and Melanie would have to wait the two days until they could make arrangements to have Miracle's body returned to New Jersey. Certainly there would be a memorial service, but Miracle had made it clear as soon as he knew his prognosis that he wanted to be cremated.

Melanie wanted to call Tommy Price. She called Vincent to ask his opinion. He thought she should wait until they could be together. For once Brian agreed with Vincent's assessment. It would only be a couple of days and they would be home. Melanie wasn't sure that was the best course of action. What if the lawyer told them something that would require them to return to Florida? They were there now with nothing to do but wait.

So, she called Tommy. He was on vacation and wouldn't return until the following Monday. His partner wasn't helpful. For one thing, there was no death certificate yet. For another, how could he be sure he was speaking with the client's daughter? She would have to sit tight. Melanie was so frustrated and desperate that she asked Brian to wait for the body while she hopped a flight home. She didn't trust Ray Rosario or his supposedly, newly found daughter one bit. But Brian was horrified by the idea. He was still a college kid. He would need his sister's guidance to get through the paperwork, making the necessary arrangements. In any case, she had the power of attorney not him.

Brian was much quieter than his sister. She was confrontational and more outgoing. He was introspective, much less likely to speak his mind. His father's death troubled him deeply. He was tormented by the thought that their decision to cut off their father from driving drove him to do something foolish. When Melanie wanted to put an end to Miracle's driving, Brian disagreed. He went along with it because he had learned at an early age that it was usually easier to do what Melanie wanted.

Brian also thought that Melanie was going to be disappointed when the lawyer explained the reason for his trip. He knew she built up in her mind some crazy scheme cooked up, not by Miracle, but by Ray, which would result in a major transfer of assets into Ray's pocketbook. On the drive to Tampa she actually said she hoped that Miracle had died before any type of transaction could be completed, as if she was relieved that he died in time to safeguard Melanie's future. Brian knew it wasn't that Melanie didn't love their father. She just had a thing about money and sometimes it overwhelmed her judgment and common sense.

The next morning, Ray, Tara and Elian met in the hotel restaurant for breakfast. Their journey was over. They could go home now. Ray sat brooding over his big deal, wondering if maybe he could delay it a few days. He needed to get back to Miami and show the other principal he had the money, or most of it. Thanks to the unexpected costs associated with their trip, the Yukon he bought, the extra hotel nights, the money he paid Sasso, he was almost $3,000 short of the $25,000 he needed. The $22,000 check in his wallet might be enough, but more likely he would have to find a way to scrounge for the rest. A week was all he had, not much time to come up with the needed three grand.

For a moment, he wondered if Elian might be willing to lend him the money. He knew the kid didn't much like him, but he was wild about Tara. Judging by the way the guy was chirping since they sat in their booth, he had obviously gotten reacquainted with her. Almost as good, Elian's father surprised him. He wasn't angry with his son for using the van to help a dying man trying for one last shot at a transplant. At least someone believed the story.

Still, it was a long shot that Elian would pony up the dough he needed, especially if he knew the real reason Ray wanted the money. The tennis shop story was true, but typical of Ray, he skipped a few steps in explaining the deal to Miracle and Tara, just as Miracle had suspected. Ray sometimes wondered why Miracle never gave him a hard time about that. His stories were sometimes downright ludicrous. Miracle never batted an eye. He just forked over the money. Why? Deep down, Ray knew why, but, unless Miracle told someone else, that was a secret that only he knew the answer to now.

Chapter 21

The waitress brought more coffee. There had been very little conversation during breakfast. Ray was ready to get back to Miami. He didn't know what to say to Tara or what to expect. Had they bonded? He wasn't sure. Without Miracle and the crisis surrounding his care, there was no longer anything to distract them. Notwithstanding the outcome, their mission was accomplished, more or less. Now they would soon be forced to face each other and decide what, if anything came next.

Ray had no experience being a father. Yet, he did feel what he imagined was a father's concern for his daughter. He wanted to talk to her, to feel her out. Did she see Ray as a dad, or was it too late for that? What did she expect from him? Ideally they could discuss all that on the ride back to Miami. But what were the chances of having a meaningful conversation as long as Elian was around, mooning over Tara?

Tara and Elian had, when they weren't otherwise engaged, talked through the night. Tara spoke her mind to Elian. She felt she was too old for him. He thought otherwise and asked for a chance. He was an intelligent guy, sensitive perhaps to a fault, but Tara was experienced enough to know he would grow out of that. Once that happened, she worried their days would be numbered.

She told him his parents were right, that the difference in their ages, while not overwhelming, might be a source of trouble later on. At 35, she said, she was too old to make a mistake like that.

Elian did his best to persuade her otherwise. He got her to admit that the feelings they had for each other were undeniable. He even acknowledged that maybe she wasn't as much in love, at least not the way he, Elian was, but whatever they had was hard, if not impossible, to ignore. Elian felt he had misjudged his father's reaction to taking the van. Maybe he was also wrong about how his parents would feel about Tara, especially after they got to know her. There was no doubt that Tara was captivated by Elian's good looks and passion for living. When he dropped everything to help her, it told her a lot about him.

As dawn broke, they reached an agreement. They would take things slowly. She wanted time to get to know Ray better, she said. And there was unfinished business that she and Ray needed to take care of. She explained all of this to Elian and he seemed to understand. There was too much happening in her life to contemplate, let alone take on a serious relationship that had obstacles of its own to contend with. While Elian lay sleeping just before dawn, Tara stared up at the ceiling feeling guilt so overwhelming she could barely breathe. She wondered for a moment if this was what it felt like to be Miracle, unable to breathe. She knew that if she told Elian about the child she was carrying, he would pressure her to get married. It would give him the last bit of leverage he needed to convince her they were meant for each other. Still, guilty or not, she needed more time.

Ray sat in the booth, fidgeting. He was ready to hit the road. He assumed Elian would give them a lift. "You guys want to get going? It's nine o'clock already. There's a tennis court in Miami with my name on it. Let's boogie."

Tara gave Elian a look. As they agreed that morning, he would not be taking them to Miami. It was time for him to go. "I'm not going to Miami this morning," he lied. "I have to get the van to West Palm Beach. We need it there."

"The Tampa Police are going to let you have the van? Ray asked.

"I called this morning. The cops released it."

"You're kidding!" Ray said. Of course, he was delighted with the news. "Can you at least take us to the rental car agency at the airport?"

"I'm sorry man. No time for that. I have to get over to the funeral home to pick up the van, dude. Anyway, the hotel shuttle can run you over there."

Ray shook his head. "I guess if you gotta go, you should do that. Adios, Elian Lopez." Tara stood to embrace Elian. They kissed, a long goodbye kiss. "Thank you again for everything. You rescued us, you know? Driving all the way from Atlanta, through the night, we'll never forget what you did for us, right Ray?"

Ray stood up. "That's right, kid. You helped my friend and I'll never forget that. It didn't work out the way we hoped it would, but without you, it might have ended in that shithole we were in back in Atlanta. Thanks, I owe you one."

Elian smiled. The two men quickly shook hands. "You still owe me $500, man." Then he and Tara walked out to the lobby and said goodbye again while Ray took care of the check. By the time he got to the lobby, Tara was waiting for him. "Guess we better get the shuttle," he said.

"We'll do that in a minute. There's something we need to discuss first. I keep thinking about Miracle and how much he wanted to see Marcia and Jagger. Before we came down to breakfast, I read the letter again, the one she sent him. Shouldn't we at least pay her a visit before we head home? Elian said we can make it to Bonita Springs in about two and a half hours."

"I don't know, Tara. What purpose would that serve?"

"Maybe Marcia saw the news about Miracle dying. Who knows? If she did, maybe she guessed what he was doing here. Don't you think she might feel better knowing for sure he tried? Don't forget, we can tell her Jagger's getting the condo too. That might make things easier for her."

"Tommy Price will get in touch with her in a few weeks. Listen, don't bet on him getting the condo. Melanie will pitch a fit when she finds out. She'll get her own lawyer, count on that. To tell you the truth, I'm tired of driving. Except for that one time in Atlanta, I haven't played or practiced for weeks. I need to get myself ready."

"Ready for what? This will take us a few extra hours. You'll be in Miami in time for dinner. You owe it to Miracle to finish his journey. You can worry about that tennis shop investment starting tomorrow." She didn't point out that Miracle was the source of the investment. Not that she had to. Ray caught her drift.

"Okay, we'll go down there, but we're not staying long. We say hello, we tell her what happened and then we get going."

"You're all heart Ray."

Ray decided to talk to Tara about their relationship on the ride to Bonita Springs. He saw no point in beating around the bush with her. A direct approach would work best. His problem was he didn't know what he really wanted. For one thing, his final week with Miracle made him wonder whether having children was worth the effort. Miracle's kids were doing their best to run his life while he tried to hold onto what was left of his dignity. Sure, they had his best interests in mind when they told him he couldn't drive anymore.

On that particular subject, he had to agree with them. In fact, Miracle asked him if he could drive for an hour or so when they were in Maryland. Tara said no, which saved Ray the trouble of disappointing his friend. Regardless, both kids were trying to put some stranger in his home to keep an eye on him. Didn't they know he would never accept home confinement as if he was a prisoner? The only thing they didn't suggest was the ankle bracelet so they could trace his every move. Well, after spending a week with Miracle, Ray knew his kids were right. He hated it for his friend.

Not having kids of his own, Ray never thought much about the power they have over you. Who but your kids could bend your will? And wasn't it yet another kid, Jagger, that made Miracle spend his last days lying in the back of a van on a doomed mission?

Still, there was no denying that he, Ray, meant something to Tara, enough for her to track him down and then willingly participate in Miracle's crazy scheme. And, she had asked for nothing in return. One of the last things Miracle said to him, just hours before he died, was, "keep an eye on her. She's lost."

Well Ray didn't think Tara was lost, far from it. But, he did wonder if maybe Miracle, with all his experience as a father, could see something he couldn't see.

"We had a hell of an adventure, didn't we, kid."

"I guess we did. I'm not sure it's over yet. I wonder what we'll find in Bonita Springs."

"We'll see soon enough. But what happens next? You found me. We got to know each other a little bit. What's your thinking about the future?"

"I don't know, Ray. It's kind of like where things are with Elian. One day at a time, I guess."

"Are you thinking about sticking around, Miami, I mean?"

"I guess so. I need to find a regular job first, one with benefits. I'm running out of money."

"Well, I should be able to help you out with that at least for a while."

"You going to scam Elian again or maybe some other suckers with your slick moves?"

"Actually, I think I'm about done with that sort of thing. I just need a big score to get me where I want to be. Only thing is, I need more money than the 25 grand Miracle gave me."

"Well, I can't help you there, Ray." Tara considered whether she should ask the question that was on her mind. "I have to ask, just curious I guess. If you're not hustling people, how can you possibly help me? Not that I would let you anyway."

Ray thought that over for a minute. "That's a fair question," Ray said. "Truth is, I have a big money match set up this week. I'm a little rusty, but I think I can handle the guy I'm playing. Once I get that done, I'm set. So, if you ever do need a few bucks, you can count on me."

They cruised along in their rented Toyota Camry, taking in the pines along the edge of the highway. Tara thought about Ray's question. He was right. She found him; they got to know each other a little. Before they met, she thought she might wind up hating him. She thought he would probably be a disappointment, just a guy who followed the sun. She imagined he would probably have a drug habit and surely he would be a heavy drinker. One who pretended to be delighted that she found him, but soon enough he would blow her off and move on. In the end, she was sure she would do no better than her mother had done with him.

In spite of what her mother told her about not knowing who her father was, she had clung to the belief that somehow her father knew about her all those years. Once she found out Ray was her father, she stubbornly held onto that belief. That way she could blame him for abandoning her. It was easier than being angry with her mother after she died for lying to her all those years about not knowing who her father was. Had her mother fessed up when Tara was younger, maybe she would have had more time to get to know him, especially when she needed him.

It bothered her that her mother preferred to let her believe that she slept around a lot, enough so that she couldn't identify who the father of her child was. How was that worse than telling her who her father was?

When she finally found Ray, he was nice to her. He treated her more like a daughter than a girlfriend from the moment they met. Maybe our brains are hard wired to know our own, she mused. She smiled thinking about the way Ray's face looked when he walked in on her and Sasso. Of course, being around him she could see reliability wasn't his strong suit, but under difficult conditions, he had performed well. He had done a remarkable job with Miracle; he handled the bad luck they encountered with an inner strength she was forced to admire.

They continued to ride in silence for a while. It was another beautiful Florida Suncoast day. The cloud formations were amazing, their shapes enhanced by the azure sunlit sky.

Then Ray decided to try again. "I'm glad you're going to stay in Miami for a while. That will make it easier for us to get together, you know, like you said; take it one day at a time."

"Right, if that's what you want. I wouldn't want you to feel obligated or anything."

"I don't feel obligated, Tara. I just feel like we shouldn't lose touch. You know something? Our trip turned out to be really a lucky break for us. We got to spend a lot of time together under difficult conditions. I was proud of you, do you know that?"

"Thanks but you shouldn't be. I just did what needed to be done, just like you did," Tara said.

"Uh huh, well I'm glad we got that time. Shifting gears, he said, "Tell me, what's going on with Elian? Is he the guy for you?"

"Maybe, too soon to tell."

"He's kind of a hothead. That Cuban blood gets up over nothing."

"Is that how you see it, Ray?"

"Hey, I'm not trying to intrude here, just making an observation," Ray said.

"Well, don't do that. I know you don't like Elian, but it's none of your business. Do not even think about getting into my life like that."

Again they rode in silence. Ray was confused by Tara's response. He wasn't telling her what to do. He wondered if this was the sort of thing he missed by not having children. If it was, he was glad he passed on that particular experience. This kid's been my daughter for a few days and already she's hurting my feelings, he thought.

The Bonita Springs exit was coming up. For a moment, he was tempted to drive right past it and head to Miami. He took a deep breath. He hated to admit it but his daughter was right.

A week and a half on the road together didn't entitle him to an opinion of who she saw or what she did. "Sorry, kid," he said, steering the car toward the exit.

"Me too," Tara said. "I want us to be friends, you know?"

"Yeah, me too. Maybe that's what we should be shooting for." He reached over and grabbed her hand gave it a gentle squeeze.

Tara reached over and kissed his cheek. "Don't get crazy on me, okay?"

Chapter 22

Twenty minutes later, they pulled into Garden Estate Park. As they pulled up to Marcia's mobile home, they saw the same depressing scene that Melanie and Brian found. The look on Ray's face told Tara he wanted nothing more than to hit the gas pedal and get out of there. For a moment, she had the same instinct, but they had come this far and they wouldn't back down now.

They got out of the car and slowly walked up to the door. "You met Marcia before, right?" Tara said. "You and Miracle talked about that the day I met him in his condo."

"Yeah," Ray was really nervous now that he was at Marcia's.

"Think she'll remember you?"

"I don't know. That was a long time ago. She might remember me." Suddenly, he felt exhausted, as if all the stress from their long journey caught up with him at once. He wished he was back in Miami, sitting at the bar in the clubhouse. He wanted to be anywhere but where he was. But he kept walking, side –by-side with Tara to the door.

They knocked and Destiny, the hospice worker answered "Hi, how can I help you?"

"We're here to see Marcia Lacy," Tara said.

"And you are?"

"I'm Ray. This is my daughter, Tara." He wondered if he would ever get use to saying those words.

Destiny gave them a long, appraising look. "Hey, you two the ones that drove that Miracle guy to Florida. Saw you on the news."

"Right, that's us," Ray said.

"Well, come on in, but before you do, Miss Marcia is real sick. She doesn't have much longer. I hope you got good news for her."

"What do you mean?" Ray asked.

"I saw the letter she wrote to Miracle, fool. I hope you're here with an idea for her son."

"Actually, we are," Tara said. "May we come in?"

"Sure. You know something, you look kind of familiar," Destiny said, pointing at Ray.

"Well, Wimbledon is going on. Do you watch tennis?"

"Yeah, all the time, I'm 250 pounds; I got 3 kids and a job that doesn't pay squat. Oh yes, I'm always watching rich people play tennis."

Ray and Tara walked into the tiny trailer. Marcia was in bed. Emaciated, her skin a sickly gray her eyes pale, it was obvious she would be gone soon. Her face told the story of a woman in excruciating pain. She was alert though, and her eyes grew large when she saw Ray. Sitting next to her bed was Jagger, his hands cradling his head. He looked up and smiled. "Are you the people that are going to watch me when mama dies?" he asked.

That's when all hell broke loose. Tara got a good look at Jagger about the same time that Destiny made the connection. "Oh Lord!" Destiny said.

Tara looked at Ray and said, "Come outside with me for a minute." She turned to Marcia and said, "Would you excuse us for a moment please? We'll be right back."

Ray followed her out to the tiny front walk. "What's up?" he asked.

Tara looked at him, reached back and slapped his face so hard the entire neighborhood could hear the crack. "You son of a bitch! How many brothers and sisters do I have? How many Ray? How could you? You knew it all along, didn't you?"

"Are you crazy? I have no idea what you're talking about!"

"Don't give me that, you asshole." She started swinging at him, landing punches on his arms and hitting his face a couple of times before he restrained her. By now, Destiny had stepped outside. A big woman, she quickly got between them and told them to shut up. "There is a mentally challenged man in there that is about to be very confused, plus a dying woman who may be finding out for the first time exactly who the father of her child really is."

"He's not mine," Ray said.

"Don't give me that bullshit; you the father alright. The boy looks just like you even with his lopsided head," Destiny said. "I'm going to get Jagger out here and take him for a ride with your friend here. What's your name, honey?"

"Tara."

"That's right. I remember now from the news. You come with me and Jagger okay? I'm guessing he's your long lost brother, if I heard you right when you were smacking this fool here."

Ray stood there, his shoulders sagging. From the moment he read Marcia's letter to Miracle, he had been afraid this might happen. It was a longshot for sure, but he knew it was a possibility. Now he cursed himself for allowing Tara to drag him to Marcia's. He always wanted to believe the baby was Miracle's. In fact, he had every reason to believe it.

When Marcia told him she was expecting all those years ago, he didn't believe her or didn't want to. Considering the circumstances at the time, he was convinced that if Marcia was indeed pregnant, it had to be Miracle's child. Since Marcia never told Miracle she was pregnant Ray let the matter drop, never saying a word to Miracle. That was one decision he never regretted. He had assumed if Marcia really was pregnant, she would find a way to get an abortion. In May of 1972, abortion was still illegal, but it was possible to get one. Ray was sure Marcia wouldn't have the baby. When Miracle showed him the letter she sent him, it sent chills down his spine.

Then it appeared he was in the clear after all. He quickly stopped worrying about it because Marcia had finally decided to tell the truth. Jagger really was Miracle's son. He was about to point this out to Tara when Destiny stepped outside with Jagger in tow. Ray took a really good look at him now. There was no denying it. Jagger had the Rosario nose, close set eyes and olive coloring. He was a father. Again; in the space of less than two weeks, he went from being a carefree bachelor, to the father of two, one of whom was mentally challenged.

At that moment, rather than Miami, he would have given anything to be back in Miracle's condo, this time refusing to take him anywhere. Better yet, he would never have gone to see Miracle. Miracle had been indebted to him since they were kids. Ray liked it that way. Now, for reasons he simply couldn't fathom, he was the one with the debt and Miracle wasn't there to bail him out. In a flash he understood that had Miracle not been sick, he would have taken Jagger in and called him his own. Knowing Miracle, he probably would never have guessed that Ray was the kid's father. And if he did, he wouldn't have cared. Miracle never saw Marcia as anything but the perfect woman. Had he been told what happened between Marcia and Ray, he would never have believed it. Forty years later, Ray had no choice. He had to see it that way.

"So, Mr. Ray, can I assume from the panicky look on your face that you get the picture now?" Destiny asked.

Ray nodded. He looked at Tara whose face offered not a trace of solace. "Well, what am I supposed to do about it now?"

"You can start by talking to Miss Marcia. And let me warn you. Be kind and promise her you will do the right thing, or you will hear from me. And you don't want any part of that, know what I'm saying?"

Ray laughed. He wasn't sure if it was Destiny's attitude, nervousness or simple resignation over what was happening to his life that made him laugh. He started to climb the steps.

"Where you going? Wait here until I come back and get you."

Destiny walked into the trailer and went to Marcia's bedside. "Honey, I promised you I would put some makeup on you when Mr. Miracle got here. Looks like it's that Ray character instead, but I promised to make you look pretty and I'm gonna do it. Let me help you sit up a minute." Destiny combed Marcia's hair and applied a little hair spray. She put lipstick on her, some rouge and even a bit of eye shadow. "You want to see yourself? I'll get the mirror."

"I don't think so. It might not be helpful right now," Marcia said.

"Good point, but you do look pretty, so don't fret."

Destiny stepped outside again. "You can go in, but don't you forget what I said."

Destiny got into the passenger seat of Ray's rental car after ordering Jagger to get in the back seat. Tara took the wheel and followed Destiny's directions. "It's too hot to go to the park. Let's go to the mall," Destiny said.

The mall wasn't too far from where Marcia lived. As they got close, Jagger got excited. "Can I have candy from that store that sells those orange and cherry slices, Miss Destiny?"

"We'll see. Did you bring any money with you?"

"No. I forgot it. I have it on the table near my bed. Can we go back and get it please?"

"I'll buy you some candy, Jagger. Don't worry about it," Tara said. She was fighting back tears. She thought, I've cried more in the last week than the last ten years.

They found a parking space and walked slowly in the heat toward the mall entrance. The Florida sun was doing its best to remind people that the Sunshine State was a lot more fun in March than in June. The mall's air conditioning was a welcome relief. Destiny started looking for a place where they could sit down, but Jagger was insistent about the candy he'd been promised. Tara checked the kiosk with the store listings and found the one with all the candy. They walked down the long aisle past several clothing stores, a shoe store and a jewelry store to Carmella's Candy Shop.

Jagger made his customary selections. Sensing this was a special occasion, he asked for an extra one. Tara looked at Destiny, who nodded her approval. Jagger was happy. They strolled down to the food court and found a place to sit.

"You mad at your father for not telling you that you had a brother all these years?"

"I didn't know he was my father until recently. I came here from LA to find him. It wasn't hard. Now I'm wondering how many kids he has, you know?"

"Uh, huh, I know, believe me I know about men like him. All charm and promises he's going to be a big man, ridiculous dreams and rides to nowhere."

Jagger was completely absorbed in his bags of candy, eating one piece out of each bag before returning to the first bag to repeat the process.

"This is such a terrible situation. Miss Marcia doesn't have but a week, maybe two, to live. They going to wind up putting Jagger here in a group home which he will hate, unless his family steps up and does something." She looked at Tara and held eye contact an extra beat to be sure she got the message.

"Actually, that's the reason we came by. Miracle provided for Jagger in his will. He left his condo to Jagger, which should help. Maybe he can be placed in a better situation."

"I sure hope so," Destiny said. "But since it turns out that Mr. Miracle isn't Jagger's father, can you be sure there won't be a problem?"

"I don't know," Tara said. She thought about Melanie and what Ray had said about her. She had her doubts that Melanie would let the revised will stand. It occurred to her that she had the will in her purse. "I need to get to a copy center. I have a copy of the will here. Miss Lacy should have a copy for her records, don't you think?"

"Back out in that heat so soon? Let's go, girl."

"Oh Raymond, I can't believe you're here," Marcia said.

"Neither can I. It was Miracle's idea to visit you. It was a long, hard trip, in the end; sad really."

"I'm sure it was. It's a shame but we all have our time. I guess his -and mine just got here a littler sooner is all."

Ray nodded. "How are you doing? I'm awfully sorry this is happening, Marcia."

"It's painful, but I'm determined to die with a little dignity, you know," she said, her eyes sweeping her tiny home.

"Did you hear about Miracle, how he died and his long ride to nowhere?"

"Yes, Destiny told me about it. She said it was all over the news. Was it true about the transplant? Is that why he wanted to come to Florida?"

"No, no, not at all. It was a story he made up to protect you in case things went wrong. He really was coming to see you and Jagger."

"I feel so sorry for him. I had no idea he was sick."

"Neither did I. I went up to Jersey to see him expecting everything would be normal, whatever that is. Instead, I found a guy sitting in his recliner tethered to an oxygen tank. He looked terrible, but Marcia, he tried his best to get here. He wanted to meet Jagger. Most of all, though, I think he wanted to see you again, one more time."

"Well, I hope he didn't have to suffer. He was always very sweet to me."

They talked for a few minutes about Miracle. Ray brought Marcia up to date on his marriages and his two children. He told her about Miracle's reaction to her letter and how it led to Miracle's decision to make the trip to Florida. Marcia's makeup ran down her cheeks, carried away by her tears.

"I feel so guilty now, Raymond. That letter was the hardest thing I ever had to write. I knew Jagger wasn't Miracle's child."

Marcia reached for her Bible and pulled out an old photo, worn and faded now. She handed it to Ray. All these years I kept this picture I had of you and Miracle standing on a tennis court. You're both so young and full of life. I would pull it out once in a while and see Jagger in you, especially as he got older."

"How is that possible, Marcia? You and I were together one time. You and Miracle were together every night. What were the chances it would be mine?"

Marcia smiled. She fiddled with her bed sheets, as if she were trying to discern a pattern in the threads that only she could see. "A mother always knows, I guess. Anyway, that's all water under the bridge now, isn't it?"

"Not quite. You still have a child with heavy duty needs," Ray said.

"As do you, Raymond, my love."

"I'm not sure what to say Marcia. I don't have much of anything to offer. I've lived my whole life on the run. At 60 I wouldn't know how to settle down."

"You never did know a thing about that did you? But we were in love once. I'll always believe that. We didn't mean for it to happen. You came to Miami to visit your friend. How long were you here for, a month?"

"I think a little longer than that, maybe six weeks."

Marcia sighed. "How could we know that the minute our eyes met we would be hopelessly in love? Tell me something. Have you ever in all these years experienced that again?"

"No."

"And yet you threw it away. Not that I blame you. Honestly Raymond, when I told you I was pregnant, I really couldn't blame you for running away."

Ray sighed. He took in the room. "You wouldn't have anything to drink would you? I could use a drink about now."

"I'm not sure. Check the kitchen cupboard to the right of the refrigerator. If I have anything, it would be there."

Ray looked and found half a bottle of Jack Daniels. It was an old bottle, still 86 proof. He found a glass and grabbed some ice from the freezer and poured himself two fingers. He took a long swallow, not quite emptying the glass. "You say I threw everything away. True, I guess, but it was a lot more complicated than that. Miracle was deeply in love with you. For what it's worth, I don't think he ever got over you. He was like a little kid when he got your letter. You know, I never thought we would be happy together if we had to live with doing that to Miracle. Probably sounds lame now, but sooner or later, it would have come between us, don't you think?"

"No, I don't think that at all. We would have been fine. He would have understood. He had a gentle heart."

"He did but I don't think I would have been able to forgive myself, Marcia."

"I wonder Raymond, what would have happened if he had made it here to see me and Jagger. Ever think about that?"

"Only now that I'm here. You have to believe me that I really thought Jagger was his, not mine. Honestly Marcia, as long as you told him Jagger was his, Miracle would believe you."

"Do you think my letter killed him?"

"Hell no, Marcia. He was dying, wasting away in his condo. He was better off going out the way he did. Believe me, he knew that."

"I was desperate. I remembered he had all that money. I had no place else to turn. Oh, I thought about trying to find you, but I assumed you were like me a dreamer, living month to month. Jagger needs so much more than that." Marcia took a tissue from the box and wiped her eyes. "Raymond, did I do a terrible thing?"

"No, not in my book," Ray said.

Ray decided to tell Marcia about the trip, how excited Miracle was about the prospect of seeing her again. He also told her about Tara; how he found out she was his daughter. He thought about telling her that Miracle was no longer rich, but thought better of it. It might make Marcia feel worse. Then he remembered the will and how Miracle left the condo to Jagger. He told Marcia.

"Oh my! He did that? That is wonderful news," Marcia said. "Maybe there's a happy ending for once. My dear Raymond, would you mind giving me a hug? If it makes you feel creepy, you don't have to. I know how I must look to you now."

Ray stood up and bent over to Marcia. He took her in his arms and gently but firmly hugged her. He willed himself to kiss her cheek. He had been sure he did the right thing by taking off all those years ago. He assumed that Marcia and Miracle would be married and their baby would cement the relationship. He had underestimated Marcia's feelings for him and her determination not to live a lie. Had he trusted their love, maybe their lives would have turned out for the better. As he hugged Marcia's frail body, he was filled, momentarily, with regret. He let go of her and she sank back into the pillow, a tiny smile on her face.

"When will Jagger have access to the money from the condo? I'm sorry. I do have to think of these things. I don't have much time left,"

"Could be months, or even a year. It depends on how long it takes to sell the condo. I have to tell you Marcia, we can't be sure Miracle's kids won't contest the will."

Marcia shook her head and closed her eyes for a moment. "What will happen to my son?" Her eyes swept the trailer, then fell back on Ray's sober face. "You can see the way we live but he's comfortable here. He knows where his things are. He feels safe here. I can't bear the thought of Jagger being cooped up in a tiny room or, who knows, mistreated."

Ray sat there wringing his hands. "I still play tennis. I have a big match coming up. If I win, maybe I can help."

"If you win? Ray can't you just take him? He's your son too. Believe me; I know exactly how much I'm asking of you. I've taken care of him for 38 years. Do you think maybe now it could be your turn?"

Ray never saw that coming. He realized he should have, but he felt he had been blindsided. "Hold on Marcia. I didn't even know I had a son until a half hour ago."

"Not true. I told you when it happened. You chose not to believe me."

Ray looked at her. He had no idea what to say to a dying woman who was being anything but rational. They hadn't seen each other in decades. She never, not once, tried to contact him about the son she knew was his. She had been content to let Miracle shoulder the burden until she discovered he wasn't an option after all. Now, suddenly, Jagger was his too. How could she ask him to take on Jagger, even if he was his son?

Even in her compromised state, Marcia understood Ray's angst. "Oh Raymond, I don't want to be unpleasant with you. I have so little time left. I've made so many mistakes in my life. You must hate me now and I don't blame you one bit."

"Why didn't you try to find me? Were you so sure I wouldn't help? Is that what you thought of me?" Ray asked, hands cupping his face. He got up and went back to the kitchen. He poured himself another ounce of whiskey and gulped it down.

"Raymond, you and Miracle stayed in touch all these years. He was married twice. Did you ever think of looking for me in all those years?"

"No."

"May I ask why not?"

"Who knows? I guess I didn't want to be tied down. Maybe I was afraid of being disappointed by someone I cared about, or worse, disappointing you." What he couldn't bring himself to say to her on her death bed was the simple truth. He loved her, but he never trusted love. It didn't last, or maybe he didn't want it to last. It was always easier to move on.

"Something brought you here, a higher power I'm sure. Just please think about Jagger, okay?"

The door opened and Destiny, Jagger and Tara walked in.

"Mama, Miss Tara bought me a lot of candy," Jagger said.

"How nice, did you thank her?" Marcia asked, wiping the last of her tears away.

"Yes Mama, I said thank you, didn't I, Miss Destiny."

"He did. He also stuffed himself with most of it and didn't offer me any," Destiny said.

"Jagger, come here son. I want you to meet someone. This is your daddy, Jagger. His name is Raymond Rosario."

Chapter 23

"So, tell me, how did your trip to Florida go?" It was Monday afternoon. Sandy came over to Melanie's as soon as she heard they were home. Sitting in Melanie's kitchen holding a large Dunkin Donuts coffee, four sugars no milk; she pressed her daughter for details, eager to know what happened. Of course, they had spoken over the phone but the lawyer in Sandy made her want to hear it again, this time with the benefit of body language, which always revealed more than mere words.

Melanie and Brian got into Newark just before noon. A friend of Brian's picked them up at the airport because Vincent, not expecting them to come home so soon, was fishing with a friend in Barnegat Bay.

"Not much to tell. We met Marcia and her son Jagger. The kid's retarded. Actually he's a man in his thirties, very sad."

Sandy frowned. "Retarded? You meant to say mentally challenged, I'm sure." She reached for an Oreo cookie. "Did Marcia give you any insight into her relationship with your father?"

"I got less from her than I got from you. And Ray, that bastard, wouldn't tell me anything either."

"So what's next?"

"Well, like I told you, I have to wait until Tommy Price gets back from vacation before I can get a look at Dad's will."

"I've been thinking about that. Would you like me to make a phone call? It's ridiculous to have to wait a week. I can't believe your father never gave you a copy of his will to begin with. Anyway, I happen to know Tommy's partner from when we worked for the Essex County Prosecutor's office years ago."

"That would be great, Mom. It's going to kill me if I have to wait. Have another cookie."

By four o'clock that afternoon, Brian, Melanie and Sandy were sitting in the office of Clyde Tate, Tommy Price's law partner. Tate was a tall, extremely thin, mustachioed man with a practiced lawyerly demeanor. The Tate and Price offices were well manicured, filled with an eclectic mix of rich looking, post modern and old world office furniture, offset by an office landscapers dream of flowering plants and trees. The wall behind the reception desk was lined with expensive filing cabinets made of fine oak, all of it eye catching and most likely intended to give visitors the impression that the firm catered to the moneyed class. In truth, Price and Tate's practice was limited mostly to real estate closings, wills and the occasional divorce case.

Clyde Tate's austere office made it clear that the attorneys had spent most of their decorating budget on the reception area. Tate had the will in front of him. "Listen, I'm going to give you a copy of the will. I assume you are aware that Tommy is the executor. I have, of course, verified that the deceased found in the vehicle in Tampa was in fact Mr. Morgan. Not that I doubted you, Sandy, just being thorough, as is my habit."

Sandy said she understood perfectly and thanked Clyde for his time. Melanie spoke next. "Yes, I know Mr. Price is the executor. This is the first time I'm seeing my Dad's will. Have you reviewed it?"

"Not thoroughly. It's been a busy day. I did notice however, that your father made a change to his will just last Tuesday," Tate said.

Sandy shook her head. This was exactly what she was worried about. Miracle, always the great benefactor, had it in him to give away half his estate to some charity at the expense of his kids. "What changes?" she asked.

Clyde Tate looked at Brian and Melanie, momentarily not sure he wanted to get into this. "I really think it would be best if you spoke with Tommy about this. I can tell you what changes were made. Certainly, you can read the language, but I have no idea why the changes were made."

"Just tell us what you do know," Sandy said, very much the attorney now.

Tate picked up the will and perused the new section "Mr. Morgan left his condo and its contents, with certain exceptions, to a Mr. Jagger Lacy, to be held in trust by Mr. Price."

"You can't be serious," Melanie said. "Why would he leave his condo to that retard?"

"Melanie!" Both Brian and Sandy said her name in rebuke at the same time.

"You're right, I'm sorry. It's not that poor bastard's fault. But why would Dad do such a thing?"

"As I said, you will have to ask Mr. Price I'm afraid," Tate said.

"With or without Tommy Price, it's not hard to read between the lines here. Maybe your father had a secret all these years. Maybe Jagger is literally a bastard child. Maybe you two have a brother you didn't know about," Sandy said.

"And that's why he was going to Florida?" Brian asked.

"Could be," Sandy said, "You both saw, what's his name, Jagger. Did he look at all like either one of you or your father?"

"I can hardly remember what he looks like. I paid so little attention to him," Melanie said. "Did you get a good look at him, Brian?"

"No. But from what I remember, I don't think he looked like anybody in our family."

"That may be the case, but the will is very clear on this. There is no reference whatsoever to any filial relationship between Mr. Morgan and Mr. Lacy. Unless you plan to contest it, the condo's ownership will pass to Mr. Lacy once the probate process is completed."

A copy of the will in hand, Brian, Melanie and Sandy said thank you and marched out of the law office in shock. On the ride back to Melanie's house, they talked about what to do next, if anything. Sandy advised them to wait until they got a full accounting of what was being left to them, aside from the condo, before taking any action.

"As sick as he was, your father may have felt it was important to leave Jagger something," Sandy said. "From what you described of his living conditions and his mother's impending death, he will probably need help."

"That sounds like a good idea," Brian said.

"Maybe so, it won't hurt to wait on that, I guess," Melanie said. "I'll bet Ray knows all about this."

"Obviously, he does," Sandy said. Brian nodded in agreement.

They kicked that around for a while and decided that Ray, who was with Miracle the last days of his life, surely knew a great deal more than he was saying. "He won't tell us anything, unless he can make a few bucks," Sandy said.

Chapter 24

Ray stood up and shook hands with his son. The younger man was smiling. "I have a Daddy now? Nobody ever said I had one, Mama. Are you going to live here with me? I don't want to leave Mama alone."

"Hush now, Jagger," Marcia said. "You won't be leaving me alone." Marcia knew immediately she had made a tactical mistake in telling Jagger about Ray so quickly. Her sense of urgency drove her to it. Still, she worried, not knowing how Ray would react to his son.

Ray shrugged his shoulders ever so slightly. He had never felt so trapped in his life. He had always been able to extricate himself from relationships that no longer interested him or suited his needs. When it was time for him to move on, he wasn't vulnerable to crying or begging. Reason and logic were wasted on him. But blood was a different state of affairs entirely. He needed time to absorb what was happening; time to think. At that moment, every instinct told him to run. He tried his best to fight it, aware of Tara's presence; Marcia's dying wish and Jagger's confusion and worry. But his only thought was he never signed up for this. He was way too old to make the kind of changes that would be required to take on a disabled person he just met minutes ago.

He looked at Marcia and said, "I'm sorry Marcia. I can't handle this. I need some time to think. Look, I'll send you some money when I can. I think it best for me to leave. Sorry, I'm really sorry."

He turned to Jagger, shook his hand again and headed for the door. He remembered that Tara had the keys. "Give me the damn keys," he said.

She refused. "You can't leave now, not like this Ray."

He snatched her purse off the kitchen counter and rummaged through the makeup, wallet, lip gloss and tissues to find what he was looking for. It was a horrifying moment. Everyone except Ray was crying, Marcia, Jagger, Tara. Even Destiny had tears in her eyes.

Ray turned to Tara. "You coming with me?"

She wanted to refuse. She wanted no part of him, but she was worried, sure that with Ray's refusal to care for Jagger, she would be next in line. She was sure Marcia would beg her to care for her brother. She felt her face flush as she contemplated her own refusal to help. She couldn't possibly take on the job of caring for a 38 year old mentally challenged man, even if he was her half-brother. She nodded her head. Yes, she was leaving with him.

They got in the car without any promises to Marcia or Jagger, and drove off. They drove all the way to Miami without either one of them saying a word. Ray dropped Tara off at her apartment. They didn't even say goodbye. He headed to the airport to turn in the rental car and pick up his car. He was tired.

Marcia Lacey slept through the night, devastated by the events of the past few days. On Tuesday morning, she asked Destiny to call and make arrangements with the state agency that would arrange care for Jagger. There would be paperwork to complete.

Tuesday turned out to be a very long day for her. Marcia's pain worsened. The morphine wasn't as effective as it had been just a few days ago. With no appetite, she was fading quickly now. She managed to complete all the necessary paperwork, but she was exhausted by the effort. She arranged with her neighbor to coordinate Jagger's move to a group home. Marcia explained to the neighbor that he was to be transferred the day she died. There wouldn't even be a memorial service. A simple cremation, her ashes scattered in the Gulf of Mexico was all she wanted. Her work done, final decisions made, she was ready to get on with dying. It was only a question now of when the good Lord would call her, she said.

On Wednesday morning though, much to her chagrin, she rallied again. She ate breakfast and even managed to get up and look out the window at her back yard. There were two orange trees that still grew oranges in spite of woeful neglect. She loved those trees and said so to Destiny. Then they heard a car pull up. A door slammed. Both women stood still, unable to even face the front door. Hoping for good news seemed a ludicrous notion.

When they heard the knock, Marcia sat in her well-worn recliner rather than climb into bed. Destiny opened the door wide. "I knew you would be back here, honey," she said.

"I had to come back, if only for a visit." It was Tara.

They sat and talked about what happened the last time they were together. Tara apologized for Ray's behavior. When asked, she acknowledged she hadn't seen him since he dropped her off at her apartment. Marcia gave Tara some details on the arrangements that were being made for Jagger. "It isn't all that bad really. The state agency does a good job, but I sheltered Jagger from so much over the years. He is very naïve, I'm afraid. I just wish he could be with people who he could be comfortable with; people he could trust. I wanted to die knowing he was with family."

Tara asked her about her letter. Exactly why did she chose Miracle over Ray when she knew Ray was Jagger's father?

"I wanted what was best for my son. I knew enough about both men to know that Miracle was much more likely to care for Jagger than Ray. And he had the means to do it. Sadly, it seems, I was right about Ray. I suppose, considering the way Miracle died, I did a terrible thing. I'm not sure I believe in heaven or hell but then, if there are such places, I guess I know where I'm headed."

"Don't say such a thing, honey," said Destiny.

Tara wondered about Marcia's decision and what she would

have done under the same circumstances. She was facing a similar situation. She realized now that her visit to Marcia was as much for her own needs as it was for Marcia's or Jagger's. She respected a mother's right to choose, but an abortion was out of the question for her. She always believed that only a woman in that situation could make the right decision given her circumstances. Yet, when faced with her pregnancy, she couldn't imagine any other choice. She would have the baby and deal with the consequences. But, could she live with not telling Elian about their child? Maybe Marcia had some wisdom to offer. Just as Miracle had said to Ray, Tara was indeed lost.

They heard another car. Two car doors slammed, which informed them it wasn't Ray. The three women looked at each other, vainly hoping they were wrong but unwilling to look out the window. Destiny got up and awaited the knock on the door.

"Hello, my name is Melanie Morgan-Cox."

"And what can I do for you?" Destiny asked.

"I would like to see Marcia."

"You Miracle's child, right? Looks like we having a convention at the Garden Estates Park today. Who's this lady with you?"

"I'm Sandy, Melanie's mother. How did you know who we were?"

"Miracle, may he rest in peace, and that fool Ray been all over the news." Destiny then lowered her booming voice to a whisper. "Y'all can come in, but you're out of here if you upset Miss Marcia. She's busy trying to die in peace. What exactly do you want?"

"We need to talk to her about Miracle and Jagger," Sandy said. "Apparently, my ex-husband left something for him in his will."

"The condo right?"

"That's right, how did you know that?" Melanie asked. "That wasn't on the news."

"His friend Ray was here. He told us about it. You gonna give it to him? The boy needs it."

"May we come in?" Sandy asked.

From where she was sitting, Marcia could hear the conversation. She was grateful to be alert. "Let them in Destiny," she said.

"You remember me, Miss Lacy?" Melanie said.

"Yes, of course. You've met Destiny and this is Tara."

"I know who she is. Where's Ray?"

"He's in Miami. Where's Brian? Tara asked.

"Obviously, he's not here. Where's Jagger?"

"He's working. Now that we've taken attendance, what do you want?" Destiny broke in.

"I'm not sure we know where to start. I'm an attorney. I know I should be skilled in matters like this, but I must say I'm at a loss here," Sandy said.

"Let me see if I can help you out then," Destiny said. "Are you here to let Miss Marcia know you won't give her no trouble about the condo?"

Melanie glanced at Destiny and stepped closer to Marcia's recliner. "Miss Lacy, we have no idea why my father would leave his condo to your son. Do you?"

Marcia looked at her hands. Her right hand was gently scratching the arm of the chair. Her left was gripping the other arm hard. "I might know why, yes." By now Marcia was resigned to Jagger's fate. She had lost hope that anyone would come to his rescue. She certainly expected nothing of Miracle's family.

"Can you tell us why then?" Sandy asked.

"I can. He was under the impression that Jagger was his son. I sent Miracle a letter asking for his help, since I am dying of pancreatic cancer."

"We are very sorry to hear that Marcia," Sandy said. "You said Miracle was under the impression that Jagger was his son. Is he?"

"No, he isn't."

"Whose son is he then?" Melanie asked.

"Why do you want to know that?"

"Yeah, that's a good question," Destiny added.

"Well, for one thing my ex-husband recently amended his will, stipulating that the condo should be left in trust for your son. Apparently, under the impression that he was Jagger's father. My daughter and I would like to help, but I think we're entitled to know more than you are telling us," Sandy said.

Marcia asked Destiny for a sip of water and a dose of morphine. The pain was returning with a vengeance now. "Alright, if that's why you came all this way, I'll tell you. Jagger's father is Raymond Rosario."

"That son of a bitch!" Melanie said. "Can't say I'm surprised."

Destiny quickly stepped forward now and got as close to Melanie as she could without touching her. "I am not going to tell you again to mind your manners. This woman is in a world of hurt. You will show some respect for her in her home. Do we understand each other?"

Sandy smiled. "Well said, Destiny; thank you. We do understand you. This is an emotional time for all of us, I'm sure." She turned to Marcia. "Tell me though, why would you tell Miracle that Jagger was his son when you knew it wasn't so?"

"I don't want to talk about that. I'm sorry." Marcia paused and took another sip of water. Then she said to Melanie, "I'm sure you knew your father was a close friend of Raymond's for many, many years. But I wonder if you know everything there is to know about their friendship."

"I know very little about their friendship. To tell you the truth, I never understood it," Melanie said, casting a wary glance at Destiny.

"Your father never told you what happened between them when they were children?"

"No."

"Did he tell you what happened, Sandy?"

"I'm afraid not."

Marcia looked at Tara, who shook her head no.

"Would you like to hear the story? Your father told it to me many years ago when we were a couple living in Miami."

"Yeah, I can't wait. My father told you this story, not Ray, right?"

"That is correct. When they were about 12 years old, just boys really, something happened that got Raymond into very serious trouble. As I recall, your father was lighting matches and throwing them over this tall wooden fence. There was just enough wind, he said, to make them die before they hit the ground."

"Really, what was on the other side of the fence?" Sandy asked.

"Well now, Miracle said the fence stood between two garages. There was a narrow alley between the buildings that had brush and trash that had been thrown over the fence from time to time. I think he said the other end of the alley was a dead end where the two buildings were connected by a brick wall. I remember him saying it was summertime and it hadn't rained for a long time. Miracle told me that Raymond came along and asked what he was doing. When he told him, Raymond said he was crazy or something like that. But as boys of that age are wont to do, Miracle goaded Raymond into throwing a lit match over the fence too."

"Oh Lord, those boys were just begging for trouble," Destiny said.

"Anyway, one of Miracle's matches did reach the ground, still lit and it started a fire. He got scared. He said he was so afraid of getting into trouble that he climbed over the fence to try to put it out with his feet. But it was too late for that. Then he couldn't manage to get back over the fence. There was a two-by-four that held the fence slats together that could have given him a boost up, but he was too frightened to see it. The fire was getting close and he started screaming. Raymond jumped up onto the top of the fence and hung over so Miracle could take his arm. Somehow, Raymond managed to help him get safely over the fence before he got burned."

Marcia took a few sips of water and wiped her lips with a tissue.

"And for that, my father gave Ray half his fortune?"

"Let's not exaggerate, okay, Melanie?" Sandy said.

Marcia took a deep breath. She needed more morphine. Her eyes implored Destiny for more. "Got it, honey," she said.

"A very bad thing happened next. You see, the police arrived along with the fire department. They put out the fire, but it took almost an hour. Miracle told me people had thrown a lot of trash in the alley over the years. It must have been a real fire hazard. One of the garages was a small auto repair shop. Some damage was done. Miracle said the owner was livid about what happened.

"Then the police asked a lot of questions, but neither boy would say much of anything. But an old woman, I remember Miracle describing her as a crone, came forward and told the police officer that she had seen Ray throwing the matches over the fence. She also said she didn't see Miracle throw anything.

Miracle told me he thought the woman had it in for Raymond. She lived next door to the Rosario's. After Raymond's father left them, Raymond's mother started spending time in a tavern. She left Raymond and his brother home a lot. She would come home drunk, sometimes not alone. The old woman wasn't crazy about having Italians in the neighborhood to begin with. Miracle thought the old woman saw Raymond as a juvenile delinquent."

"Oh this is getting interesting. You been holding out on me, Miss Marcia," Destiny said.

Marcia put her finger to her lips. Destiny nodded, chided for the moment. Then Marcia continued. "Raymond refused to say anything in his own defense. When Miracle was questioned by the police without Raymond around, he denied throwing any matches over the fence. He told me he was afraid he would get in trouble. Well, being from what people used to call a broken home, plus the old woman's eye witness testimony, Raymond was put in reform school for a year."

"I'm sorry, but that's bullshit. My father would never have done anything like that," Melanie said.

"You know something? I asked Miracle if he had any idea what it had been like for Raymond in that reform school. I'll never forget this. He said, 'I asked Ray once. He told me, you don't want to know.' Anyway, I wasn't there and neither were you, Melanie. Who can say now? What I can tell you is that when I knew him, your father was haunted by what he did. I hope he was able to forgive himself before he passed."

"Then why would Ray still be my father's friend if he did that to him?" Melanie asked.

"You would have to ask Raymond that question, I'm afraid."

Melanie was ready to launch into a diatribe about Ray, but Destiny stepped closer to her again with a look that would scare a pro football linebacker.

Tara sat quietly, her hands in her lap. She was beginning to understand Ray's relationship with Miracle more clearly now in light of the story Marcia told them. She was also beginning to realize that Ray, having been abandoned and neglected as a child, probably wasn't capable of maintaining long term relationships. In one way or another, both his parents had abandoned him, and his friend let him take the rap for something he didn't do. Trust would always be an issue for him. Her mother was naïve when she fell in love with Ray and probably too young to grasp what she was up against. And Ray, who hated life stories, probably gave her mother very few clues to work with. She had fallen in love with the wrong man.

But Tara believed in redemption. And more than anyone she had ever met, her father needed to be redeemed.

Chapter 25

Finally back in Miami, Ray was ready to get down to
business. His big money match was coming up on Saturday
morning. It was his chance to finally put some money away. All
he had to his name was a two bedroom condominium on Biscayne
Boulevard near the JFK Causeway. One of the thousands of
victims of the Florida real estate debacle, he owed more on his
mortgage than the condo was worth. Beyond that, he had about ten
grand in a Roth IRA. Not much for a lifetime spent on the tennis
courts in more places than he could begin to remember. And now,
those days were over. His knees hurt constantly from the pounding
they took year after year. Too, he always had to worry about skin
cancer from all those years in the sun. And, at 60, he no longer had
the energy for constant travel. His road trip with Miracle brought
home his growing distaste for life on the road. He was over it, the
bad food, strange rooms with lumpy mattresses and strange faces
in elevators.

The opportunity to put all that behind him fell into his lap
just a few days after he took Elian's $500. He had been talking to
friends for a few years about opening a tennis shop. They all told
him the same thing: It's a very competitive business. According
to his calculations, which he worked and re-worked constantly, he
needed about $100,000 to open the doors, but felt he could do it for
less. Getting the money he needed though, seemed as unlikely as
an invitation to the International Tennis Hall of Fame. Then he got
lucky.

As was his custom, he had been sitting at the air conditioned
bar at the tennis resort after he gave a few lessons. Through the
large windows that overlooked the tennis courts, he watched a

young guy playing a match and struggling to hold on. He managed to win a tie breaker and then headed to the showers. A newcomer to the club, he seemed to have an entourage. Ray had seen the kid play one other time. It was obvious he could play the game. Certainly, he was very good for a club level player. Ray guessed he was in his late twenties. He asked around about him and learned that the kid was new to the Miami tennis scene. One day when Ray was chatting with a waitress at the resort, he learned that the guy was from South America. The waitress told him he was visiting Miami for a few months. His family was very wealthy, she said.

The next day, Ray ran into him at the bar during the cocktail hour and introduced himself. The guy's response was cool. He said, "Hello, Ray Rosario. I'm Armando De Rossi." Then he turned back to the wide screen TV to watch the finals of the French Open.

Ray ordered a drink and sat down next to him. He offered a few comments about playing in the French Open on the famous red clay.

"You actually played in that tournament?" Armando asked.

"Once, but I didn't have enough experience on clay. I got bounced the first round."

"I saw you play on clay at the club. I guess you learned how. You're a pretty good player for an old guy."

"Well, I could beat you without breaking a sweat, even if I let you serve every game," Ray said.

Armando laughed. "I've seen you taking advantage of the suckers around here a couple of times now. You sucker them all, letting them serve every game. It's funny man."

"I don't sucker anybody. They all think they can beat me and sometimes they do," Ray said.

"Yeah, until you play for money. Then your game improves. You give tennis players a bad name, man."

They bantered like this for a while longer. Armando told

him he was an amateur champion in Argentina. After a few drinks, Armando got up and left to join a few friends for dinner. There would be no further conversation beyond a grudging acknowledgment they offered each other in the form of nods and thin lipped smiles across the room until their paths happened to cross two weeks later. It was a Saturday afternoon. Ray had just taken down yet another sucker, this one a university professor. He spotted Armando in the locker room. Since they were there alone, Ray decided to try his luck.

"So, you're a young guy about 28, I'd say. Think you could beat a 60 year old man with a bum right shoulder?"

"First of all, I'm in my 30s old man. And yeah, I know I can beat you."

"Seems to me we know different things."

Armando laughed. "You can't hustle me, man. We play a match and you probably hurt yourself. Don't want your small change, viejo."

"Care to make it interesting?" Ray asked.

"What's your idea of interesting, $500? I spend that for breakfast, man," Armando said.

"How much do you want to play for?" Ray asked.

"Go away old man. You can't afford it."

Now Ray wasn't a fool. He realized the guy might be trying to hustle him. He stuffed his clothes and towel into his tennis bag. He was calculating the odds. De Rossi was 30 years younger. That counted for something. And for all Ray knew, he might have deliberately played below his ability for Ray's sake. Ray had done that himself many times. But there were certain things that were hard to fake when you were under the watchful eye of a seasoned pro. He might have a few shots up his sleeve that he hadn't shown yet, but whatever he had, Ray was confident it wouldn't be enough to overcome Ray's savvy on the court. Besides, he was hungry. He decided to bite. "Why don't you let me decide what I can afford, joven. What's on your mind?

"I'm thinking $25,000, best three out of five like, Wimbledon," De Rossi said, wanting Ray to know he knew exactly who he was dealing with.

"That's a lot of cabbage, my friend."

"Like I said old man, you can't afford it. You should stick to the CEOs and sales reps you like, down here on vacation. Maybe they don't mind dropping a few hundred bucks to say they played a famous touring pro with a broken wing."

"I didn't say I wouldn't take the bet. I'll need a couple of weeks to put it all together is all."

The $25,000 purse decided, Ray began negotiating the other terms. They would play early in the morning. He wanted odds. De Rossi balked at that until Ray pointed out that even with those odds the young man wouldn't be playing for much beyond pride. "With all your dough people are going to think you're afraid if it's even money." Ray skillfully goaded the younger man into three to one odds to make up for the huge age difference. He appealed to the young man's vanity, his sense of physical superiority. As sharp as De Rossi was, he couldn't resist the chance to put the old man in his place, exactly what Ray wanted.

If he beat this guy, he would win $75,000. De Rossi barely blinked an eye. He really did come from a family worth at least a billion dollars. Ray also told him it would have to be a best of three sets match, again due to his age and the Miami heat. De Rossi smiled at that one and nodded his agreement.

Finally, since Ray couldn't serve, he asked to start each game at 15 to Love, giving him a one point advantage at the start of each game. But De Rossi balked when he heard that, saying if Ray wanted a point advantage to start each game, he would consider it, but the odds would drop to even money. De Rossi had a demand of his own. He insisted they play on a hard court which would favor the younger man. Since Ray had no doubt he would win regardless of the playing surface, he agreed. He also dropped his request for a one point per game advantage. The three to one odds were irresistible. He wanted the biggest financial score he could get.

His only problem was coming up with the $25,000 he needed to secure the bet. Franco, the guy who ran the pro shop at the tennis club agreed to hold the money. His take was a grand to be paid by the loser. They set the date for two weeks later to give Ray time to raise the money. He wasted no time arranging a trip to New Jersey. When he mentioned to Tara he was going, she offered to go with him. He leered at her a little, but she set him straight immediately. He laughed, kissed her cheek and said never mind.

The next day he took her to lunch at the club. She asked again if she could go with him. He had already decided to invite her, but she saved him the trouble. He actually regretted the come on he gave her. Experienced with women, he knew she wasn't the type to give it up easily. And, he sensed she would never get cozy with him. He agreed to take her along anyway because she was good company. Of course, he didn't tell her why he was making the trip.

Miracle was always good for the money. He had never turned him down. This time though, he would be asking for more than Miracle had ever given him before. Ray decided to insist it was a loan he would repay. He knew better than to tell his buddy what he needed the money for because Miracle was never one to take what he would term a foolish risk.

To Ray's mind, this match was a lock. That's not to say that Miracle would have been impressed. He could never understand the beauty of a con job no matter how well it was crafted. Better to tell him he needed the money for a tennis shop investment. In any case, after this match he would be able to retire from the hustle and really invest in something that would give him a steady source of income. He even considered asking Miracle to be his partner in the venture.

But when Ray saw him, he was shocked by Miracle's condition. He never imagined that his friend might be sick or dying. The guy had always been healthy. Nor did he think for a moment he would wind up trying to transport his friend to Florida.

The odd thing was that Miracle's illness made getting the money a snap. No need to request a loan or a partnership. Almost as strange was reconnecting with Brooks Riley in South Carolina. He told Brooks about his big match of course. Brooks loved it and suggested they might be able to do some business together if he won that kind of cash.

On the other hand, Ray was still in shock about both Tara and Jagger. In his wildest dreams he could never have envisioned discovering at 60 that he had two grown kids.

Before Jagger, he thought maybe he could build a relationship with Tara. She was an adult and fully capable of managing her life. She was a nurse; she could take care of herself. But Jagger was another matter. Ray knew he could barely manage his own life. How was he going to take responsibility for an adult man who needed regular supervision? Of course, stiff arming Jagger probably cost him his relationship with Tara. So he was back where he was before he went to New Jersey, free as a bird. So be it. He thought he could handle that.

But it wasn't that easy and deep down, he knew it. He was having trouble sleeping He was having nightmares about Marcia. Miracle had been right, of course, Marcia wasn't the love of his, Ray's, life. But she was special. She had a good heart and a patient soul. She had fallen in love and it frightened him. He learned the hard way long before he met Marcia not to trust love. It was never permanent. Even if his feelings for Marcia could equal what she felt for him, he would have walked away. Miracle was his best friend, and in the long run, his only friend. No one would ever understand the friendship between the two men. It was true that Miracle had saved his own skin and let him pay the price for something Miracle did. Having actually gone through reform school, even as a kid, he realized Miracle was in no way tough enough to have handled it. Ray was always a scrapper, quick with his fists and street smart. He held his own in reform school. Sure, he took plenty of abuse from older boys and guards alike; much of the experience quarantined from his conscious thoughts.

When he was released from reform school, he went home and was put back in school with other kids from the neighborhood. Some parents told their kids to stay away from him. He was a troubled boy and a trouble maker. Mr. and Mrs. Morgan never discouraged their son's friendship with Ray. In fact, Mrs. Morgan felt almost as much guilt as Miracle did because she was sure that Miracle had not told the truth. For obvious reasons, she never pushed Miracle for the whole story.

Miracle stayed away from Ray on his own accord. He couldn't face him. But one day, Ray cornered him in the school playground and gave him a good beating. The next day, they were friends again. As things got worse at home for Ray, he found himself having dinner at the Morgan home on a regular basis. Mrs. Morgan welcomed him with open arms. By the time they were in high school, he was sleeping on the floor at Miracle's house so often that Miracle's parents bought him a bed. As he got older, and Mrs. Rosario's drinking got worse, she dropped her objections to Ray staying with the Morgan's.

By the time Miracle was a senior at the University of Miami and Ray was a sometime touring pro, they stayed in touch mostly through occasional letters they would write. When Ray came to Miami, Miracle was the first person he called. Naturally, Miracle introduced Ray to Marcia. Ray could see how crazy Miracle was about her. She was a beauty. Ray had met his share of beautiful women on the tour, but Marcia was something special. Her lovely complexion, dark red hair and angelic demeanor, mesmerized him. She was outgoing too, which seemed to complement Miracle's quieter personality.

Ray was in town for a tournament and some exhibition matches. He stayed with Miracle and Marcia who were living together. One afternoon, after practicing his game for the upcoming tournament, Ray returned to the apartment expecting to find Miracle.

But his friend had a couple of late classes that day. Marcia was there. They talked a while, smoked a couple of joints and drank some wine. As flower children of the times often did, they decided to have sex. Marcia believed monogamy implied ownership. She hated that, she said. As it turned out it was more than sex and they both knew it immediately.

They were on fire, bonding instantly. Suddenly, Marcia wanted nothing more than to be with Ray, and only Ray. He was crazy about Marcia too, but he had been crazy about a woman before. He knew his feelings would cool down. They always did. Settling down wasn't an option for him. Knowing how Miracle felt about Marcia made Ray feel terrible about what he'd done. Miracle was deeply in love with Marcia. He confided in Ray that he had proposed to her several times. He wanted to marry her, but in spite of Miracle's wealth, Marcia put him off.

Ray hung around for another month after that, keeping a commitment to play in an exhibition match and finishing up a stint giving lessons at the famous Palmeri School of Tennis. He did his best to stay away from Marcia, making sure he got back to the apartment after Miracle and Marcia were in bed. He got up early and left when Miracle did.

On the day before he was leaving town to catch up with the tour, Marcia cornered him again. This time she followed him to the school and met him in the parking lot. She told him she was pregnant, but Ray quickly laid down the law. He told Marcia to leave him alone. He insisted that if she was pregnant the baby was Miracle's not his. That was their last conversation until he saw her on her deathbed. And Ray never gave it any thought after that until he saw Marcia's letter to Miracle.

Now almost 40 years later, Ray was astonished that one afternoon of lovemaking could come back to haunt him. He did his best to put Jagger and Tara out of his mind. He had a lifetime of experience in putting behind him what he found inconvenient. He did his best to ignore the voices in his head. It was a battle he was sure he would win. It had always worked before. Why should this time be any different?

He spent as much time as possible on the tennis court that week. He practiced hard, working with a tennis pro who had helped him out before. He played a couple of practice matches and even squeezed in a few people who wanted 30 minute lessons.

He didn't see Armando De Rossi play at the club or anywhere else that week. Not that it bothered him. Ray was convinced that Armando De Rossi had exaggerated his accomplishments on the tennis courts of Argentina.

Chapter 26

Marcia Lacy finally succumbed to the ravages of her cancer just after midnight on Friday. Jagger was asleep, but Destiny, sensing Thursday afternoon that the end was near, decided to stay over. On Thursday night, just before dinner, Marcia's neighbor stopped by to check on her. Destiny asked her to sit with Marcia and Jagger while she made arrangements for her children. She was back by 7:30. She sent the neighbor home. The woman was obviously uncomfortable watching over a dying woman. Destiny had seen the death rattle many times before. To the uninitiated, it was a startling revelation.

The hospice staff, sensitive to the situation, arranged to have the body quickly transferred to the crematorium. Destiny was exhausted, but before she went home she called Tara to give her the news. But Tara spent Thursday night with Elian, the first time they had seen each other since Tampa. Her cell phone had been turned off. She heard about Marcia's passing over a cup of coffee Friday morning.

My brother's mother is gone, she thought. She had been doing a lot of thinking since she visited Marcia and Jagger. She was troubled by her seeming lack of empathy for her brother. After Melanie and Sandy left Marcia's, she and Destiny talked. Destiny told her that Jagger's life would never be the same. He would be living with strangers, all of them mentally challenged. The thought made Tara cry. At this stage of her pregnancy, Tara noticed she cried easily. Still, Marcia was sweet. Tara wished the woman could have died in peace, secure in the knowledge that Jagger's future was assured.

Tara wanted to help, but she had no idea how she could do that. Financial assistance was certainly not an option, nor was it a solution. During her visit with Marcia and Jagger, she learned that what Marcia really wanted for Jagger was to live with family, relatives he could learn to trust and people Marcia could trust. Above all, she did not want her son taken advantage of in any way. Money alone simply wasn't a substitute for love and caring support. After Ray's abrupt departure the other day, Marcia realized that Ray probably wasn't capable of taking care of Jagger. But here was Ray's daughter, who also happened to be a nurse, sitting in front of her again, obviously wanting to help in some way.

But Tara wasn't prepared to turn her life upside down either, not without Ray's help. Marcia didn't come right out and ask Tara to take Jagger. She didn't have to. As soon as Melanie and Sandy left, Marcia dozed off. Destiny didn't waste any time. First, she made them some tea and put out the cupcakes Tara brought.

"I am glad you didn't put these out while that daughter of Mr. Miracle's was here," Destiny said. "She don't deserve even a ten day old cupcake. Bad news is what she is."

"I think she's more confused, or maybe frustrated, than anything else," Tara said.

"She's probably mostly thrilled the boy isn't her brother is what she is."

"That too." They both laughed a little.

"So you came back here. I can't say I was exactly shocked to see your pretty face again, girl."

"I know. I had to come. It's weird finding out you have a brother."

"Let's talk turkey, Tara baby. Jagger's Mama is gonna be gone real soon now. Can you take him? Maybe that Ray character will come around and help out."

"I just don't know. It's so much responsibility. I have to think about it."

"You know honey, there's more to Mr. Jagger than you might be seeing. Oh, I know he looks like a simple creature but he's more complicated than that. He thinks he should be married, Lord knows why, and he wants to go see the Tampa Rays baseball team play. Watches them all the time, knows the players and roots for them," Destiny said. "There's still time for him. With a little help, he might surprise you."

"I'm sure you're right Destiny. I just don't know if I'm what he needs now or even if I have what it takes."

"Well, you think on it, but don't you go underestimating yourself. Thing is, you don't have much time," Destiny said, nodding over to the bed where Marcia was sleeping.

When she got back to Miami, Tara spoke with Elian about it. He saw immediately how upset she was. "Listen to me baby. If this is something you want to do, I will be there for you all the way down the line. You want to take him in, we'll figure it out, I promise." He told her he would find Jagger a job in his company.

What he didn't grasp was that Jagger couldn't really be left unsupervised for very long. Tara doubted that Elian really understood that caring for Jagger would be full time, a very long term commitment. Tara thanked Elian for being so sweet. She was actually bowled over by his offer. In spite of what she learned by observing the heartbreaking outcome of Marcia's choice, she was leaning away from telling Elian about the baby. But Elian's reaction to Jagger's situation gave her reason to reconsider.

Her heart rate actually jumped when she heard Elian's words, but she was also aware that such an arrangement might tie her to him in a way she wasn't prepared for, at least not yet. She wondered about that too. Was she more like Ray than she realized? Was she afraid of commitment? Her first marriage was a disaster, lasting only a few months. Sure, her husband had been an animal, but deep down she wondered if it was her fault that he behaved the way he did. Did she subconsciously push him away?

Yet, she found Elian appealing in so many ways. There was a distinct physical chemistry between them. They just seemed to be on the same page about what they wanted out of life. The age difference bothered her, but was that just an excuse not to commit? Now, with a baby on the way, she was about to learn the meaning of commitment, shared DNA with Ray be damned.

While Tara was listening to her message from Destiny, Elian was making their breakfast. He put a plate of scrambled eggs and toast in front of her. She pushed it away.

"You just told me ten minutes ago you were starving. What's up with that? I just made you a good breakfast."

"I'm sorry. Marcia Lacy died early this morning. I just can't help thinking about Jagger. They'll probably take him to that group home this afternoon."

"Sorry to hear that, honey. You have a decision to make. Like I said, I'm ready to help and, if you get the condo money, you can buy a place, you know, just for the time being."

"The time being? What does that mean?"

"You know what it means. Sometime down the road…"

Tara looked at Elian, stood up and said, "Sorry, I knew what you meant. I'm just really stressed right now. Anyway, forget Miracle's family. His daughter Melanie isn't going to give up $250,000 now."

"How do you know that?" Elian asked.

"I was there. I saw the look on her face when she found out Jagger wasn't related to her. She acted like she was pissed off at Ray, but I could see she was relieved. She was off the hook."

"Did she say that?"

"Of course not. But she and her mother got out of there as soon as they could.

"That doesn't necessarily mean they won't help. Don't forget they would have to contest the will. Miracle's family is screwed up right now. The man left town and died. Now they've discovered there's a change in his will. Give them some time, girl. They might surprise you."

"I think you're dreaming, but I hope you're right. Maybe you wouldn't be so optimistic if you saw Melanie at Marcia's. Very cold, you know?"

"Cold is not good," Elian said.

Tara picked up a piece of toast and took a small bite. "I just remembered something she said before she and her mother left Marcia's. As she was leaving, she made a comment like, 'it's too bad Ray wasted so much of my father's money all those years. Maybe he could have used some of it to help his son now.' Can you believe that?"

"I still say give her some time. Anyway, if Jagger needs a lawyer, we can help him out."

Tara smiled. She had a sad look on her face. She stroked Elian's arm. "He's my brother. I have to at least see him before he goes. Will you come with me?"

"Sure. Eat some breakfast. You're going to need your strength, baby girl."

You don't know the half of it, Tara thought.

Saturday morning looked like an ideal morning for a tennis match. There was no wind to wrestle with. On the other hand, as early as it was, 6:30, it was already getting hot and humid. Even during the warm-up, which wasn't very taxing, Ray could feel the sweat dripping down his back. He would have to do his best to beat this guy in straight sets. He realized a third set might be more than he could handle in these conditions.

Armando De Rossi, on the other hand, looked cool. He had a very relaxed air about him. When it was time for the coin toss, he took exaggerated steps to reach the net. Since the agreement was that Armando would serve every game, the toss was to decide which side of the court, north or south, the winner would select. On that morning, there wasn't a particular advantage to be had on either side. There was no wind and the sun rising in the east would affect them equally. They also agreed that since De Rossi would be serving every game, points would always be called based on how many Armando had first. A 15-30 score for example, would mean

Ray was in the lead.

When Ray called heads and won the toss, he initiated his first bit of gamesmanship by electing to let De Rossi choose the side he preferred. In effect, he was telling his opponent that it didn't matter. Ray would win the match regardless of what De Rossi did.

The money was safely in the hands of Franco, the pro shop manager. He was already a winner, guaranteed a thousand bucks, no matter what happened. Ray had to scramble to come up with the difference between the check he got from Miracle for $22,000 and the rest of the cash. He called Brooks and persuaded him to put up the remaining $3,000, assuring him he would get his money back. Brooks laughed and said, "Okay, but Angelina can never know about this. You better win."

The first three games went by quickly. Ray, a terrific returner of serve who could still hit with power when he had to, had little trouble sending his opponent back and forth from one side of the court to the other. He hit the ball high over the net with a tremendous amount of topspin, which made the ball jump off the court's surface and quickly bounce high so that the best his opponent could do was hit defensive shots. In spite of his status as an amateur champion in his native Argentina, De Rossi had only played one other tennis pro that had actually been on the professional tour.

With a three nothing lead, Ray relaxed a little, which he soon remembered is always a mistake. Four games later, De Rossi was ahead 4-3, and Ray was feeling winded. It was beginning to dawn on Ray that Armando De Rossi was a much better player than he had been led to believe. He wondered if the guy he saw playing just a few weeks ago knew he was being scouted. Perhaps he had deliberately played beneath his capability. That was a tactic Ray was certainly familiar with. And while De Rossi was not a professional, he was obviously good enough to adjust his game on the fly.

Ray also wondered if those first three games he had won so

easily were just another attempt to lull him into complacency. If this guy was a hustler, he was pretty good at it. Starting with game four, De Rossi had had no trouble handling Ray's topspin returns and groundstrokes. He not only got to every ball Ray hit, he came to the net whenever Ray, forced to play defense himself, hit a short return. The guy had great reflexes and quick hands. Ray was in trouble and he knew it.

But every player, even the best in the world, has a weakness. And as Ray well knew, the pressure of having to serve every game eventually becomes a chore for most players. De Rossi had a good serve. He was skilled at moving the ball around, varying spin and speed. But, as Ray expected, when he was able to easily return most of Armando's serves, the younger man started going for too much, trying to overpower Ray. He began having trouble getting his first serve in. That forced him to rely on his second serve which was good but nothing special. Ray took advantage of that, and evened the score. Then he went up 5-4 in the next game. If he could win their tenth game, he would be up one set to love.

As is customary, the players switched sides on odd number games. At 5-4, the two men went to their respective benches to get a drink and towel off before switching sides. As they passed each other, Ray used another tactic that sometimes worked to his advantage. He said, "Armando, you're serve's gone south of the border on you. I'm sure it will get better though." This was intended to keep his opponent's mind on the problems he was having with his serve. Armando just smiled and shook his head.

Ray sat there thinking about the next game. If De Rossi did get his mojo back on his first serve, he would be hard to beat unless Ray could come up with a better strategy. What De Rossi clearly had going for him was his youth and superior speed. Ray considered all this as he headed back out onto the court. He decided to take a chance. Another weakness he noticed was that the guy tended to berate himself a little if he got beat by one of Ray's shots. When the match resumed, Ray stepped well into the court to wait for the serve, rather than a couple of feet behind the baseline where he had been standing, out of respect for De Rossi's power.

The strategy worked, at least on the first two points. Irritated that Ray wasn't respecting his youth and power, De Rossi over-hit the ball and double faulted twice. On his next serve though, De Rossi eased up and placed his serve on the T that separated the deuce and advantage sides of the court. Since Ray was standing so far in, De Rossi had no trouble scoring an ace. Ray was now ahead 15-30.

He went back to his customary position to take the next serve. De Rossi hit the ball out wide and Ray got there a bit late. He attempted to return the serve down the line, but missed. Now it was 30-30. De Rossi's next serve was inexplicably weak. It looked like a watermelon to Ray. He creamed it. De Rossi never even made a move toward the ball. He was ahead 30-40. It was set point. Ray's luck held as De Rossi, seeking the element of surprise, eased up on his first serve again and Ray surprised him with a drop shot that just cleared the net and died. Ray was ahead one set to love.

Ray was happy and relieved. His confidence surged. He felt sure he had the psychological edge, with a one set lead and he wasn't that tired yet. He got out of his sweat drenched shirt and put on a new one, drank more water with a bit of a sports drink mixed in. He ate half an energy bar to get ready for the second set. He looked over at Armando who was standing off to the side with his girlfriend. They were laughing about something. Ray wondered if the guy really cared about winning. He was definitely playing it cool and casual.

The second set didn't go the way Ray thought it would. In his experience, guys who managed to play well enough to keep it close for one set were secretly satisfied simply to have managed to hang in there with a much better player, especially a pro. A psychological victory of sorts had been won just by keeping it close. Ray would really pour it on early in the second set to demoralize his opponent. And that usually led to a collapse, although Ray always made sure the guy won at least two games later in the set to keep them from feeling they had been hustled.

That didn't happen against De Rossi. The younger man played outstanding tennis, taking every advantage of his youth and speed to win. He was also having one of those moments that even low level club players occasionally have where almost every shot he tried worked to perfection. De Rossi won the second set 6-1. They were tied one set apiece and would have to play a third set.

As they walked past each other to change sides, De Rossi smiled and said, "You are pretty good for an old man. I mean that, you're still good."

Ray realized Armando was returning the favor with his own remarks. And he got to Ray a little because he didn't expect it from De Rossi. He couldn't believe he hadn't seen it coming. Rich or not, the guy wasn't going to throw away seventy five grand. He really believed he could beat Ray. Well, there was no point in berating himself. He had another set to play. Instead, he shot back. "Armando, you ain't seen nothing yet, but you're making it hard on me. Very cool, I like it that way," Ray said.

In spite of his bravado, Ray was really worried now. He knew De Rossi's strategy would be to make him run in the last set, to hammer him with power serves, take him out wide and then come to the net. He was going to need every trick he ever knew just to stay in the match. He really was beat. The sun was shining now, bright and hot. The temperature was already 90 degrees and there was no cloud cover. He had to find a way to win the first couple of games, he told himself. He had to shake De Rossi's confidence and rebuild his own in the process.

And then, out of the corner of his eye, just before the last set was about to start he saw Tara and Elian sitting down on the stands on the other side of the court. He saw Elian wave, but he wasn't waving at him. He was waving at De Rossi. He looked over at De Rossi, who was smiling broadly. These two knew each other. Did that little bastard Elian set him up? He looked back over at

Elian and Tara. He saw something else that almost made his knees buckle. Jagger was with them. He was wearing a Tampa Rays baseball cap and sunglasses, but no doubt about it, that was Jagger sitting next to his sister Tara.

Ray called a time out. He walked over to them and said, "What's going on, Tara?"

"We came to watch you play. It was Elian's idea. We brought Jagger along, too."

"Hi daddy. Are you playing tennis?" Jagger said.

"Yes, I'm playing tennis," Ray said. He leaned into Tara and whispered, "What's he doing here?"

"Marcia died yesterday morning. I'm sorry."

"You picked a hell of a time to spring this on me, kid." Then, turning to Elian, he pointed his finger at him and said, "You little prick. You sent De Rossi looking for me didn't you?"

"No way,man. He's just a guy I met here at the club."

"What are you talking about?" Tara asked.

"Let Fidel here explain it to you. I have a tennis match to win."

But De Rossi was still sharp. He easily won the first two games, serving three aces, all of them wide so Ray had to run far to his right just to reach the ball. The angle De Rossi was getting on his serve was just too much for Ray.

When the third game started Ray decided to try moving up into the court when De Rossi served to see if he could unnerve his opponent again. When De Rossi saw this, he laughed and hit a perfect serve directly into Ray's body, causing Ray to hit a weak return that landed in the net. It was 15-love. Ray's first instinct was to go back behind the baseline, but he thought better of it. He decided to stay put and see what might happen.

De Rossi smiled again, but this time he served the ball into the net, as he did with his next three chances. Four serves in a row into the net and suddenly, it was 15-30, Ray's lead. DeRossi got his next serve in, but Ray was ready and he pounded it to DeRossi's backhand. Then he ran to the net and dropped Armando's return just over the net for the point. He wound up winning the game, but he also realized that he could no longer afford to stay at the baseline to conserve energy. If he had any chance to win this thing, he had to be more aggressive, heat, be damned. Now Ray would charge the net.

On the changeover, Ray sat and tried to block all thoughts from his mind except winning the set and match. The money's the thing, he told himself. But he couldn't resist looking over at Jagger and Tara, his children. As soon as he saw them together, it registered. He understood exactly what was going on. Tara brought Jagger to Miami with her to force his hand. The poor guy really looked lost even behind his sunglasses. Seeing him again, Ray was afraid he was defeated, outfoxed by his own daughter. Tara would never let him get away with running away. Finally, he had met a woman who could make him tow the line. And it was his daughter. He toweled off, drank some water and headed back onto the court.

He wasn't sure how long he could keep going to the net, but it was working, so he kept it up. And it was effective. He won two of the next three games to even the score to 3 games each. De Rossi rallied after that and won the next two games, hitting passing shots that Ray couldn't reach as he ran to the net. Armando was one game away from winning Ray's 25 grand. And Ray knew he couldn't let that happen. Whatever he decided to do with Jagger, he was going to need that money.

On his first serve in the next game, De Rossi decided to charge the net. And Ray, who had tried a few lobs unsuccessfully early in the match, felt he had no choice but to do it again. He hit a beautiful lob over his opponent's head that landed just inside the baseline and won the point. Then De Rossi double faulted again. Ray fed him a couple of more lobs that landed in hard to reach spots and now it was five games to four, De Rossi. He was still just one game away from a win.

Ray was exhausted now. His legs were cramping; he felt

like he was dehydrating. Sitting on the bench he wasn't sure if he could continue. But Jagger and Tara were sitting in the bleachers shouting words of encouragement with Jagger repeating whatever Tara said. He was having fun. They were counting on him. He had to find an inner strength, maybe beyond anything he ever felt before. He looked at the people sitting in the bleachers, most of them probably unaware of what was at stake. His eye caught hold of a guy, around 40 years old, beefy and mean looking. For some reason, that guy reminded him of one of the guards at the reform school he attended. The resemblance was eerie. Immediately, Ray picked up his racquet. He willed himself to get off the bench and return to the court. A very mean guy, who knows, maybe the bleacher guy's father, beat him up and did things to him he evicted from his memory. He remembered now. He had the inner strength.

The two men went at it with everything they had. De Rossi had mostly pride at stake. The son of a wealthy and doting man, losing wouldn't change anything. The money meant nothing to him. Ray won the next game by sending every shot to De Rossi's backhand, which up to then, had held up pretty well. But Ray knew about the unique pressure a player feels when its time to close the deal and win the match. Most players tend to get cautious; subconsciously hoping the other guy will make mistakes. Only the very best can pour it on even more to finish off their opponent. Armando wasn't that strong. His backhand finally started to waver and soon they were tied, five all.

De Rossi rallied though, relying on his serve again to win the next game. Then much to De Rossi's chagrin, Ray, seemingly from out of nowhere, finally found a way to cut off De Rossi's wide serves and send them whistling down the line for winners. They were tied 6-6. By previous agreement, they would play a seven point tiebreaker.

Ray asked for a bathroom break. De Rossi wasn't crazy about it, but he couldn't very well refuse. Ray took the opportunity to change his shirt again. He drank as much liquid as he dared without overdoing it. He felt refreshed.

The tie-breaker turned out to be almost anticlimactic. Ray, who had hit the ball hard and deep whenever he could during the match, decided to mix things up, hitting looping shots with heavy topspin to push Armando back behind the baseline and then following up with drop shots and lobs to win points. It worked. When Ray managed to win the first three points, with ease, his new style of play got the better of Armando. The heat was also wearing him down now, affecting his judgment and the discipline to remain focused. Now De Rossi, trying to catch up, started to take the high risk shots, the same kind that had worked almost perfectly in the second set. But his execution faltered. He managed to win three points in a row and then, Ray shut the door. He won the tie breaker 7-3 and along with it, the match.

When the match ended, Armando De Rossi quickly came to the net. He congratulated Ray and told him he was surprised he could stay in there for three sets. "You surprised me, Viejo. I think perhaps I misjudged you."

"Listen Armando, you gave me as much as I could handle. On another day, it could have gone the other way; I mean that."

"Maybe so, perhaps we can play a rematch before I go back to Argentina," Armando said.

"You bet, kid. I'll play you for $500 whenever you want."

Both men laughed. They shook hands. As he was walking into the pro shop to get his winnings, Ray marveled over the way Armando De Rossi handled losing seventy-five grand. He couldn't begin to imagine what it would be like to be casual about that kind of money. Had he lost his twenty-five grand, Ray thought he probably would have tried to swallow a tennis ball whole. He wondered if his opponent would have played better and maybe won the match if he was playing under pressure, something more than bragging rights.

Chapter 27

Elian was cruising along Alligator Alley, Tara seated beside him. They were headed to Bonita Springs. The couple held hands and tried to spot alligators near the waterway alongside the highway. Although Tara never said so, Elian was sure that Tara planned to take Jagger back to Miami with her. That's why he took the SUV instead of his Corvette. He could pack a few of Jagger's most important things in the back of his vehicle. Then, about five miles before they reached Marcia's mobile home park, Tara said, "I think I've made a decision, two of them actually."

"Okay, if I guess?" Elian said in a playful tone

Tara smiled at him. "Well, one should be easy. The other is going to rock your world."

"Sweet. You're going to take Jagger, right?'

"Right, I'm taking him. It's funny, I only knew Miracle for a few days and yet, he demonstrated such courage and determination. I really admired him, you know?"

"No question you're going to need some courage girl," Elian said. "You realize what you're taking on? I mean we talked about it and I meant what I said about helping out, but most of the responsibility is going to be on you. I hope you're not counting on Ray to help. He's worthless."

"Elian, please don't say that. You don't know him. I watched him and saw how he took care of Miracle."

"Yeah, for money."

"No, that wasn't it. He already had the money. I watched him clean Miracle up after he had an accident in the van. Listen, I've done that sort of thing for a living. I would have taken care of it, but Ray told me no."

"Seriously? That's a surprise. Why would he do that?"

"I asked him that later, when Miracle was asleep. He said, 'You're not just a nurse to Miracle. He would have been embarrassed to the max if you had to do that for him.'"

"Elian laughed. "I can't imagine Ray wiping his friend's ass like that. Served him right."

"Elian?"

"No, no, I get it, girl. I hope you're right, really. Just remember Jagger isn't some road trip that ends after a few days. Now, what's the other decision? You gonna move in with me?"

"You should have quit while you were ahead. I do have something to tell you though."

"Right, the second decision, can't wait to hear it. So tell me then."

"Elian, this has been a week like no other for me. For better or worse, I have a father now after all these years. And I'm about to have an older brother I just met move in with me. That's a lot to absorb. But there's something else even bigger and more important going on. I'm also going to be a mother."

Elian looked at Tara, his eyes so wide you might think he discovered an alligator in the back seat of his SUV. He pulled over onto the shoulder of the road. He made a point of putting on his hazard warning lights. "Time out, Tara. I'm really confused here. What exactly are you telling me, babe?"

"Maybe I should have said it another way. You're going to be a father, Elian. Sorry, honestly, I am."

It was Destiny who vouched for Tara as Jagger's next of kin. Arrangements hadn't been completed yet for Jagger's transfer to the group home. Since the state agency was overwhelmed with cases, they were eager to cooperate. Tara made it clear she was willing to give it a try, that if she couldn't handle it, she would turn Jagger over to the state for placement in a group home. The case manager was a friend of Destiny's. She promised to hold open a slot for Jagger for a month but no longer. After that, he would be back on a waiting list and his case would no longer be considered an emergency. Tara signed some papers and just like that, she had custody of her brother.

They loaded some of Jagger's things into the back of Elian's SUV. A legal aid worker was working on getting Marcia's mobile home cleaned up and hoping to find a buyer. The proceeds, if there were any, would go into a trust fund for Jagger. Marcia had done a good job under the circumstances, taking into account all the details that would have to be handled once she was gone. Just two and a half hours after they got to Bonita Springs, Elian, Tara and Jagger were back on the road to Miami.

Jagger was frightened by the sudden changes and it showed in his demeanor. He clung to an old baseball mitt and he started asking questions. The case worker gave Tara several tips on how to handle Jagger. She also cautioned her that she would need to be patient with him.

Once they got on the road, Tara quickly got an idea of just how much patience she was going to need. She found she had to explain to Jagger several times where they were going and why. She reminded him they were related. She asked him if he had any friends who had a sister. They stopped to get gas and have something to eat at the Miccosukee Service Plaza run by the Miccosukee Indian tribe. After he ate lunch and picked out a couple of candy bars, he calmed down. "You came to see my mama before she died. You bought me candy at the mall. You're a nice lady."

When Tara told Elian he was going to be a father, he was thrilled. He was also terrified. There was no time to really discuss it. They pulled into Garden Estate Park less than five minutes after Tara gave him the news. He loved Tara, no question about it. Now though, driving back to Miami, only half-heartedly following Tara's conversation with Jagger, it dawned on him that he was tied to her in a very permanent way. Suddenly, he had a few doubts. For one thing, if they got married, something his parents would certainly demand, it wasn't just a baby. Her mentally challenged brother was part of the package too. And, while he had really pressed Tara to move in with him before she mysteriously disappeared, the equation was different now even without a baby. In the back of his mind, in spite of his comments about Ray, he hoped the guy would step up and take custody of his son. That would be the ideal situation. Well, now that there was going to be a baby, Ray would have no choice. He would have to take Jagger. Tara's story about the way Ray took care of Miracle also gave him hope.

Once Jagger settled down, they drove quietly for a while, each one waiting for the other to say something. Finally, Tara couldn't take it any longer. "Tell me what you're thinking," she said. "I'm not planning to put any pressure on you, if that's what you're worried about."

"Did I say I was worried?"

"The word worry is stamped on your forehead."

"It's a lot all of a sudden, you know? A child, your brother, a crazy father, you hit me with a lot of stuff girl."

"Sorry."

"Does Ray know you're pregnant?"

"I haven't told him."

"What does that mean? Is there someone else who might have told him?" Elian asked.

"Miracle knew." Tara told Elian about the pregnancy test Miracle found in the bathroom.

Elian didn't know what to say next. He never dreamed it would come to this, but Ray, his seeming nemesis, was probably the guy whose help he needed most. Well, he knew where to find him. He would take Tara and her brother to see the big tennis match.

Chapter 28

It took a while to count the money, 750 $100 bills. That done, he headed for the clubhouse to take a shower. On his way there, he saw Tara and Jagger. "We're so proud of you," Tara said. Ray noticed that Jagger was holding his sister's hand. Ray couldn't help noticing the way Jagger looked at her. He would have to have a talk with him, he thought but then he realized he didn't have the slightest idea of how you deal with a mentally challenged adult. He was overwhelmed by how much he didn't know. He actually said aloud in a low voice, "Is it possible to grow up all at once when your 60?"

"Better late than never, Daddy Ray." Tara had heard him.

Ray smiled. He was about to flip her the finger when he remembered yet again she was his daughter. For a guy who had spent most of his life being cavalier with women, he was turning out to be an old-school father. "Meet me in the restaurant. I'll be there in 30 minutes," was all Ray said. He took a long shower alternating hot and cold water. His life was about to change in ways he couldn't fathom just two weeks ago. He would have to have a long talk with Tara. He wasn't about to take this on all by himself. The money would help, but he realized it was only a start. There was a lot more involved with being a family.

As he was getting dressed, his cell phone rang. It was the same number he had seen at least five times now during the last week. The caller never left a message. He figured it was probably a reporter from the tabloids looking for a story. He had already seen one headline in the supermarket claiming Miracle was actually Jesse, Elvis's twin brother. He hadn't died at birth after all. He decided to take the call so he could get whoever it was off his back.

"Mr. Rosario? Hi, my name is Tiffany Dearborn. I am an

assistant producer for the news show, Perspectives. Have you heard of it?"

"Everybody's heard of it. You want to interview me about Wimbledon?" The Wimbledon finals were scheduled for the next day.

"That might be a small part of the story, but what we're really interested in learning more about is your recent road trip with your friend Miracle Morgan. We believe Mr. Morgan's story might be captivating to our audience."

"Really? Why is that?" Ray asked.

"Well, we have reason to believe that there is more to the story. We've spoken with Mr. Morgan's daughter, let me see, oh yes, Melanie,

"I see."

"The family doesn't believe that Mr. Morgan went to Florida for a lung transplant. Can you comment on that?"

"I can, but I'm not going to."

"Mr. Rosario, Melanie said if we wanted to know what really happened we would have to talk to you. Would you be willing to tell the whole story?"

Ray correctly guessed that Melanie didn't say anything about Jagger because of Miracle's will. Sandy had instructed her to remain quiet about that until they had some time to think about their options. "Would I be paid for my story?"

"Oh, I'm sorry, no. We don't do that, but I can tell you that sometimes a good story like this one will lead to other opportunities like a book contract or made for TV movie. Can't promise, but it is always a possibility."

"That sounds like a long shot to me," Ray said.

"Well, there's only one way to find out," Tiffany said "As I said, it depends on the story. I think Mr. Morgan's journey has excellent possibilities. We could also highlight the uphill battle people who have pulmonary fibrosis face."

Ray had seen at close range what a pulmonary fibrosis patient faced. An uphill battle was no way to describe what Miracle had been up against. It was more like trying to beat a nuclear arsenal with a bow and arrow. "I need to talk it over with my family first. Why don't you call me back next week?" Ray almost laughed when he told Tiffany he had to speak to his family. He was surprised that the words made him feel good.

For so many years, the man had lived his life more or less on the run. On the run from women, on the run from big opportunities –after all why else would he ever get involved in a rugby match at a moment when he could have made history in the biggest major tennis tournament in existence?

He thought about Miracle too. Here was a man who tried to do the right thing. He didn't always succeed but he kept trying. Even at the end of his life, Miracle tried his best to be helpful. He must have wondered whether Jagger was really his, but he never hesitated for a moment. He was quite prepared to pay for a crime he didn't commit. Maybe that was the point. If he suspected Ray, which was certainly possible given how irritated he was when Ray called Marcia the love of his life, it was his chance to finally, once and for all, pay back his debt to his friend.

The biggest difference between Miracle and Ray was easy to see. As a man, no matter what happened, Miracle never ran away, especially from himself. He knew it couldn't be done. Ray thought it could; until now.

Showered and dressed in shorts, an ivory Tommy Bahama shirt and sandals, Ray walked into the tennis resort's restaurant and got another surprise. Several people sitting at their tables having lunch gave him a round of applause. Apparently, a few of them knew about the money match. Some had arrived at the resort early to watch, sitting in the cool restaurant, eating breakfast and drinking coffee while Ray and Armando sweated it out. One guy pulled him aside before he could reach his table and jokingly said, "You buying a round for the house?"

When he got to the table, he saw Elian sitting there. His face flushed. If Elian set him up for a fall with De Rossi, Ray would never be able to trust him. He would never accept him as part of his family regardless of the way Tara felt about him. Elian anticipated Ray's reaction. And he knew he would have to make peace with him if he really wanted Tara. He said, "Congratulations Ray. I'm glad you won."

"Easy to say now isn't it, when your shot at revenge is gone"?

"You're wrong Ray. Armando and I played a few times but I wasn't in his league, no way, man. But I swear I had nothing to do with your match with him. The only thing he ever asked me was who you were"

"So you didn't try to set me up?" Ray said.

"No, I didn't. I'll admit I'm surprised you beat him," Elian said, grinning, "but like I told you, I'm happy for you."

"Ray, leave it alone. You won." Tara's tone was sharp, but her eyes were pleading.

Ray relaxed. "There's nothing to leave alone. Elian and I are cool, but I'm keeping the $500 I won from him." Both men smiled.

He had won a lot more than money. He was about to start a new life with children who just might learn to like him and maybe love him a little. Jagger would be a constant reminder of what he, Miracle and Marcia gave up, but maybe that wasn't entirely bad. And, while he couldn't honestly say he had strong memories of his relationship with Dana, the way she raised Tara would give him a growing source of contentment. She was a fine woman, much better than he deserved.

Too, he would see Brooks about going into business together. And, he just might be able to wangle a book or TV movie deal. He thought about how a show like Perspectives might even encourage, or force, if necessary, Miracle's kids to help out and let Jagger have the proceeds of the condo sale when it happened. Miracle would have liked that.

What was it that Miracle had said not long before he died?

That he was going to keep breathing for a while. Yes, keep breathing and see what comes next.

He looked at his children, Jagger and Tara, and felt a sudden rush of pleasure. Life was good.

And then Tara had more good news. He was going to be a grandfather.

Acknowledgements

I have many people to thank for their generous assistance and unflagging encouragement as I wrote this book. First and foremost, I have to thank my beautiful, loving and courageous wife, Nancy for making it easy for me to spend the time required to write. She is also my first editor, finding errors in logic, consistency and grammar. She worked hard and never complained even after reading my work more times than I can count.

This book would not have been completed without the encouragement of my friend Candy Barone, who read the first six chapters and insisted I keep going. Paul and Mary Ellen Palmeri read while I wrote, contributing numerous ideas and above all motivation when I needed it.

Mindy Eberhart, BS, RRT, CRT, former colleague and one terrific friend took the time not only to read the manuscript to ensure I got the clinical aspects right, she returned it to me with helpful copy edits. Pulmonologist, Carlos Remolina, MD, a lifelong friend also gave me important insights into idiopathic pulmonary fibrosis.

Tennis pro, Robbie McCammon, USPTA who continues his outstanding work as an instructor and tennis coach in Tennessee, read Keep Breathing and made exceedingly useful suggestions regarding the story's pivotal tennis match.

As with any undertaking that involves storytelling, it's possible that some of what I've written may not strictly adhere to the guidance I was given. Any inconsistences related to diseases or the delivery of patient care, tennis scenarios or the intellectually challenged, are solely the responsibility of the author.

I must also mention two people who have graciously

reviewed all of my books and offered sage advice. I owe a great deal to Brenda Albright and John Anderson for their time, patience and above all friendship. I cannot imagine writing a book without having Brenda or John read and edit it for me.

Other friends who made important contributions include Ed Kays and Kevin Wronko, Esq. I cannot thank them enough for their help.

I also want to say a special thank you to Ellen Bennett for her outstanding work, especially in designing the book's cover. I am more than grateful for her willingness to help.

Finally, I want to remember Frank Euston, to whom *Keep Breathing* is dedicated. He fought the good fight, but pulmonary fibrosis took him from us much too soon. Throughout the writing of this book I felt Frank's presence from heaven, coaching me, frequently pointing the way forward. Shredagavis Frankie.

About the Author

A native of Newark, New Jersey, Len Serafino lives in Nolensville, Tennessee with his wife Nancy. He is the author of the novel, Back to Newark and Sales Talk -how to power up sales through verbal mastery. He can be contacted at lserafino@comcast.net.

* * * * *

A portion of the net proceeds from the sale of each book will be donated to the Pulmonary Fibrosis Foundation. Learn how you can make a donation to the Foundation through www. pulmonaryfibrosis.org